# Rooms

## Bob Stegner

Cover Illustration and Design

Greg Opalinski

# DEDICATION

*This book is dedicated to my father and mother for their encouragement and faith in me and to Magda and Kendra for their hard work, support and belief in Rooms.*

# TABLE OF CONTENTS

# FORWARD

It was Zeer's third lifeglobe experience, and she was hopeful and looked forward to the change when she'd arrived on R-131. She was a habituate, and she had come to work in a new training center and experience this newly constructed lifeglobe. It was incredibly massive, and its architecture angular and unique.

The person whom she'd be working with was named Tal. He had an excellent reputation for running a very professional center, and she had met him over the vids before taking the job. He'd seemed to be an interesting and serious person who also had a good sense of humor. She was looking forward to working with him.

Zeer had also come to R-131 because of the reputation of its Rooms' circuit. She had been a player since the first settlement that she'd lived on. She'd always longed for adventure, and in addition to being a habituate had also studied yoga and meditative mind control. All of these skills, along with her experience, had given her the edge that made her the elite Rooms' player that she'd become.

However, after living there, working at the training center and playing the Rooms' circuit for two years, she'd started to sense the same longing that had always set in after the newness of a move had worn off. She'd enjoyed her work as well as her fellow habituates and clients. She was basically content, but the limits of living within a structure, no matter how large and beautiful, were creating the same sense of monotonous confinement that she'd experienced before. She'd tried to shake it off but couldn't.

One day, though, her life was immeasurably altered when she received a very unique and unusual gift.

# 1
## R-131

Lying quietly awake, Rad looked through multiple transparent barriers to the world outside. The night was coal black and still, as the wind, sand and silt no longer pummeled the exterior of the lifeglobe. A calm had set in following the violent storm that had raged on for days on R-131. At the edges of his sleeping area, the artificial glow of the nightshines sent out faint waves of light, giving it what should have been a warm, comfortable feeling. He was safe and protected from this harsh planet, living in a beautifully unique and new home, and the people that he'd met since his arrival seemed content and excited to live here. He should have been as well. However, despite his surroundings, Rad carried inside an unease and a sad loneliness that permeated his nights and his days.

***

This particular move had been difficult for him. It had meant a full year of traveling in sleep-modem, and even though he still enjoyed the adventure, each move had affected him more. He was continually searching for a new career, a unique adventure, anything, hoping that he could find what was lacking in his life.

His latest home here on planet R-131 was located almost ten thousand light years from Earth, and because of its recent construction, the architecture and design were innovative and technologically advanced. It had been made of alloys of varying strength and texture that created its arched support system, and all of the materials used in its construction were, as with most of the settlements in the galaxy, indigenous to the particular planet where it was built. It spread over several hundred square kilometers and was an octopus on the landscape.

Although very modern and beautifully built, this lifeglobe's basic form and function was still similar to most of the others. However, there was one difference that made R-131 unique. Word had spread among many of the elite Room players that this particular lifeglobe possessed one of the most dynamic and difficult holographic game Rooms ever conceived, and countless players were gradually relocating here in order to have a chance to experience what was coming to be known as "*the* Room." It was said that a woman, referred to as the "old one," had designed it, steered the Room and handpicked her players. There were multitudes of Rooms dotting every colonized lifeglobe, but the gossip about this one persisted.

Rad had heard about this Room as well, and as he considered it, his mind started racing. He was wondering what it would be like to play this famous Room, but then he stopped himself and thought out loud, "Enough! I can't start obsessing again – not again..."

***

It was morning, and Rad threw down some food and rushed out the door to get to his first council meeting. He noticed Zeer, a woman he'd met outside his apartment only days earlier. She was kneeling down to pick something up in the hallway. Her body was taut underneath the towel that robed her frame. Even if he hadn't known, it would have been easy to tell that she was a trainer, a habituate. She was extremely strong. Her muscles, although not as bulky, easily matched his in pure tensile strength. Her face looked vibrant, which, inside a lifeglobe, took tremendous commitment.

She caught his eye. "Good morning," she said, while looking through the slightly wet strands of tawny hair hanging in front of her eyes and noticing Rad's slim, strong build, black hair and his blue, wide-eyed gaze.

"Morning. I met you a few days ago outside our building, but I didn't tell you my name. It's Rad."

"Mine's Zeer. You're my neighbor then?"

"I guess so!" Rad laughed. "I wonder if there's anything interesting on the vids today. Have you looked yet?"

"I have, but don't worry you haven't missed anything," she said. "There was just some news about a theft last night and lots of adverts about all the Rooms here."

Rad was doing pretty well until that point, then he nervously asked, "I...I was wondering if...if you were doing anything for lunch? Could we meet somewhere?"

"I can't. I'm sorry."

"Okay. Maybe another time," he said.

"We'll see," she responded with a smile and then went back inside.

Rad wasn't surprised by her answer. After all, he'd just recently met her, but he *was* disappointed. He was drawn to her. She seemed intelligent, had a wondrous smile and he could also sense an aura of secrecy about her. Even that simply made her more exciting. He wondered whether or not she might be a player. He would love to spend some time with her and get to know her. Maybe he'd have another chance.

***

Arriving at the council meeting, he introduced himself and was greeted by everyone. The meeting began, and Rad had hoped that his job on this new lifeglobe might somehow be more interesting or just different in some way; but as the discussions continued, it didn't even seem like he had changed planets. He could tell that the work that he'd be doing here would be just as mundane as what he'd done on all of the other lifeglobes.

To Rad, it seemed that having a governing council was a very archaic custom, especially considering the highly efficient super technologies that had been developed over time to run and maintain the lifeglobes. Governing councils were simply less and less necessary. However, having such a council had been a custom that had originally come from the first colonists who had left Earth several hundreds of years earlier. The custom had continued on each new lifeglobe and had become very important to the inhabitants as it gave them a place to voice their concerns and grievances and helped them feel secure in these out-of-the-way settlements. There seemed to be a need to know that every lifeglobe had an order that could be depended on for safety and

3

well-being, and it gave them a connection to the Earth, even though it had been abandoned long ago.

By night, though, these same people who needed the security of their council also had an insatiable need for something new, something out of the ordinary – anything to break the monotony of working and living inside such an isolated and confined space. Rad wondered, *'Why is there always this dichotomy, this strange yearning that we all have?'* He was constantly questioning and probing his existence, wondering, thinking, obsessing...

He laughed at himself as he realized that he was doing it again. His parents had always tried to get him to relax more. He smiled as he thought of them. Their teachings, even after all of these years of separation, still crossed his mind at times. He hadn't thought about them for a while. He missed them.

***

After the meeting that day, Rad decided to take his parent's advice. He hopped on his speedcycle and toured his new home. The lifeglobe was massive and covered many square kilometers so using his favorite mode of transportation would allow him to see it all more quickly and give him some needed exercise as well. He'd brought his speedcycle with him from his last assignment. He was always surprised at how light and efficient it was, and he even knew the history of its development. It was very much like what used to be referred to as a bicycle, only the speedcycle was much more efficient and a great deal faster. It had a computer assisted ride and propulsion system that, as you pedaled, would actually push and accelerate your momentum, and the ultra-light v-frame could cut through the air and eliminate most of the wind resistance allowing him to travel at amazing speeds.

He pushed himself, accelerating and cycling as fast as he could. The air rushing past his ears created a comfortable sound; one that was foreign to most people living in a lifeglobe, but it made Rad smile.

The sky of R-131 seemed to contain a misty haze that

4

evening as he pedaled hard and glanced up through the transparent roof. He'd heard that it didn't rain here but that there was a small amount of water in the atmosphere that was acidic and toxic and could sometimes be seen as a light mist or cloud hovering above the surface of the planet. For some reason, recalling this made him think back. A truly free and open sky was something that he had only experienced once. He stopped for a moment and remembered.

He had been living on a settlement where he'd received his first assignment after leaving the lifeglobe where his parents had raised him. It was a lunar planet with no atmosphere. Rad had walked outside the lifeglobe one night in his survival suit and had dared to shut off the system and open the optical face of his headgear for less than a minute. He remembered it very clearly and could still feel the rush of air from his suit and see the unobstructed view of the horizon and stars in the distance. The experience had been extremely frightening and yet magnificent at the same time. The cold had been severe, threatening to freeze his skin. His lungs had ached from the need to inhale, and his eyes had clouded rapidly with exposure to the elements. He'd become light-headed and dizzy in seconds; his head had pounded and ached from the rapid change in pressure. But even with all of this, the experience had made him feel extraordinarily alive. It had been a rush, more exhilarating than anything he had ever known. He'd only been exposed to the elements for a few seconds before closing the face of his helmet and re-pressurizing his suit, but being out in the open, unblocked and free, had been something that he would never forget. Everywhere he had ever been, there had always been the necessity to look through something, always needing to be protected from the "out there." *Everyone* was always protected from the "out there."

He climbed back on his bike and continued on. Speed! Concentration! He pounded the pedals of his speedcycle. Velocity! Danger!

Rad reached the outer rim of one of the many radial arms

that extended from the center of the lifeglobe and slowed down. His muscles were hot from the pounding and exertion, and his skin was cool as the air had brushed over the exposed parts of his body. The reality was pure and simple. He headed back. His large smile said it all.

\*\*\*

The next two days would be free-days for Rad. He had finished with the council meeting in the afternoon and was looking forward to them. It would be time that belonged to him and no one else.

Just as he began to feel the freedom of his time off, his thoughts returned to Zeer. He had seen her again a few days earlier and had asked if she could show him some of the Rooms on R-131. He'd mentioned to her that he didn't want to get back into the room circuit as seriously as he had in the past, but he did enjoy the camaraderie and the fun, and since she had lived there longer than he had, he was wondering if she could introduce him to some Rooms. Her answer, though, was disappointing. She said that she wouldn't be able to, then looked through him and walked away. Her mind seemed to be somewhere else, and he thought that he'd heard her whisper something just as she left. It didn't completely register, but he thought that she had mumbled something about wondering if he'd "...found it?" 'What could she have meant?' It intrigued him. She was beginning to drive him a little crazy, but he needed to move on and enjoy his time off. He just shook his head and walked on.

# 2
## The Door

Rad had decided to begin his first free-day evening in a small and cozy pub that he'd heard about in the Center. It was called "The Club" and was very much like all of the other pubs on R-131 except that many of the best Room players would gather there on free-days or evenings and discuss the latest rage on the market. The other reason that it was unique was because it had one special section in the back that was dedicated specifically to the history of the Rooms around the galaxy.

As he entered, the place was buzzing with conversation and filled to the brim. All of the tables were full except for one by the door. It had three chairs, two of which were taken. Rad walked over and asked, "Can I sit here? It's the only free chair that I can see in the whole place."

One of the men sitting there said, "Sure. My name's Simon and this is Tal."

"My name's Rad. It's loud in here, huh!" he hollered. They both smiled and leaned in as Rad sat down.

Rad hadn't met either Tal or Simon before that afternoon, but as they talked, drank some of the local brews and got to know each other, it wasn't long before he felt completely comfortable with them.

"This lifeglobe is incredible, Rad. It has all of the best Rooms: 'Starpassage,' 'Freeball,' 'Void,' '6th dimension.' God, I love it here!"

Rad smiled. Simon was definitely an enthusiastic person. He'd probably been born that way. His eyes were darting around looking everywhere as he talked, and he was tall, thin and moved in an easy way. He had an infectious smile and seemed very intelligent. Rad liked him.

Tal, on the other hand, was an immense brute about two meters tall and obviously a habituate like Zeer. He seemed much more calm than Simon and had a slight grin on his face as he asked, "So you two, I was wondering? Are we going to go to one of those really strange Rooms tonight?"

Rad couldn't help himself. "Strange Rooms? What do you mean, Tal?"

Simon poked Tal in the side, "Stop that, Tal, Rad's new here. You don't want to scare him away!"

"Don't worry Rad, we won't go to any of *those* until you've been here a while," he said with a wink.

Rad finally got the humor, and they all laughed. Up until then, Tal had been a lot more serious and reserved than Simon, and with his immense size, Rad had simply not expected his sense of humor.

As they all got up to leave, he knew then that he liked both of them and that it probably wouldn't be long before they were all good friends. Somehow, he felt they already were.

Rad and Tal started walking toward door, but Simon stopped them and motioned for Rad to follow. He did, and Simon took him to an area near the back of the pub. The bookshelves and walls in this room were filled with many pictures, articles and books. Simon said, "Look at the sign up there, Rad."

Rad looked up and noticed what it said, 'The Galactic History of Rooms'. "I'd heard that this pub had a room like this, but I had no idea that there would be this much in it."

Tal then escorted Rad over to a particular article that hung in a frame on the wall and said, "Rad, this is our favorite artifact. Everyone that comes to this pub for the first time reads it. It's sort of an initiation. It's nothing big, but it does summarize what the Rooms are and where they came from. I'm glad Simon remembered to bring you back here. The article isn't long. Go ahead and read it and then we'll head out."

Rad simply shrugged and said, "Sure," and began reading.

Conceived in the bosom of the late twenty-second century, the Rooms evolved from the need for a variety of stimulating types of entertainment for the colonists who had left Earth and inhabited various celestial bodies, the first of which was Earth's moon. Many of the original colonists felt that these Rooms were just a fad. They believed that the discovery of an Earth-like planet would eliminate the need for them. To date, though, no such planet has been discovered, and the Rooms have existed and evolved technologically for over five hundred years. They have become a common sight on almost every settlement in the galaxy and a techno-cultural phenomenon, time-specific to this age of the human condition. Many believe that the advent of these Rooms brought a uniqueness and sanity to the all too commonplace environments of the lifeglobes.

The current Rooms now consist of a completely three dimensional, holographic experience controlled by super-computers and nanosensor technology. The player, or players, if chosen by a Room, can control, to a degree, what happens during a game, and these games have outcomes, which are as varied and real as life itself. They are usually in the Center of the settlements and are extremely popular with the inhabitants.

The difficulty of each Room depends upon the type of game, the level of the technology and the sophistication and experience of the individual player. The better the player, the more control they have. The weaker the player, the more the Room plays them. The realism can be frightening at times, and if a player is not prepared or plays a game beyond his or her ability, they could be injured. This happens rarely, though, because upon entering a room, the participants are usually screened to make sure that that particular Room is safe for them. There is still an element of risk, though, which heightens the allure of the Rooms, the participant's enthusiasm and the competitive nature of the Rooms.

So go out, enjoy yourself and have fun playing the Rooms on R-131.

As Rad finished, he laughed and asked about the hand-written sentence that had been taped to the bottom of the article.

Simon answered, "Nobody knows who put it there, and no one's ever taken it off so it's just become a part of the article. I think we all feel it just works as a good finish to it. What do you think?"

"I love it!"

Tal added, "Okay, so let's go out and do what it says!"

***

The three new friends walked up to a set of stark black doors and could see their reflections glaring back at them. There was a vibrant blue light above the doors that they knew was counting and screening participants for anomalies. The Room would allow them in when ready.

They had all agreed that tonight the first room they would visit would be "Quad." It was a multidimensional game that was not only popular for its amazing interface but also because of the way that it adapted to each player.

Tal tapped both Simon and Rad on the shoulders as he noticed a change in the blue light. The dark door disappeared, and they entered a circular room filled almost to capacity. They were ushered into their seats. Glancing around, Tal and Simon pointed out the number of elite players in the Room. Rad's nerves were beginning to surge. He could sense the excitement. It had been a while since he had been in a Room, and tonight, he just wanted to watch and feel the exhilaration of the experience.

They walked forward and sat in floating body-chairs, each with an ordering platform attached. If anything were needed, a person could simply touch a sensor. Whatever was desired would be delivered immediately. The room itself was dimly lit and decorated in soft, deep blue colors. It was like a theater-in-the-round, with the Focus, or the area of engagement, accented with lighting and placed below the audience in the exact center of everyone's attention.

A voice asked the crowd to be seated. The lights were dimmed, except for the Focus, and a small but firm humming sound hushed the expectant players and grew in intensity and volume, a crescendo that everyone there could sense.

All at once the room exploded in a brilliant array of colors and simple but intense music. Rad's body seemed to become part of the experience as he felt a tremor pass from his feet to the top of his head. The Room was beginning to engage and choose its first player.

It all stopped suddenly as the surroundings turned pitch-black, and a single word, "Quad," pulsed continuously and diminished in volume from the middle of the darkness. Rad didn't know what was going on in Simon or Tal's mind, but he was shaking from the anticipation and the adrenaline.

As the single pulsing word passed into oblivion, a small light grabbed Rad's attention. A voice seemed to reach out, "One has been chosen." The glow from the solitary light grew and expanded, and a single figure appeared seated in the Focus area. The player stood. The chair glided away. The game began.

***

After his normal six hours of sleep, Rad awoke very slowly and felt exhausted. Even though he had been an elite Rooms' player before coming to R-131, it had still been quite a while since his last experience, and sometimes, like this morning, it was very difficult to recover from a night of multisensory immersion, even if you weren't chosen; and Quad had been one of the most elaborate Rooms that Rad had ever witnessed. R-131 was everything that he had expected. The players who participated directly in the game were superior, and the holographic imagery was remarkable. 'But now, after the excitement has worn off, why do I feel so empty, so sterile?' It was as if the technology had somehow robbed him of some aspect of his humanity. He'd had this feeling before.

Rad rose up on one elbow and snuck a look outside through sleepy eyes. The miasma of a typical lifeglobe morning stared back at him with metal and glass collected into endless curves and shapes. R-131 was riled again this morning. A huge storm was beating against the globe, but it had no meaning for him. He was secure, protected. His head then turned, and he panned his sleeping area. It didn't seem to matter whether he was looking outside or within his home. They had something in common. Something was missing. He was drained.

Just then, he saw a call coming in on his vid-screen. It was Simon. "Rad, what a night, huh! I just thought I'd check to see if you'd like to come out with us again tonight."

"I'll think about it Simon. I'll get in touch with you later. Okay?"

"Okay."

Rad knew that Simon was disappointed, but he just couldn't give him an answer right now. He was still trying to shake off the strange feelings that he'd had when he woke up and decided that he needed to eat something and then go out for a ride. He needed to feel the air and hear it move again.

\*\*\*

Balanced and ready, the power in Rad's body was about to be transformed once more into speed and movement. He placed his foot on the pedaling device, rested his back against the support and...felt a tap on one shoulder. He was about to tell Simon to knock it off when he noticed the configuration of the hand and arm that had done the nudging. He was extremely surprised and delighted.

"A beautiful machine, this speedcycle."

Rad's heart was in his throat. Zeer, with her brilliant eyes and a big smile, was standing alongside him. Somehow he'd managed to say, "Thanks..."

"I've noticed that you seem to ride almost every chance you get. Could I try a short spin?" she asked.

Rad recovered. Her comments had given him the chance to get his thoughts together. "Sure. Uh...have you ever handled one of these, though? They're sort of old-fashioned. Most people don't understand why I ride it. I'm not sure I always do either."

"I think I understand, but, no, I've never ridden one. I've worked with a simulator at the training room, though. I think I can handle it."

Rad gave her a short demonstration, adjusted the fit for her and let her go. She seemed to become part of the cycle almost as soon as she sped away. He could tell that she sensed the same freedom and love for speed that he did.

Returning, she had a slightly red face and a bright smile

originating in her eyes. "I love it! Feeling the air moving over my skin was wonderful. I can see why you ride."

"Not many people really understand my preoccupation with it. It's new to find someone who can relate." She beamed at Rad. It gave him the confidence to continue. "Zeer, the other day when I spoke to you, you seemed to be either disinterested or preoccupied. Why did you decide to open up to me now? It wasn't just my speedcycle...was it?"

"No, it wasn't Rad. I've just had a feeling about you, and I noticed you at one of the Rooms last night."

"You were at Quad too? What did you think?"

"It wasn't as impressive as it would have been to me several months ago, but it definitely was a step above most of the other rooms here. The players that experienced the Focus seemed to gain the most from the experience, but that's as it usually is, isn't it. There were some excellent players, though."

"You're absolutely right about it being the best for those that were chosen. It must have been mind-boggling for them. Although, I'm still new here, and it definitely had an effect on me as well."

"Did it leave you feeling somewhat strange, though?" she wondered.

"You too! I can't quite put my finger on the reason why."

Zeer reached into the pocket of her garment and grasped something. "Another reason that I'm here is that I've been asked to give you this."

"A book. I don't understand?"

"I don't think it will take you too long to figure it out, Rad."

"Does this have something to do with what you whispered when I saw you yesterday?"

Zeer just smiled. "It's getting late Rad. I need to go. I might see you out tonight. Look for me." She moved away.

Now his brain was full of all kinds of thoughts, and he wondered, 'Someone had asked her to give this to me?' His eyes ricocheted from watching Zeer walk away to the book and back again. He didn't quite understand what had just happened, but one thing he did know was that he needed to ride. He dropped the book into one of the side panels of his bike and sped off.

*\*\*\**

The half-light of the moon was coming up as the nightshines were gleaming along the paths of R-131. Evening seemed to be just a darkened extension of another collection of hours on the lifeglobe. The paths were extremely well groomed. There was no trash. The air was clean and sterile. The buildings were architecturally beautiful but also cold and unalive - the same textures, the same colors, the same three-dimensional shapes staring blindly back at you. However, within that bland environment, no matter where Rad had lived, he had always been thankful for the variety in the people - their faces, their dress, their independence, their laughter and their emotions. And now, it was evening again, that specific time of day when excitement, freedom and self-expression blossomed.

He knew that he had to go back to his job tomorrow, so he'd decided to go it alone tonight. He walked, popped into some clubs, had a few drinks and people-watched. He was enjoying his solitary trek among the throngs of the lifeglobe.

He stepped out of the last club for the night and decided to stay out just a little while longer. He wasn't ready to go home yet. He moved away from the Center and began to explore. There were never really any areas of a lifeglobe that were completely dark, but Rad did venture into an outer section that was dimmer and had very few people. As he moved further from the Center, the sounds of the nightlife behind him had become a muffled roar in the background, evaporating more and more with each step. He kept walking deeper into the solitude, enjoying the quiet and the lack of light. He hadn't felt this serene in days, but then within his peripheral vision, he noticed a faint glow some distance down a long side path. It seemed out of place. He hesitated for a moment and then moved toward it. He was curious.

The pupils of his eyes settled and accepted the velvety semi-darkness as he reached the source of the light. It spread onto the path in front of him from beneath an old wooden door with a round handle made of burnished bronze. He had never before seen anything so large that was completely made of wood. He had seen smaller objects, but nothing like this. It must be priceless. He stroked it gently. It was warm and smooth, and the light that came from the space underneath wasn't strong or harsh but had a golden radiance that almost seemed alive. He reached down and touched the light and ran his fingers along the door's handle but then pulled back. He felt as if he was intruding. This seemed to be a very special place, and whoever was behind that door belonged here, not him. He walked away.

On his way back home, the congestion of the lifeglobe pushed against and was counter-balanced by that one path, that one door. Rad was drawn to it. He was tempted, lured... He was nuts! His mother had always known that he was a romantic, an extra-sensory fanatic. But there was something...

It was late, and he finally arrived back in his apartment. He crunched down into his chair, and turned on some music. As he listened, his thoughts gnawed at him. He was pondering whether he should have walked away from the door or not. 'What was behind it? Who was in there? What were they doing?' Then he noticed the book that Zeer had given him. It lay on the floor next to his chair. He reached down. The cover was old and soft. It felt comfortable in his hand. He opened it. The yellowed pages were blank. He stared.

# 3
## Change

Shar was now old and ready, her last cycle all but complete. She paused for a moment and looked down upon her acolyte who was still asleep. She then raised her eyes and glanced one last time at what had been her home for the last one hundred fifty years. The simple earthen bowls were neatly stacked against the shelf next to the back wall; the grasses and herbs had been gathered into piles of commonality, and the fire's comforting glow reflected in her eyes. This was a warm backdrop to the beauty of the starlit, crisp night that was framed by the entrance to her home – a cave, which was the very womb of her magnificent planet.

Shar walked quietly towards the opening, holding in her hand her sphere - the one that had accompanied her throughout her life. She turned her head one last time. She knew Fawn was complete. Wrapping her fingers reverently around the sphere, she walked further from the cave toward the shadowy trees in the distance. Once she was far enough, she held up her hand. The light from the sphere grew, encompassing her. She rose into the night and sped skyward, a comet-like flash into the heavens.

*** 

The thoughts and memories of her mentor were uppermost in Fawn's mind. She had been with her just yesterday, sharing and living her life. Now, Shar was gone. She had prepared Fawn for her departure, but it was difficult. She remembered Shar's last words from the night before. "Fawn, you came to me an unadorned tapestry from an ancient culture of mistrust, greed and misunderstanding. You were a lump of fire-burned earth not yet formed and shaped, yet with the willingness to be molded. You have felt death, destruction, and the cry of a beautiful planet smoldering in its innocence. You have lived with me for a long while, and our mother has shown us life, completeness, unity, and best of all, the wonder of chance. You will never die. You will cycle and to cycle is life."

Fawn had been taught and made to feel whole. She had learned and experienced the mystery, the gut wrenching reality that, after the learning, became truth. She sat propped against her bed knowing that at this moment she was old and young at the same time. Shar was gone, and she knew that she would never see her teacher again, but she also knew that Shar would always be part of her, as surely as if she were still here.

Fawn placed her fingers amongst the pebbles of dirt, sand and rock at her feet. She breathed the molecules of her master's breath, and allowed the colors, shapes and shadows to enter the receptors of her vision.

Moving slowly, she left the womb. Her eyes shifted skyward, and a tear crossed her face as she looked into space, remembering Shar and what she had taught her. The planet of her ancestors was, for all intents and purposes, dead, but this planet and she were vibrant and alive. It was now Fawn's time to go forward and share the knowledge.

Holding the sphere that was now hers, she connected; the energy surrounded her, and the soft flesh of the soul of her being rose and moved over the planet's surface towards the Learning Cluster. She was alive and new. Her next cycle had begun.

***

Rad was shocked when he saw the news on his vidscreen. Zeer was the main headline. She'd disappeared and hadn't shown up to work for many days. Her friends, although she had few, were alarmed and had brought it to the attention of the lifeglobe patrol. An investigation was taking place, but at this point, there were no leads.

He leaned back with a feeling of helplessness. He hadn't even gotten to know her, yet she had been an important part of his thoughts. Rad was stunned. He tried to imagine what had occurred. She was an intelligent, beautiful and strong woman. He couldn't believe that she would ever place herself in a position of weakness or vulnerability. He could still see the brightness in her eyes after she had ridden his speedcycle. He could still sense the feeling of her hand as she laid the book in his.

Rad called the information control officer for the council. He told him that there had been a death in his family, and he would not be in that day. He just couldn't.

He had to do something to take his mind off of Zeer. He really didn't know her, but he was drawn to her. He cared about her. 'What had happened?'

***

"Tal?" Simon was in a light-hearted mood, as usual.

"Yes?"

"Rad's a player, and I know he's a good one. He's been holed up at work and in his home for too long. Do you know what's wrong with him? Neither one of us has known him very long, but I like him and hate to see him become a loner. That could be dangerous here."

"I haven't seen him much since the night that we all met, but I agree with you."

"I was thinking that we might be able to take him out again. Have you heard about the new game that everyone's talking about?"

"No."

"It doesn't even have a name that I know of, but it's said that all of the others, including Quad, don't even come close to its difficulty or intensity." Simon was getting fired up again with the thought of a new Room.

"I know what you're thinking, Simon. You want to introduce Rad to this new Room. You probably have a good idea. Where is it?"

"I don't know!"

"What? You get me hooked on your idea and then tell me that this Room is so famous that you don't even know where it is!"

Simon knew that Tal was often disgusted with his nonchalant attitude about details, but this wasn't his fault. "Now wait a minute! Nobody knows where this Room is because that's

18

part of the game. It's located somewhere in our lifeglobe, but when the Room is actually played, there's never an audience. The people who *have* played seem only to be the top players, and we both know that R-131 has drawn more than its share of famous players recently."

Tal was somewhat intrigued. His analytical mind posed the next question. "I've heard about an 'old one' who steers one of the Rooms here. Could she be the maker of this one?"

"The people who've played have mentioned her but never in very concrete terms. The Room is always dark. They've seen what seemed to be a female's shadowy appearance, but that's it. You have to realize, too, that when they arrive they're somewhat disoriented."

Tal looked confused again. His body language told Simon that he needed more information.

"The disorientation is caused by the fact that none of the players have ever figured out how they arrived at this Room or how they left. Pretty freaky, huh!"

"People play and don't know exactly where the room is or exactly what they did when they played, and no one knows when or if they're going to play it or not. Sounds like a good one to stay away from to me. I do have to admit that I'm curious, but this all seems pretty strange."

Simon was almost drooling, "I know. I want to play, and the only way that I can figure out how to do that is to prove my abilities against some of this lifeglobe's best. How about tonight?"

Thinking about Rad again, Tal said, "I'll check back with you later. I'm going to go see if I can talk to Rad."

The massive black, white, and grey edifices of R-131 created an eerie perspective as the two men separated and moved in opposite directions. Simon sauntered away easily with thoughts of the evening to come; Tal was more deliberate, sensing the windless sounds of the lifeglobe and thinking about Simon, the strange new Room, and Rad.

# 4
## Insight

Tal had decided to go over to Rad's place and talk with him, but as they sat down he ended up doing little more than listening. It was obvious that Rad's spirits had lifted. He'd explained that he was just feeling down about what had happened to Zeer. Tal understood. He'd known her, too, and was very concerned, but he could tell that Rad's worry had come from a different type of attachment. He had obviously felt something for her. Rad then brought up the idea himself of going out to a Room that evening. Tal was surprised and pleased to see Rad excited about getting out. It would be good for him and help him focus on something else. He seemed ready, even intense.

They contacted Simon and all met at The Club again. They discussed what Room they would go to that night, and they all agreed to go to Quad again. There was some discussion of the other Room that Simon had talked about, but it was obviously something that a person couldn't actually choose to do.

As they walked up to the entrance of Quad that night, they noticed the blue light again. It blinked. They waited a moment, and the black doors disappeared. Tal and Simon watched Rad walk forward with a determination that they hadn't noticed when they'd been there before. They both had a feeling that he was an experienced player. They would probably find out sometime during the evening.

The three had arrived much earlier this time and sat close to the front. The chairs cradled their bodies, and the round platform in the center of their vision drew their attention even more this time than last.

Rad's eyes were glued to the soft light above the playing area. He pushed a button on the console of his chair. A drink appeared. He placed it to his lips, never moving his eyes, and drank. He seemed to relax. He was ready.

The preliminary chain of events began just as last time, except that everyone knew that a session in Quad, once it really began, was never the same. Each was different and totally dependent upon the player in Focus.

The lights dimmed. The humming began. Everyone tensed, wondering who would be chosen. The crescendo was the key that Rad had watched for, then the eerie music. He prepared himself.

In the many Rooms that Rad had played on other planets, he had educated himself with skills that had helped him become an elite player. He was highly trained in a variety of ancient techniques of mind and body control as well as some more recent developments in quantum physics. All were extremely useful in order to be able to pit one's self against the millions of scenarios that a highly technical room was capable of sustaining.

As the power of the room began to move through his body, he was able to shut off the feeling from the lower part of his legs. This stopped the surge and allowed him to withstand being taken over by the room as he had before.

Suddenly, at the height of his concentration, there was a tremendous flash, much larger and more brilliant than during his first experience. He began to rise with his chair. He looked down. The rest of the people in the room were laid back as if in a trance - heads drooping, eyes shut, seemingly unconscious. He was fully aware.

The room had become pitch-black, and he felt his chair descend smoothly and settle somewhere in the darkness. The pulsing of Quad took over. The light slowly filled his eyes. The game had begun.

As the light increased, Tal and Simon had come out of their trance and opened their eyes. They were astonished. The thrill of this choosing far surpassed the many that they had witnessed before. There was tremendous energy tonight, and to add to their excitement, Rad was the one in Focus, calm and ready.

The room began spinning. The voice that steered the room was ever-present in their minds. Rad could sense Quad's probing, which he had to control in order to play well. The crowd was able to see and feel what was happening to him. They would sense every journey that he would take and experience every struggle between he and Quad.

The spinning was accompanied by a burst of what appeared to be meteor showers. The showers materialized mostly in the stage area with sparks tailing off into the audience. Rad could hear cries from the onlookers. He grabbed control, and as he did so, the sites and sounds of the audience in the room vanished.

The meteors showers stopped, darkness surrounded him for a split second again, and the hologram changed. He was standing on a lunar planet – desolate and dry. His clothes had been somehow transformed into the normal protective spacewear usually worn outside a lifeglobe. He was simply alone. It was still. Stars were in the distance. He remembered then that he'd been there before. He reached up and lifted the visor on his headgear - a mistake. Air rushed out. He couldn't breathe. Panic gripped his every nerve. He couldn't move. The realism was horrifying. He was flat on his back, pressed against the lifeless soil. He was dying.

Tal and Simon could sense the struggle. They yelled to stop the game. It was intense. It was unyielding.

Rad, from somewhere within, made a conscious choice. This was not real. He closed his eyes and began communicating directly with Quad.

Darkness. Silence.

The spectators felt an immense struggle - two wills pitted against each other - a psychic tug-of-war.

Energy. Release.

Quad reciprocated the communication. "So where do you want to go? You've taken control. It's your choice."

Rad issued his desire. Quad obeyed.

Speed was the essence of the next level of Quad. He was traveling at a tremendous rate and was riding a beautifully crafted speedcycle. The onlookers could feel the rush and were with him on the lunar surface. It was magnificent, with shades of multiple colors and open, unscreened sky. Everyone was involved, hushed, and ecstatic at the same time. Rad moved with the grace and agility of an exquisite trainer on a well-designed machine. He had won. He had steered the game and traveled across an amazing planet at speeds beyond his comprehension.

He came to a stop, tilted his head slightly backwards and closed his eyes. The game ended. Sweat poured down his face. Standing in the Focus area, Rad could now see the onlookers as they roared and cheered with enthusiasm. Somehow, he had made the game move his way. A voice said, "Thank you for playing Quad. You have been given a score of one million. That is the highest score that has ever been awarded. Your name is Rad. It will be remembered."

The armchair onlookers again went crazy. What a night!

***

During the next several months Rad, Tal, and Simon paid many visits to Quad as well as most of the other rooms on R-131. It had become almost as much of an obsession with Tal and Simon as for Rad. The two less experienced players were gaining in knowledge and ability daily, although Simon more so than Tal. Rad was still far beyond their capabilities, though, as he was a level 1 player. Simon had reached level 5, Tal level 7. It wasn't that Tal couldn't have been as good as Simon. He just didn't have the time or inclination to commit to being an elite player. He was already an excellent habituate and helped run the best training room on the lifeglobe. That took tremendous dedication.

During this time, the rumors of the infamous mystery Room were still circulating. More and more players had been chosen and had had very similar experiences: the memories of tremendous exhilaration, the realization of the unique honor of being chosen, and no real idea of the Room's location or the exact circumstances of their arrival or departure. None of them had had more than just a vague sense of what had happened to them. These were the connecting threads that ran through all of the narratives at night places and private sleeping quarters across the lifeglobe. As the number of participants increased, players began piecing together what they thought to be a clearer picture of what this mysterious Room was about.

Everyone believed that the Room, steered by the old woman, contained several levels of play, but no one had heard of a single participant who had made it past the first level. No one had ever returned to play a second time. It was terribly frustrating, defeating, difficult and exciting to the participants. They all agreed upon one thing, though. The graphics of this particular Room were the most glorious of any that existed. The colors, the depth, the clarity, and the exquisite realism were unbelievable and excruciatingly frightening. It was not just an illusion. It felt real.

All of the stories were beginning to haunt Rad. He was, by far, the most sought after player on R-131. His skills were envied by almost everyone, and those who did not envy him hid their jealousy with bravado. The owners of the Rooms solicited his expertise. He was offered special incentives to play certain Rooms. They knew that if they could beat him or keep his scores low, the value of their individual enterprise would double. These incentives added up to all of the free-days that he could ever want, and financially, it came to the point where he really didn't need to work for a living. He had pushed his skills further here than on any other lifeglobe, and since R-131, by reputation, had the preeminent Rooms' circuit of any lifeglobe, Rad had become a celebrity. He was a star. That was the problem. He was who he was, and yet, he had not played the old one's Room.

Along with that frustration, Zeer's disappearance continued to have a profound affect on him, so he immersed himself in the Rooms - the one thing that he swore he wouldn't do again. The emptiness that he felt, even in the midst of all the glory and notoriety, was growing. His colorless, odorless surroundings, ever-present and monotonous, were closing in and suffocating him. He wanted to yell. He did. He screamed in fact, as he road the only form of sanity that existed to him - the speedcycle. *'Why was that simple, scintillating machine so important, and why does it bother me so much that one oddball Room hasn't accepted my talents, and where is Zeer?'*

During his travels from one lifeglobe to another in search of some meaning beyond himself, he had cared for many women. He had loved, held and shared thoughts and time with those who

24

possessed tremendous minds and egos. He had not sensed, though, in any of them, the calm strength that he had felt in Zeer. He realized that he didn't really know her, but he had learned to always trust his feelings, not only when competing in a Room, but in life as well. The two definitely had similarities. The training for one gave him strength for the other. He simply missed what he could have possibly had with her. He missed Zeer.

***

Simon left his home and was out for a walk. He glanced up and noticed a storm pounding on the protective shell of the lifeglobe. He knew that outside the dome the temperatures were bitterly cold, and it made him shiver just thinking about it. He unconsciously wrapped his arms around himself and continued on.

With every step, he was thinking about the mind-boggling array of experiences that his latest habit had engendered. The universe did not seem as big. His wildest dreams didn't seem as important, and his smile was not as easy or simple as before. In one way, he felt more fulfilled because of his new accomplishments and knowledge, but he also felt more alone and frustrated. His striving had bread a need for even more. He felt confused.

He sat down in the middle of the night, gazing up at two of the three moons that belonged to the tug and pull of R-131, and in that quiet moment, he thought about the men and women who had traveled so far throughout the Milky Way for hundreds of years now. All of them, including everyone on this lifeglobe, had had one ancestral home. They had all come from Earth, and it had been a blue diamond in the midst of a universe of many magical and alluring planets. None, however, in recorded history, had ever been inhabited by the variety and number of brilliant and exuberant forms of life that had existed there. The many stories and compu-tales that Simon had listened to and viewed during his life now journeyed through his active mind. He wished that he'd been able to see and experience that wonderful place.

And with that thought, his eyes moistened and suddenly shards of color blasted across his vision. Without any forewarning, his body was forced onto the hard pavement. He ached to open his eyes but couldn't. His head pulsed, and the sensations in his extremities softened; his entire body had become numb. He panicked with the thought of insanity or disease creeping through his soul. As the moments passed, though, he felt himself give in and relax. He lost consciousness and slept.

***

Slowly Simon awoke and raised his head. He was lying on a luxurious material of some kind. He did not have any pain and was able to function almost immediately, except for a slight drowsiness, which even now was leaving him. He sat up and became aware of a spherical light nearby. He reached down and cradled it in his hands. It's light was warm and calmed him. From the glow of the sphere, he noticed that he was in a room, although its exact features were obscured. He was startled by a simple tender touch. A hand had reached out of the darkness in front of him, caressed his fingers and folded around the luminescence that he held.

Feeling the hand, his first thought was that he had been kidnapped or whisked up onto some Ramjet to forever travel without a name or home. He started to speak, but as his lips parted, he stopped himself. Somehow, he felt the need to remain silent and watch.

The glow between his fingers intensified. His captor, or friend, whichever it might be, was clearly visible. She possessed the eyes of a temptress - vital and yet soothed by lines of ever-present humor. Her hair was long and flowing. The tender brown coloration changed shades in the light as she moved. Her clothes and body language demonstrated serenity, strength and warmth.

The light continued to grow in intensity, but the room still remained dark, with only the immediate surroundings becoming more distinct. She looked directly into his eyes, and in so doing, her features became even clearer. There was power cradled

26

within the softness of her face. She was not young or old, but she was strong and vibrant. Simon was entranced.

She spoke in low musical tones. "Simon. You are part of all. Your knowledge is great, yet it is hidden from you. You are surrounded by the cosmos, yet you are alone and lonely. Look into your hands and stand on the shoulders of the universe."

He looked down, losing himself in the brightness, escaping into the void. He was pulled and tugged deeper and deeper into the radiance, imperceptibly at first and then with increasing velocity. He was becoming a vibrating molecule, a glorious neutron, a rushing cosmic ray speeding through space.

Simon had become the purest sense of being. His physical body gone, he just *was*, his vision clear and precise.

He burst from the brightness into the black void of space. Almost within seconds, he viewed the tremendous power of a supernova. It exploded within the periphery of his vision - gases moving, collecting, swirling. He saw moons as they circled in elliptical swells around huge planets. He was a witness to the universe. He was the universe. Traversing from galaxy to galaxy, solar system to solar system, planet to planet. He was an interstellar wanderer of immeasurable distances. It was more than anyone could hope to absorb or understand.

His movement slowed. In the distance, a spiral galaxy seemed to be his destination. In one of its twisting arms, near a moderately bright sun, were several planets. Each reflected their sun's brilliance with a different aura. One in particular was the size of a pin; yet millisecond-by-millisecond, it was rushing to fill the expanse of his sight. Rushing! Hurtling!

Panic! He would explode on its surface, its beautiful blue surface. It yanked at him with ever-increasing power. His breath was gone, his eyes glued wide. He would surely die.

The fear subsided temporarily as he passed through a thick layer of cold, damp clouds. His respite was short lived, however, as he emerged with the planet's surface accelerating toward him. A massive mountain was below. It was exploding, and he was heading straight for it. The unbelievable speed of his forward momentum carried him closer and closer to the planet.

"Where am I? Why am I here? This is starting to scare the shit out of me?"

He screamed! He was thrown directly down the mouth of a wide, gaping, active volcano. He was doomed.

The sounds, the power, the heat, the violence! A planet was reshaping itself from within its own bowels - a life-giving killer. He would be burned into soft ash, slowly transformed into a hard swirling rock, fossilized. He reeled.

"I can't stand this! What do you want? I want out! Free me!"

Silence.

# 5
## Obsessed

Somewhere in Rad's semiconscious mind he heard knocking sounds, an opening door and steps shuffling hurriedly as someone zigzagged the furniture. He rose up on one elbow and glanced through half-asleep eyes.

"You'll never believe it. I was chosen. Me! She called me. I don't think I made it all the way, but... it was incredible! Rad...!"

"OKAY, stop. You know how bad I am in the morning. Hold on a minute." Rad smacked his lips and shook his head in an attempt to get rid of his overnight cottonmouth and wake up. "Could you get me a glass of water?"

"Sure." Simon ran to get the water. He was definitely being Simon.

Rad wondered, *'What was this all about?'*

Simon hurried back into the room and handed Rad a cup of water. Rad looked up, smiled, shook his head and took a long, slow drink. Simon's impatience was showing.

"Now, talk to me." Rad prepared himself for Simon's excitement.

"I experienced it!"

"What 'it'?"

"*The it*! The Room! The old one! The old woman! She called me, chose me. Without any warning, I was there. I was out last night. I sat down in the southern perimeter. I'd been walking and thinking. With your help, Rad, my eyes have been opened about my home, this world, the universe, the possibilities that exist. The Rooms have expanded my mind, but last night I was lonely. I felt a need to be by myself and think. I sat down. I could feel the night and the quiet of the outer perimeter. It gave me a chance to think, and then it happened. I closed my eyes. A flash of color and light seemed to surround me and then I was there."

"Where?" Rad was astonished, jealous, interested and eager to hear it all. The Room, the old one who didn't seem old, the glow in Simon's palms and the fantastic journey - it was hard to believe. A key had to exist, a key to the reason for the existence of this room. The realism must have been extraordinary. It wasn't hard to see it in Simon's eyes. Rad picked his brain. There had to be a certain action, a set reaction, some reason for Simon being chosen. He probed and searched Simon's brain.

Simon reached the point in his recollections where he shared his tremendous fear with Rad. It was visible. Rad gazed down at Simon's hands. They shook with the force of what he'd experienced. Rad was enthralled. Simon had witnessed the beginning of a world, the joy and power of a living, changing, diverse cosmos – birth and life.

With his hands shaking and his mind spent, Simon sat silently. Rad glanced past his friend and through the outview of his sleeping area. Their brash, sterile world was a lifeless rock compared to the beauty throughout creation, compared to what he had just heard. Simon had stirred some old memories in Rad - his longing for a world such as the one of his ancestors - such as Earth – was resurfacing.

"Simon, that must have been mind-blowing!"

"Yeah, without a doubt, but I'm exhausted now. I've got to go get some sleep. We can talk more tomorrow. Thanks for listening to my hysterics, Rad."

Simon left. The room was now silent, but Rad was filled with questions. 'Would he ever find this magnificent Room? Was it just a game? Who was this temptress that led Simon there, and why was it that Simon had been able to remember everything in such detail when others couldn't?'

***

Three weeks had passed. Tal and Simon had gone back to Rad's quarters many times to discuss what had happened, but to no avail. They searched but couldn't find him even though they had run into several people who had either seen or talked to him recently. As they questioned them, it seemed that he was on some solitary mission in search of those who had experienced the magical, illusive Room. Rad had evidently ended his nightly Room treks in lieu of rambling in and out of nightspots and conversations in search of something only clear to him. One night they did gain a glimpse of him as he flashed down a back street on his speedcycle, but he was gone before they could react. They went home wondering, thinking, remembering. Rad had affected their lives, but he was becoming a memory, a shadowy mythical memory.

\*\*\*

Simon missed Rad but went ahead with his life. He continued pursuing more and more Rooms, becoming better and better at them. He was now a level 3 player. His reputation had increased week by week, while that of his mentor and friend was fading, except for the rumors about the ever-seeking, ever-curious maniac on the speedcycle.

Tal, on the other hand, felt the loss of his good friend more deeply. Rad had a spirit, which Tal could not easily forget. Simon was continually catching him looking down streets, swinging his head around at sounds and glancing into nightspots hoping to catch a glimpse of his old friend. He was a serious man, friendship a serious matter.

\*\*\*

Tal had grown up with an instant power over everyone that he met. His huge muscular frame also possessed a graceful strength. He had a mild sense of humor, a gentle touch and a somber intelligence that many admired. He was a caring man who never abused his strength and was seldom angry. If he were aroused, though, he could be dangerous.

It was late in the afternoon, and Tal was moving through a group of people who had gathered to listen to an impromptu concert. It was a free-day for many, and you could often find small groups performing near the Center. Their music matched the hard and sharp edges of the lifeglobe's architecture. A firm, quick rhythm pounded into his eardrums, while the melody was hidden in synthetic sounds and counter-melodies of digital instruments and affected voices that echoed off the curved clear ceiling of the lifeglobe approximately four hundred meters in the air.

The sounds around him neither mesmerized nor moved him. The sensual feelings of the individuals collectively in the crowd held his interest far more than the pungent counterpoint pounding upon his ears. He had left his living space in a shadowy mood, and there he remained.

Resting his powerful buttocks on the steps of the council building, he observed the festivities and yet remained separate. As he continued to watch, though, he noticed heads, interesting bodies, arms, smiles, laughs and dance-like movements. It seemed that he could never pass up the alluring nature of the opposite sex.

His eyes focused on one particular woman. He observed her movements, read the obvious body language and searched for the not so obvious. She glanced his way. For a split second, she reminded him of Zeer. Closing his eyes and quickly shaking his head back and forth with unbelief, he looked again. He realized that it was not Zeer but a good friend named Lon. Both he and Lon had known Zeer from the training center. A smile crossed his mouth as he chuckled at his serious mood. Lon waved. Tal returned the wave in kind. Maybe things weren't so somber after all.

His knees tensed to stand. His mood had changed, and he'd decided to become part of the day after all. He moved toward Lon. She grinned. Tal quickened his step and reaffirmed his change in mood. He straightened to his full height and grinned back.

Striding positively toward Lon, something moved across Tal's peripheral vision. His eyes shifted, and he saw two individuals that were conversing near the outer circumference of the gathering. Tal slowed his walk. One of the women...no, that wasn't right. The one talking was female; the one listening intently was male. The woman was gesturing with her hands and leaning forward as if she were speaking with passion. The listener was an unkempt sort. His dark beard was shaggy, his clothes definitely early-rag, but his face appeared eager.

Tal felt a light touch on his arm. He glanced around. "Just a moment Lon," and looked away again.

"What is it, Tal? Do you see somebody you know?"

Not looking back but grasping her arm gently to let her know that he didn't want to ignore her, he said, "There are two people way over there. One of them looks familiar. I think..."

He and Lon shuffled through the large crowd in the direction of Tal's eyes for a few moments. Lon was still clinging to his arm as they moved. Suddenly, a burst of speed from the powerful man jerked Lon's hands loose. She was surprised and watched him literally split the crowd in two as he raced ahead. She followed.

Fifty meters, forty-five, forty... The happy free-day gatherers now recognized the commotion before Tal reached them and moved aside to let him through. Thirty-five, thirty... He had lost sight of the man and the woman. He was keying on just getting through the crowd as quickly as possible. There, he could see again. The woman remained. The man... Tal stopped. He looked rapidly in all directions and spotted the painted rags of an individual flying away on a speedcycle. The woman glanced curiously up at Tal as he turned towards her.

"Do you know who you were speaking to?" Tal was panting slightly.

The woman seemed a little nervous. "I don't know his name. Why do you ask?"

"I believe that was a friend of mine. I'm worried about him. I haven't seen him for quite some time. What were you talking about?"

"Is he in some kind of trouble with the council? Are you part of the globe-patrol?"

"No." Tal grabbed hold of his emotions and his breath. He used a habituate breathing technique. A slightly audible sound could be heard as some air passed through his nostrils. "He's a friend. Were you giving him advice? It seemed like you might have been explaining something to him."

"It was not advice I was giving. Rather, it was information about something that is extremely important and dear to me."

"Yes?" Tal's voice resonated as a question.

She seemed calmed now. "I am one of the chosen..."

That simple statement was all that Tal needed to hear. Everyone on R-131 knew the meaning of those six words by now. She had played the Room. Rad was obviously obsessed with the desire to be one of the chosen. He had accomplished more than any other Room player on R-131, and yet this one pearl, this one illusive gem continued to escape him.

Tal talked with the woman a while longer, but she obviously didn't remember a great deal about her experience. Simon had told Rad and he much more about the mysterious Room. *'What was it that Rad was trying to learn? What was he searching for? Was it possibly some key, some consistent piece to the puzzle that would allow him to be able to be chosen? Maybe he was just trying to find clues to the whereabouts of the Room so that he could simply introduce himself as a logical competitor for the old one.'*

As he finished speaking with the woman, Tal again felt a very familiar tug on his arm. It was Lon. She had allowed him to have his space and work out the problem that was obviously intense before asserting herself. He carefully closed his hand around her elbow. She understood. He needed her. He needed a friend to talk with, a woman to understand. She closed her eyes and nodded. They walked off holding each other and talking as Tal remembered the wild-eyed look on Rad's face. He was consumed. He was addicted. He was obsessed.

# 6
## Rad

Rad pushed aside the hair that was constantly in his eyes while he shuffled through pages and rummaged the archives in the Hall of Records. He was irritated, agitated, curious and on the verge of enlightenment. He was working towards a clue - the one tie-in that would make this whole thing reasonable, understandable. Simon had been chosen. Thirty or forty others that he knew of had gone through the experience. No one had returned for a second try. No one had ever gone past the part of the Room where Simon had stopped. And Rad, he had not even had a glimmer of being chosen. *'Why?'* He sometimes wondered if it could have somehow been the company that he kept, his position of prominence in the governing council or possibly his success as a Rooms player. *'Could that have kept him out? What was the common thread woven through those who'd been chosen? Was he pushing himself towards insanity?'*

As he sat there, a thought flashed through his mind, *'Zeer.'* He had not thought of her for some time, although she had remained somewhere in his subconscious. She had not been found. *'Would she have scoffed at his fanaticism? Would she have quietly walked away from him, shaking her head and wondering what had turned him into the madman that he'd become? Why was he so possessed?'* He didn't know, but he was consumed with the need to determine why.

He glanced down the aisle past the rows of terminals through a small outview in the large hall and let his mind wander. Besides the all-consuming purpose that had overtaken him during the last several months, there was one other aspect of his existence that continually gnawed at him. It was the stark emptiness of the ever-consistent patterns that surrounded him. The government, which he had been a part of, was sickeningly consistent from Outpost Q-422, to B-127, to X-701. The nightspots, the eating rooms, the pavement, the slab-curved buildings, the transportation, the living quarters, the art, the music - all of these were molded into the image of a sterile and bland conformity. The plants were the same as any that he had seen on the last four lifeglobes. The air smelled and felt identical to that of his last home. The people...the people, as always, were the one thing that still possessed some irregularity, some diversity, some interest for him. Their appearance varied. Their speech patterns showed originality and individuality. Their emotions could not be predicted, and their needs and interests were somewhat different. Every human was still unique.

Rad was close to complete exhaustion. He hadn't slept for days, had not eaten properly for weeks. He had moved with tremendous intensity towards something that he could not truly define or understand; but move toward it, he did.

Glancing down at his cloak, he noticed in the pocket the small leather book. It was the one Zeer had given him so many months earlier. Quieted by the exhaustion, he reached for it. The soft cover immediately brought back memories of the night that he had seen the wooden door. He opened the book. He hadn't done anything with it since that night. The cool lights in the hall, the hard chair and the table were part of this moment, but not part of Rad's consciousness as a shock moved through his body. Next to his right index finger on the very first page of the book, one word had appeared. The old leather cover came alive in his hands with the discovery. The one single word was "Earth." Visions and memories welled up, and the lonely word assumed a power of its own as he read it over and over again. Consumed by the experience, Rad lowered his head onto the book, closed his eyes and fell into an exhausted, fitful sleep.

# 7
## Zeer

Zeer's conscious feelings were returning. Smell was the first sensation that returned. The membranes within her nose literally screamed with the onslaught of unusual aromas. She had little control of her body. Light-headedness persisted. The lids of her eyes were stiff and heavy. Soft crackling and rustling sounds began to creep into her vague awareness. Her strong body was trembling. She could feel now that she was lying on a comfortable and luscious material. Her hands and facial muscles began to move. Uncontrolled at first, but then with more effort, she was able to reach up and run her fingers along her neck, chin and face. Dull but growing sensations had begun surfacing throughout her body. Alive. She was alive.

'*What was that?*' Another's touch carefully moved across her brow. Her eyes still refused to open. The sensation calmed her more as the movement edged down and touched her eyes. They were fingers. She could tell they were fingers. A flush of increased sensitivity moved through her, caused a shiver and then subsided. The lids covering the pupils of her eyes separated achingly. Strands of mucus ran through her already cloudy vision and a subtle glow appeared and etched itself within her consciousness. It became brighter by the moment and seemed to completely encompass her with serenity and warmth. Raising her shaky head, the light drew her in. It possessed a recognizable appeal. She laid back - her gaze still affixed on the glow, and she realized that the numb feeling was now rushing away. Her normal faculties, if anything would ever be normal again, were returning with uncontrollable tenacity and strength causing her to gasp.

A warm broth was held to her lips. She drank. Her vision had not returned completely, but touch, hearing, smell and taste were vibrant and intense as each stimulus fed each reaction.

The light persisted as the only visual signal that she received. The soft welcoming touch returned, and it, along with the surface that she lay upon, made the experience no less confusing but definitely less stressful. For some inexplicable reason, Zeer felt at home. Tenderness and care surrounded her.

She was being brought back to life with gentle loving concern. The kind touch moved over her living limbs and across her torso. At this point, the realization crystallized that she was unclothed. Her mind reacted and her body tensed, but the light eased her fears and opened her even more to her surroundings. Her breasts filled with warmth, as they were lightly brushed by a hand, which moved along her body and massaged her torso, her legs, her arms. It was as if she could feel the passion of her own conception. Giving into the love that was communicated through touch and the ever-present glow that surrounded her, she accepted and returned that love.

The glow from the soft light then diminished but remained. A tear slid from her eye. She was content. They held each other close and laid together, both covered now with an extravagant blanket. With her eyelids closed, Zeer fell into a natural and welcome sleep. She slept for many hours.

***

Ever since Zeer had risen up on one elbow and the sleep had left her eyes, she had been gazing quietly at her new surroundings. She was located inside what looked to be a large domed cave. The walls of the enclosure were made of solid reddish-brown rock that was rough in texture but was softened by the movement of flickering light upon them. There was a small fire alight near her bed. It felt unbelievably soothing. Zeer was mesmerized.

She rose up off her elbow, pulled the luscious cover up over her body, and began to sip the warm nourishment, which had been given to her by the man whose shadow was dancing across the hardened dirt walls. She didn't know his name. They had not spoken since she had awakened. She wasn't afraid of him. She had, almost without thought, begun feeling close to him. She was alive, and her memory and sanity were returning.

He spoke quietly to her. "Zeer, you're awake. I'm glad. My name is Dominie. I'm from the Learning Cluster here on Loon."

The words startled her. She had not expected them. She looked up from the bowl. He had walked over and was sitting barely a foot away. He was smiling. Zeer returned his smile, somewhat sheepishly. She was beginning to recall her awakening. "Thank you for waking me so slowly. Your touch was very comforting." She felt warm, not only from the broth and the fire.

Dominie noticed her unspoken thoughts. "It's our way Zeer. You are the first for many years who was not born on Loon. We shared to ease your migration and to begin your cycle. Loving and sharing with our energy spheres engaged is how we embrace life, how we learn about and touch each other. It brings us joy and connection. We share freely and bond with each other. As I said, it's our way. It's an important part of life."

"Thank you. It was definitely a unique greeting. If your goal was to help me relax, it worked. I feel calm, but I do have many questions."

"Yes? Let's begin with the first."

"How did you know my name?"

"We've known you were coming for a long time."

"Where am I, and what is Loon?"

"Loon is the name of this planet. It is some fifty light-years from your old home and is located in a different sector of the Milky Way Galaxy."

Her eyes radiated wonder. At the moment, that one statement was almost too much for her to fathom. The colonization of the galaxy, at least to her knowledge, had occurred using only sublight speed spacecraft. She had been on R-131 just yesterday. Fifty light-years...?

Recognizing her puzzlement, Dominie left for a moment and then returned with some clothes, which were similar to his. "All of your questions will be answered in time. For now, if you could put these on, I'd like to show you something."

Taking the clothes, but still bewildered by the answer to her question, Zeer attempted to put them on. Dominie tilted his head and smiled. "Watch me."

Bending over, he pulled slightly on the front of each leg and lifted. The front of the garment separated from the back. He lifted the front of it over his head; the garment was hinged at the neck. It fell to the ground. He wore no undergarments, and yet the clothes fit snug and supported him even while moving. It was a beautiful garment, and Dominie was an extremely well built man. As a habituate, Zeer could tell that his mind and body were in harmony. The skin that covered his body was a light brown, somewhat darker than what Zeer was used to. He had strong but calm eyes that were nestled in a framework of long tawny hair. The color was similar to hers.

"Thanks. I think I can do it." With some effort, she got into the garment. Dominie helped her adjust it to fit. "This material is similar to the blanket you used to cover me. What is it?"

"It's a blend of many different fibers. I'm not sure of the exact process. Only the Weaving Cluster could explain that to you. It's called living cloth. '"Duds" is the common name we use for what you're wearing."

"Duds?" Zeer couldn't help but laugh.

Dominie laughed, too, but then asked, "Will you come now?" He seemed anxious.

"Yes, where?"

"This way."

They walked away from the domed area and into a short tunnel. Immediately Zeer shaded her eyes. Brilliant sunlight came streaming through the opening at the end of the tunnel.

Dominie took her hand. They stopped; the light was brighter than any Zeer had ever seen. "You are about to experience the real, the true. Your cycle has begun. Prepare yourself. Zeer, please look at me."

She immediately raised her gaze to meet Dominie's and felt a flush of mellow calm. She knew that all that she'd been taught, all that she had found out about herself and the Earth, everything that had become part of her from the Room and from working with Fawn on R-131 was about to become real. "I'm ready." They walked toward the light and emerged.

"Unbelievable!" That single, awesome thought traveled into the air rushing past Zeer's lips. Her head slowly moved back and forth in disbelief as her eyes squinted from the brilliant light. She was frozen in her tracks and knew that this moment would affect her forever. "This is astonishing!" She wanted to say something more, shout something more, but sensory overload had simply overcome any words. She was being bombarded with multi-sensory sights, sounds and smells. She kneeled down and put her hands into the moist, warm earth beneath her feet. She held it up close. She saw grains of rock, the tiniest of living creatures scurrying through the debris and bits of dead plant fibers. It was living earth. Never in her life, except during her experience in the Room, had she ever seen this. However, that was a Room, and this was reality on an amazing planet in her own time. Finally, she stood up, looked skywards and took a deep cleansing breath. It was the most important, the best thing of all - open, blue sky – no barriers.

Dominie stood aside knowing that Zeer would need some time. He watched for at least an hour as she walked into the woods near the cave - pausing, looking, touching and examining her new home. She had the look of a young child. He smiled as she found a small stream, cupped her hands and trickled water over her face and onto her feet.

Zeer looked back at Dominie and beamed. She stood and walked back to him. Sitting in front of him, he lifted her chin and looked into her face. A tear glistened on her cheek as she spoke, "Thank you. Thank you for opening this world to me."

"Welcome to Loon, Zeer. You were ready, and you do belong here. Your tears are welcome, and as they drop on the soil, the mother recognizes you. Thank you for being here." Dominie held Zeer close. He felt her joy. Neither of them would ever forget this day.

"Now, you have a long way to go in the next several months. You have much need for knowledge and understanding. There is someone here who will take you on that journey." He then handed her the sphere that was in his hand. "Please, take your sphere with you. It's yours now to keep with you always. Come with me."

He took her by the hand. They walked around the opening of the cave and down a slope. They continued on for about two hours until reaching the edge of a clearing. On their walk, they had spoken little. Zeer was still in a daze – still taking in her new world.

They both heard a sound. Dominie let go of her hand and motioned for her to walk ahead into the middle of an open field. As she did, she noticed that there was a person bent over mumbling to himself. He seemed to be picking plants out of the ground and didn't seem very pleased about doing it.

Zeer looked back to ask Dominie who he was, but he was gone. She was confused but knew that it was important that she meet this person.

"Well, you'd better get over here. I need some help with this."

Without thinking, Zeer found herself on her knees taking orders from someone she had never met before.

"For you to learn isn't going to be easy. Fawn said that you had the essence, and were ready, but she isn't the one who has to hold you by the hand, guide you, and keep you from getting into trouble... "

"Wait a minute! Who are you anyway? And don't talk that way about Fawn."

He stood, and stood, and... He was huge. He was almost as big around as he was tall. Zeer's eyes gaped.

"My name is Landree. I'm one of the leaders of the learning Cluster. You're under my wing now. Look at this." He held a small plant up to her eyes. She looked. It didn't seem that she had a choice. "In the center of the tiny flower, on this tiny plant, is a living universe. Do you see it?"

"No... You know you may be huge and important for some reason, but why are you being such a pain in the butt? Why are you treating me like this?"

His hard stare softened. His belly moved in spasms as he laughed. He turned her around, patted her on the hand and chortled, "I hope the pain I've caused didn't hurt too much."

Zeer laughed too. This old man reminded her of her grandfather. "Landree, you do have a soft side. I think I might be able to learn from you."

He smiled, "Yes, Zeer, I hope so."

# 8
## The Scree

After helping Landree with his plant study, Zeer and he returned to the cave. Landree referred to it as the womb of Loon, and they sat together on the blankets. He took a glowing ball out of one of his pockets, which looked identical to hers, and he placed it on the floor in front of them. After a moment of silence, he touched the sphere. An exact replica of Loon was projected in front of them. Landree used it to guide and help Zeer understand as he began to teach her about her new home. She was shown the many different biomes that covered the planet: rain forests, forests of greens, red forests, short grass tundra, grasslands, savannas, woodlands, deserts, plains and oceans. Many of the names she could recall from the reading that she had done in her leather book about Earth. The forms of plant and animal life were different, but the interdependence on oxygen, carbon dioxide, water, and nutrients was the same.

After her introduction to Loon, she and Landree made many trips over the surface of the planet. They continued to return to the womb to rest and refresh themselves along with using it as a place to discuss what she had been learning and what was to come. On each trip out with Landree, she was immersed in the ecology of Loon. She touched, smelled, tasted, encountered and learned to feel a deep reverence for the microscopic as well as what she could experience with her own senses. They studied food webs, natural genetics, rhythms and cycles within the environment, the understanding of mutual aid, predator-prey relationships, the rise and fall of populations and how the culture on Loon worked with, not against, their environment. As the seasons passed, her love for life and nature grew, and she felt and shared Landree's passion for this exquisite world.

In all of her travels across Loon, Zeer had never seen another person, and even though Landree spoke of his society's obligations and duties, she was beginning to wonder if anyone besides Landree and Dominie lived on Loon. She had broached the subject with him many times, but he'd either ignored her completely or told her to concentrate on the project at hand. She persisted, though, and one day Landree agreed to take her to his Cluster. It was time for her to be with other Loonites, but first he insisted that she meet the Scree. After all she had learned and experienced, she, very truthfully, was more interested in meeting the people of Loon than another organism. However, she also knew that Landree was responsible for the love and knowledge that she now possessed, and she respected him greatly. She agreed.

***

The next morning they had some nourishment and collected their things for the day's journey. Walking out of the cave, Zeer stopped to close her pack. Landree continued on and walked behind some thick bushes near the cave. She heard a slight humming sound. From behind the shrubs, Landree came out, riding in a small, streamlined and transparent bubble. The vehicle was suspended in the air with this huge hulk of a man inside. He smiled a sly grin and waved for Zeer to get in. During her time with Landree, she hadn't been transported in any way, other than using the energy sphere or by walking. She shook her head and smiled. As she stepped into the bubble, she said slyly, "You do use machines!" She had just assumed that it wasn't their way.

"During the time of your first cycle, we do not allow ourselves to handle anything that cannot be made simply by hand with the materials that are available. The one exception is the energy sphere, which, as you will learn, is actually a very important part of who we are. We use this time to concentrate on the power of our mother, feel her pulse and watch the life-blood course through her veins. As we relearn the names of the plants and animals on Loon and watch them interact with the life-giving suns that surround our planet, our lives regain the power and joy that sustain us. We are not stewards who merely take care of Loon. We are Loon. Cycling sustains us, but an organism that is truly alive must move ahead spiritually, physically and mentally.

That is where technology comes in. Yes, we do have machines, super-computers and nanotechnology that interact with our spheres, and we have created many gadgets that aid us in our daily lives. We also have spacecraft, such as this bubble-chair, for local travel, and we have developed mental powers that are far superior to our ancestors. However, we've done all of this with a care, love and understanding for living within our environment and within a dynamic universe. Anyway, enough explanations, you know by now that I can get carried away." Landree laughed. "Now, come with me."

They moved over the land slowly. The vehicle gave them an unobstructed view as they journeyed that day. They traveled level with the treetops, and Zeer, as she had been trained, noticed the successional changes in habitat as they moved away from the mountainous ecosystem near the cave in the direction of Sholar, the great ocean of Loon.

Nearing the ocean, an abundance of estuaries came into view. These were the breeding grounds of Sholar, where the salt-water tides and fresh water from many rivers mixed within the tall grass on the coast. Landree seemed to be moving toward a particular beach near one of the estuaries. He set the vehicle down.

He lumbered out onto the sand and moved toward a small spit that ran out into the water. Zeer followed. He took a long tubular horn from the vehicle. They walked to the end of the spit; the moisture and smell of fresh brine were everywhere. It was a clear day. The sea floaters were hovering and creating the sounds of the sea. Today, puffed clouds dotted the sky. It was warm; a slight breeze came in from Sholar. They sat together at the edge of the water near the end of the spit. The water lapped their ankles.

Laying one end of the horn into the water, Landree placed the other to his lips and blew in short rhythmic bursts. Zeer could not hear any sound but noticed bubbles rising to the surface. Landree blew into the horn for a couple of minutes, his big cheeks puffing out as he expelled each breath. He asked Zeer to take out her energy sphere. Guiding her, placing his hands around it and her hands, he helped her engage the sphere. It began to radiate and glow. It felt warm, and she could sense its connection; a comfortable pulse entered her body. They sat silently. Zeer's eyes were wide and open. Landree's were closed. They waited.

***

A significant amount of time passed. Landree was rock solid in his serenity and concentration, but Zeer was beginning to fidget. She raised her gaze and looked out across the ocean. There, a short distance from shore was a huge broiling on the surface of Sholar. Zeer could hear puffs of air and observed great shafts of water blown upwards. Suddenly, a gigantic body shot from beneath the surface into full view. It filled her vision. It was at least sixty meters in length. It was a deep grey color with triangular shaped fins halfway down its length on the lower part of its body. It possessed a tail that was much larger than any single animal that she'd seen on Loon. Yet, with all of its mass, it had propelled itself completely above the ocean's surface, its mouth agape. Several of Zeer could have jumped inside. She couldn't help herself. She stepped back and screamed!

Landree opened his eyes. "Quiet Zeer. Kneel down."

"What...what is that?"

"Scree."

Landree placed the horn back into the water, blew a different sequence into the horn. Stopped. Waited.

Several of the huge creatures moved close to shore. As they did, Landree continued to hold Zeer's hand with the sphere in it. She was incredibly apprehensive at this point, but he had never given her any reason to doubt him. He encouraged her forward, and they began walking further out into the surf. When the water was waist high, he let go of her hand and said, "Lower the energy sphere into the water. Hold it tightly." He had never allowed her to use her sphere until that moment.

Zeer cupped it firmly between her palms and did as Landree suggested. Her hands and limbs were shaking from the cold of the water and from the fear of the unknown. The huge creatures were but a few meters in front of her. Landree then asked her to open herself, to breathe and allow her mind to listen. He had taught her the meaning of self-awareness and energy flow. She breathed in and blew out. She could feel the sphere's influence entering her. She felt stronger.

Landree whispered in her ear. "Zeer, speak to the Scree."

"My...name...is...Zeer."

The Scree spoke to her. "Zeer, mine is Calna. I sense your fright. Look into my eyes."

Right in front of her, the head of one of the Scree broke the surface of the water and rose up, towering above her. She forced herself to look into its eyes.

"You have fear in you. Release it. I will teach you."

Zeer willed herself to relax. She listened and learned from Calna about the geological history of Loon and about the Scree.

During the billions of years that brought Loon to its present state, the Scree's development transpired through a series of interactive events. The double star system that warmed and lighted Loon's surface, was located a particular distance from the surface of the planet. A combination of the gravitational pull and energy from those suns, the violent explosions on the surface of Loon and the strong pull of the two orbiting moons around Loon created its atmosphere. As that atmosphere deepened, the hydrosphere on Loon began to grow. Water was literally being pulled from the rocks and lava. The moisture then condensed and collected in the layer of gases above the planet. These gases acted as a greenhouse, collecting heat and moisture. It wasn't long, in geologic time, before the rains started.

As the hydrosphere developed, more and more showers began pummeling the surface of Loon. Sholar was being born. With the birth of the great ocean, the ability of its new atmosphere to hold in moisture and heat and the continuing source of energy from Loon's two suns, life soon followed.

The basic process was similar to Earth's metamorphoses, although the exact mixture of gases within the atmosphere and the make-up of Loon's crustal plates were different. Life on Loon soon began to broil at the edge of the sea in the tide-pools and in the small, moist and muddy crevices on the land. The evolution of life on Loon had begun, and with it, the chance events that lead to the eventual development of the Scree.

Life on land was abundant, but no one creature had taken that step towards truly advanced intelligence that man had taken on Earth. Through thousands of mutations and the abundance of food sources in the great ocean of Loon, the Scree moved forward on the evolutionary chain with tremendous speed. Their ancestors were much smaller but with the size of their skull, the lack of predators and the fact that their food source, a plant called pludides, was abundant gave them the edge to begin their climb to dominance, not only in size but also in intellect.

The Scree developed a communal living style, which they have fostered and continued for thousands of years. They have few enemies, but they maintain a constant population out of respect for Loon. They are still vegetarians, by choice, even though they could easily develop ways to kill and consume prey. They migrate as nomadic tribes to the areas in Sholar that, at varying times of the year, hold the greatest amounts of pludides. They are a proud and sentient species with an undying reverence for their home and for life.

Zeer sat on the beach exhausted. She was still gazing incredulously out toward where she had met Calna. Her body was shaking as the breeze robbed her of valuable moisture. She had no idea that she might be in danger, never having been exposed to the elements to this degree. Landree was beside her and placed a blanket around her.

"The Scree were so...calm...so...serene. I'm in awe. I've just met another life form with human-like intelligence, with emotions, beliefs, hopes and dreams. Their intellect was incredible. They have so much to teach us. How did the people of Loon ever find them and start communicating?"

"It took many years. After we arrived, we first had to create our own settlements and culture so that we could survive on Loon.

We had noticed the Scree and observed their habits, but it took over a hundred years before we were aware of their intelligence. At that point, our Science Cluster had developed a way to communicate with them. That was an incredibly important moment for us and for the Scree. We have learned a great deal from each other, and now we coexist – the Scree being superior within the realm of the great ocean of Sholar, and we on the land. We love and care for their home on Loon, and they honor us with the same reverence for the land. We understand our interdependence, and ideologically, our cultures are similar."

Landree stood and gave Zeer his hand and helped her up. He knew that it was time to get her out of the elements and back to his Cluster. She was reluctant to go. She had witnessed a new life - the kind of life that man had been searching for, for centuries.

Zeer and Landree walked slowly back to the bubble-chair. It was still floating over the beach. Without a word, they each grabbed onto the handholds, stepped inside and traveled to Landree's Cluster - the Learning Cluster of Loon.

\*\*\*

A tear passed over Dominie's cheek as he watched the interaction between Zeer and the Scree. He had seen and felt the emotion that had overtaken her. He smiled and thought about how the Scree was such a proud and respected species.

Dominie had kept in close contact with Zeer's education. She never knew, but at the end of each work period he had communicated with Landree. Through Landree's thoughts and mental pictures, transported via the energy sphere, Dominie stayed informed. He'd come to respect Zeer's intelligence, her curious nature and the deep passion that she had developed for Loon. She had grown in the ways of the cycle in a very short time. All of the Clusters were honored by her. Fawn had chosen well.

\*\*\*

The Loonites who were part of the Learning Cluster knew

that Landree and Zeer were on their way. They had begun to prepare to welcome her. It would be a once in a lifetime celebration, as she was the first human to come to Loon who had not been a direct descendent of those born on the ship from Earth.

Landree nudged Zeer and pointed, "We're nearing the Cluster."

Zeer strained her eyes. All that she could see in front of her was a typical coniferous forest on a southern slope with a large grassy meadow nearby. She didn't detect anything unusual. She had assumed that she would see large buildings or some other evidence of human civilization, although, during her time on Loon, she had never seen anything of the kind. Even so, Landree was becoming visibly excited with a huge smile wrinkling his eyes.

The vehicle slowed and swooped closer to the trees. Below them, clearly visible, were hundreds of people. Behind them, was the glint of what looked to be some type of reflective material imaging the surroundings, including the incoming vehicle containing Landree and Zeer. The buildings of the people were literally in the hills with glass-like, reflective facades opening to the world around. No wonder she had never been able to see them. The structures of their society were part of their world and mirrored their environment.

The bubble-chair landed. The crowd pushed forward. The two were greeted with open arms, smiles, and feelings of warmth and love. Zeer was overwhelmed. She had not seen more than two humans at a time for many cycles. She simply went with the flow, carrying an interminable smile on her face. Someone grabbed her arm, swirled her around and planted a warm, loving kiss on her cheek. She stepped back and looked. It was Dominie. She wrapped her arms around him. It was great to see someone else that she recognized and cared for. The sun was bright - the day beautiful. Zeer was filled with love for her new home and the astonishing gift of knowledge that had been given to her.

The celebration went on for many segments. Representatives from most of the Clusters of Loon were present, and many other Loonites were able to experience the gathering and welcomed Zeer through the use of their own energy spheres.

The celebration was filled with laughter, food, games and many, many stories. All of which were a joy for the people to share with Zeer and were a means by which she was able to learn more about them. It seemed that the sharing of their history and collective knowledge were a huge part of their culture, and at the end of the day's celebration, Zeer sat down and put to paper much of what she had learned that day.

All of the Loonites in every Cluster were descendants of the original immigrants from Earth. These immigrants were a chosen few who had been conceived in the dead of space within an experimental spaceship. A group of people from Earth had formed a plan in which they had built an experimental galactic ramjet that they had hoped could travel at or slightly faster than the speed of light. The ship was run totally by computers and robots. When it left Earth, there was not a single human on board. The ship's cargo had been the DNA from many of Earth's so-called legends, leaders, greatest poets, scientists, engineers, artists, musicians, athletes and geniuses. A few randomly chosen genetic representatives were thrown in for variability. The mission was to search for a habitable planet in Earth's galaxy - one that could sustain life as Earth had. If one was found, the robots and computers were capable of starting up a small colony of Earth babies from the genetic material maintained on the spacecraft. The craft would then orbit the planet until enough was learned about its environment, and the humans had grown to an intellectual and physical age capable of dealing with the problems of colonization and beginning a new society. The immigrants were the first generation on Loon. The members of all the Clusters were the descendents of those immigrants.

The Loonite civilization had developed ways of clustering their talents. There were those who were great learners. They collected the knowledge of Loon and stored it in an amazing super computer system that was tied to each individual's energy sphere. They also passed on that knowledge to the young and old, as learning was a life-long, continual process. There were other Clusters as well. There were the Building and Engineering Clusters. The members of those had developed ways for the people of Loon to survive by living within the energy limits of their environment, using the power of the suns and other renewable sources to meet the demands of their population. There was a Healing Cluster, an Agricultural Cluster, an Environmental Study Cluster, and a Technology Cluster, along with many others. All of them had, as their consuming and overriding philosophy, the importance of working together to preserve and enhance all life on Loon. They loved and cared for their home and for each other.

***

Zeer was sitting in her apartment thinking about her life. She had been on Loon for many cycles now and was filled with wonder at the quality of her good fortune. Out her window was an exquisite land. As she looked out across her new home, she could not help thinking back on the past. She thought of the lifeglobes, the planets, the wandering and the barren nature of all those places she had lived. She also recalled the devastating history of Earth that she had experienced after being chosen by Fawn for the Room and the unbelievable beauty of the struggle and diversity of the people who continued to survive all over the galaxy. These people were living on planets whose ability to sustain life was negligible at best. They endured because of their ingenuity, creativity and determination. But just surviving wasn't enough. On every lifeglobe, the people continued to search for diversions to give more meaning to their lives. She understood more than ever now that the Rooms had been created for that purpose. But the real dream was the drive to move on, to find that speck of dust within the gigantic scale of the universe that would, as Earth had once done, provide the human race with another chance to live free and open on a living planet.

As Zeer pondered all this, she looked out at the stars. It was calm outside. Sholar, a short distance away, ebbed and flowed upon the land. The sound was always near as this Cluster was just a few hundred meters from the ocean. Zeer reached inside the pocket of her garment and pulled out an object. It carried memories that were still very strong to her. She immediately thought about Rad. He had been in the back of her mind for a long time.

She looked again at the object. It lay open on her lap, its leathery cover smooth and worn. She opened it. The pages were covered with hundreds and hundreds of words. It was a book, an open book, a teaching book, a book of life. At present, there was only one other like it in the universe.

# 9
## The Room: Level 1

They grasped Rad's shoulders lightly but firmly enough to support him. His head lay on the table between the rumpled sleeves covering his arms. Tal and Simon had discovered Rad in the Hall of Records. A friend had noticed him and contacted them. He was unconscious. Their concerned, persistent jostling aroused him. A leather book fell from his grasp. Tal put it back into Rad's pocket. His half-awake speech was nonsensical as they guided him outside and into an air-cab.

After arriving at Rad's home, they undressed him. His tattered and dirty clothes and his body reeked from several weeks of frenetic activity, spilled food, sweat and the lifeglobe. They gave him a bath of sorts and laid him on his bed, covering him with a blanket. He barely woke during the process and was out again. Tal laid Rad's clothes aside and checked the pockets. He found notes scribbled with names, numbers and nonsensical words as well as the unusual book that he had placed there. He put everything that he'd found on the stand next to Rad's bed. Tal and Simon sat on the bed looking down at their friend. He lay there weak and haggard. He had lost weight, and his face was bearded. The change in him was discomforting.

Hours passed, and during that time Tal and Simon had been able to wake Rad enough to give him small amounts of food and drink and bring in a healer to check him over. Their suspicions were confirmed. He was simply suffering from exhaustion and a slight case of malnutrition. He needed rest, liquids and food. They decided that they would continue to take care of him and watch over him; Tal would stay one day and Simon the next. They were determined not lose him again or let him out of their sight. Every once in a while he would try to wake up. He kept mumbling. They couldn't make out what he was trying to say. In the state that he was in, it didn't really matter. They simply continued to watch over him and wait.

***

It was late in the day, and Tal had just come back to give Simon a breather. Simon was asleep in a chair outside of Rad's bedroom. Tal walked over and touched Simon on the leg. "Are you awake?"

"Uh...sure, sure. You're back, huh?"

Tal held his index finger up to his lips and whispered, "We ought to do something with those clothes. I can't stand their smell any longer. I'll get them out of his bedroom and put them down the cleaning shoot."

"Yeah. Okay." Simon struggled forward, placed his hands on his knees and rubbed his eyes. "What time is it? How long have I been here?"

"About twenty hours."

The living area, outside Rad's bedroom, was cast in darkness with small eye-level lamps spreading enough light for Tal and Simon to see where they were going in the room. Rad's food dispensing device and techno-entertainment wall gave off minimal light as well, but the mood and feeling in the room were somber.

Tal entered Rad's darkened bedroom. He felt his way around and followed his nose to where Rad's clothes were laying. He began gathering them up to put them into the shoot, and as he did so, he thought of the book that he'd laid on the stand near Rad's bed. Books like that one were extremely rare, and he'd made a mental note to take a look at it when he had a chance. He walked over to where he'd placed it and glanced down. The piles of paper and notes remained, but the book wasn't there. Bending down, he looked under the stand to see if it had fallen beneath, but to no avail. He immediately thought of Simon. He picked up the final piece of clothing and walked out of the bedroom. He looked over at Simon who was sitting, drinking tea. "Where did you put the book, Simon? I'd like to take a look at it tonight."

"What book?"

"The book that we picked up when we found Rad."

"I don't know where it is. It's got to be here somewhere."

Simon stood and helped Tal look. They raised the lighting

in the room to help. They moved a chair, searched the counters and checked all of the living area. Then they turned to go back into Rad's sleeping quarters. As they did, they heard Rad groan. They rushed into the dark room. The pupils of their eyes struggled to adjust, and in their rush, they misjudged the location of Rad's bed and both of them stumbled onto it. The bed was empty. Rad was gone.

***

Harsh and cool surfaces broke through Rad's wall of unconsciousness. A murky light ushered in a sense of reality as the foggy wall lifted. He was groggy but awake. He sat on the ground with his back against an unopened doorway in an ally. Another building's outer surface stared back at him. He supported himself with his palms by pushing down against the pavement; small indentations of rock and dirt creased the skin of his hands. He shook himself, waking up but not really knowing where he was.

As suddenly as his consciousness had returned, he noticed a woman's hand reaching out for his. He looked up into her smiling eyes and accepted her help. He was still weak, shaky and confused, but he stood as she supported him. She had one arm around his waist and the other holding his forearm. She gently urged him to turn around and said, "Let's go in, Rad."

'*How did she know my name?*' But just as he had asked himself that question, he saw the door in front of him. It was "the door"...the brown wooden door that he'd seen months ago! Surprised and still confused from coming out of such a deep sleep, he watched her turn the bronze handle and followed her inside.

The room was dark yet very warm and comfortable. His eyes settled. "Uh...who are you? Why am I here?"

The woman did not answer. She sat him down on a supple, luxurious rug, then turned and walked off in the direction of some hand-woven curtains hanging from the ceiling of the room. She passed behind them, and Rad watched her obscured figure as she reached down into a box. When her hands came

56

back up again, one seemed to glow, the other held something solid.

The glow from her hand was familiar to him and gave him a feeling of peacefulness and confidence. The light held his attention, and while he watched it, the woman returned. Sitting down with him, she held out a bowl of liquid. Taking it, Rad felt somewhat wary, but began drinking from the bowl. He felt his stomach growl. His appetite was returning, and he found the broth to be warm and delicious. It was spiced in such a way that its flavor exploded in his mouth. She smiled at his wide eyes. He ate ravenously.

"I've waited for you for some time, Rad. You've put yourself through a great deal during the last few months."

"I don't know you. How do you know me, and what do you mean you've been waiting for me?" In between gulps, he was looking into her eyes as if the answers to his bewilderment were there.

"Eat and we'll begin. Then you'll understand."

She laid a small glowing sphere on the rug. It seemed to exude some part of her, some connection to her. She walked away. Rad finished eating and continued to stare at the light. He felt somewhat unsteady again and decided to lie down for just a moment until the woman returned. His heavy eyes wouldn't be denied. They closed, and he slept hard and deep - the rest of a warrior at the end of a long battle.

***

Awake again, Rad felt much better than he had for a long time. His vision was extremely acute and his senses tingling with awareness. He heard footsteps and looked up to see the woman coming back into the room. She kneeled in front of him. He looked at her more closely now. He tried, but could not distinguish her age. She saw him looking and smiled. She asked him to sit directly across from her with the glowing sphere in the palm of his hands.

Rad did as he was asked. Then she spoke, "Are you

ready, Rad?"

He hesitated and gazed back at her, and before he could respond, his journey began.

His consciousness exploded outward through the universe at tremendous speeds, while his body had been reduced to the microscopic. At that moment, the thought came to him that he must finally be in the presence of the old one, the one who steered the Room. The realization was bread from the many hours of his maniacal search - the many interviews, his obsession and the hours upon hours of research. He had finally been chosen. At least, he thought he had.

The reality in front of him took his breath away. He was passing through the same stages that Simon and many other lucky travelers had experienced. He prepared himself. He knew that he would not have a chance to continue on and play the many levels of this Room unless he could somehow survive the first, but what was the final test of this level. Obviously, know one, at least know one that he knew about, had found out. He did everything to relax. His single-celled journey continued.

In the swirling stellar view that was passing through and around him, a blue dot appeared, just as it had for Simon. Rad's mind grasped the meaning instantly as it swiftly focused in front of him. It was Earth - a spherical, blue, precious pebble on a black velvet stage. Leaping past Earth's sun, his speed increased radically. Earth's details began leaping toward him as he flew faster and faster towards its surface. He was trying to understand and control his terror and the heart-pounding thrill of this Room. He breathed, or at least tried to breathe. He wasn't sure that a single molecule traveling at the speed of light through space needed to, but he attempted it – needed it. He trembled and did his best to remain as focused as humanly possible, placing the experience at the forefront of his mind, not his fear.

Clouds, coolness and air all rushed by as Rad entered the Earth's atmosphere. On the descent, he was changing. He was gaining substance and morphing back into his original form. Directly below, the Earth was evolving in massive explosions of energy. He was present at its birth. Immense volcanoes were erupting all around, boiling lava into the sea.

Faster and faster, Rad sped downwards, and now he could see it. Directly in front of him was the mouth of a single volcano, the one that Simon had experienced. It was enormous and angry. He knew that he was going to be thrust into its fathomless depths. Within seconds, lava and ash surrounded him. He set his jaw to the task. Death and life were there. He was thrown into, sacrificed into, the Earth.

Heat. Red light. Yellow. Black. The fierce explosions were searing and burning his flesh away. His descent continued; he was being catapulted deeper, reduced, melted down, changed into his simplest form.

Then darkness and silence arrived like a hammer blow, and in that darkness, the part of him that still survived curled into a ball and floated within the very bowels of the Earth. His heart slowed. His mind began to accept his surroundings, and a real, live, living planet caressed and accepted him in return. He was humbled and touched by joy. He was home.

Shaking from the experience, Rad slowly opened his eyes. He had returned from his journey and was lying curled into a ball on the floor. In front of him, the glow from the sphere in his hands was dancing across the face of the old one, and she spoke to him with her eyes. She illuminated him with love. He rested.

***

Clutching the silk-like bed cover in his sleeping quarters, Rad was shocked to find himself home again. He could still see the old one's face burned into the retinas of his eyes. For just a few seconds, it seemed that she was there. He clumsily rose up and sat on the edge of his bed. He remained there for a long time gathering his senses. Then through his muddled memory, he recalled that Tal and Simon had been with him, helping him to recover. He stood to give them a call on the video-link, but as he did so he heard someone rushing into his room. In front of him were his two friends.

"My God Rad, what's going on? We heard you moan, then

we checked to see what was wrong. You just disappeared. What happened? This is really strange!"

"Okay, okay Simon. Give him a chance." Tal did his best to calm the excitable Simon.

Rad motioned for both of them to sit down. He was trying to organize his thoughts. They sat down, looked toward Rad and both gasped at the same moment. Simon pointed at Rad. "That's incredible! Look at his eyes. They're burning inside. Rad go look at your eyes."

Rad stood and looked into a mirror. Somehow, he knew what was happening. The Earth, old Earth's fire, was still burning inside him. He knew what to do. "Come here," he said carefully. Rad understood that at that point both Tal and Simon would be somewhat leery of him, but despite their apprehension, they drew near. Rad asked them to stare into his eyes. As they did, he sensed something inside one of his pockets. He reached down and found a small, smooth, warm sphere. His hand tingled with its touch. Keeping that hand inside his pocket on the sphere, he reached out with the other and had them place their hands around his. Rad felt the energy from the sphere grow and surround them. They shared as Rad passed on to them what he could, without saying a word.

They all sat down after the encounter. Rad's eyes had ceased to burn, but inside he knew that he was a different person.

"You were there Rad? I knew that you were destined to find the Room." Tal had carried a burden of worry for several months, and to find Rad, lose him, and have him return again affected him deeply.

"Yes I was."

"I knew it. I knew it. Could you believe it? Fantastic, huh! The memory has faded for me, but when you shared with us, it all came back. How did you do that? I think you passed, Rad. Can you survive another level of that game?" Simon was incredibly perceptive and, as usual, very passionate.

"All I can think about now, Simon, is getting more rest, eating some good food and then going for a ride on my speedcycle after I recover. I need some time to think and try to absorb what I've gone through."

"I've never asked if we could before," Tal said with some reluctance, "but I was wondering if we could ride with you. I think I can get some bikes and suits to wear from the training center. We'd like to come." Simon agreed.

"The company would be great. No one has ever asked before. Sure."

Tal and Simon left to get the bikes, and Rad lay back on his bed, knowing that some more rest would be incredibly welcome at this point. Before nodding off, he thought of his friends and was looking forward to riding with them. Both of them had been so good to him, each in their own way.

***

Tal and Simon returned after a couple of hours and woke Rad. He felt much better. His friends had picked up some of his favorite food, and they all ate, talked and laughed about recent events. It was great to catch up on life and get ready to ride again.

Rad adjusted the speedcycles to fit Tal and Simon, and they were just about to leave when Rad went back into his sleeping quarters to get his cycling gloves. He glanced down at the covers on his bed once more, thinking back to their feel when he awoke. Lying on top of them was his book. He must have had it with him in bed during his recovery. Between the extended time in bed and the excitement of the Room, Rad hadn't thought of it for a while. It lay there and seemed to beg him to pick it up. He laughed at his flare for the dramatic that had developed over the last few months. He picked it up and also took the energy sphere from of his pocket. He casually looked inside the book. The pages no longer had just one or two words. They were completely full, each and every page. He couldn't help his disbelief. He sat down for a moment and gazed at the pages, but he knew that right now he simply couldn't deal with this, too much had happened. He needed to clear his mind. He stood back up, slipped the book and sphere under the covers, pulled his helmet on and went out to ride with Tal and Simon. There would be time to figure all this out later.

# 10
## Into the Desert

Rad stopped for just a moment and looked back at the lifeglobe. From this perspective, it was infinitesimal and fragile in contrast to R-131, which itself, was simply a tiny nugget in the universe. The planet seemed endless as Rad's footprints marred its surface. In a way, he felt ashamed to be stepping on the barren soil outside his home. The original settler's tracks had been blown away long ago. His seemed virgin. The moons were out tonight, following his progress as he ventured toward the Sharp Mountains, at least a two-day traverse from the lifeglobe.

Through his visor, R-131 was a study in black and white. A canvas covered with shadows, lines and stark scenes of hostile intent. Its minimal atmosphere served to burn up the meteor showers attempting to broach its crust, but deep craters still gave evidence to its explosive past. Rad continued on, using the light on his helmet, skirting obstacles and stepping carefully across the virgin soil. In his mind, he felt exposed, even though he was protected by his survival suit and helmet. He knew that any malfunction or mistake could cost him his life. Of course it was dangerous to exit the safety of a lifeglobe alone, but the experience was already worth it. Being outside brought an authenticity that he could never experience from within. He was alone in the wilderness of this planet. Hardly anyone in recent history had traveled this far on foot. Rad felt alive.

\*\*\*

Five days earlier, Rad had tried to go back to the Room to meet the old one. He now knew the location because of the wooden door and felt that he had to get some answers and needed to understand why he'd been chosen, what connection this leather book had to his experience and simply what all this was about. When he arrived, he'd knocked but no one answered. He'd tried the handle, but it was locked, so he sat down and waited, but no one arrived.

While sitting there, Rad realized that if he couldn't ask the old one his questions, then he would have to use the one thing that he'd been given and find his own answers – the leather book. There must be some connection between that book, the Earth and the Room. He decided to leave the lifeglobe and get away. He needed to be alone – completely alone - somewhere where he could immerse himself in study and seek out the answers that he needed. He'd recovered quickly enough from his last ordeal, and the speedcycling that he'd done with Tal and Simon had helped him to get ready for another strenuous and lonely journey.

Because of his previous association with the government and the inner-workings of this lifeglobe, he had made friends within the maintenance crews on R-131 and had convinced one of them, a woman named Shee, to let him borrow a survival station for his journey. This included a small hand-drawn cart to transport it and an oxygen interface that would last for about two months for one person. He gathered enough food and water for more than a month, took with him a small compu-tablet with 3D-maps from the original computer imaging of the planet, various other survival paraphernalia and the well wishes of Shee. He had not told Tal or Simon about his latest escapade and didn't want to have to tell them about the leather book.

Before leaving, he also downloaded information on the ancient arts of mind control and meditation, writings on poetry, everything he could find about Earth, a series on current quantum physics and finally some information about the techno-history of space travel and the human search for another Earth-like planet. He wanted to have everything that he might need.

***

Rad's trek was solitary, yet free. He needed to learn. He needed to understand his origins, what had happened on Earth and what it was to be human. He needed adventure. He needed to feel.

His first encounter with the old one and the Room had changed him. He knew that change was part of everything in the universe. People changed. The lifeglobes changed, breaking down after a time and needing repair. This planet changed. Tal changed. Simon had changed. Zeer...she was gone. That was a change. *'Why did he have such longing? Why?'* For now, he simply needed to stop thinking and put one foot in front of the other. This would be an important journey.

\*\*\*

Gone again. Tal and Simon had come to terms with Rad's latest disappearance. The news had spread throughout the lifeglobe about the crazy man losing it one more time. The big question was, *'Where was he?'* The news' vids buzzed with speculation. Out of necessity, only Shee knew that Rad had left, and he had asked her to let Tal and Simon know in a couple of days and tell them that he was okay. He just needed some time.

"That guy's strange, Tal. We get him back. Help him. He seems fine. Then the old disappearing act again."

"He's searching Simon. The contact with the old one, his experience in the Room and his long search has had an effect on him. I think we just need to let him be who he is and go on living our lives. That's important. We can wonder, but it's his life. I know we'll see him again."

Simon shook his head. He did understand, though, more than he let on. After all, he too had experienced the Room. It had affected him greatly. All he had to do was close his eyes, and he remembered it as if it were just happening. He thought of Rad and believed as Tal had that they would see him again. *'What changes would there be in him?'* He wondered.

\*\*\*

Naked. The freedom of nudity anywhere, even if it was inside a small survival-dome was exhilarating and joyful. Maybe it came from when we were children, or maybe it was simply from not being confined by our clothes, but it was stimulating and helped Rad think. Within his temporary new home many kilometers from the lifeglobe on R-131, he read, consumed and devoured unbelievable amounts of information and ideas. The Earth, once a living breathing entity, had been filled with such promise. Life had boiled on its surface, floated within its oceans and even survived deep inside its crust. Its evolution sustained the ebb and flow of succession and the delicate balance and interdependence of ecosystems. The growth and demise of the human culture and of the planet itself had been cultivated and nurtured by mistrust and hate, racism, religion, greed and power. The warning signs were there. The gadflies drew blood with their counsel, but the human species continued to fuel the race towards the destruction of this jewel, this one-in-a-billion planet.

As Rad meditated, a tear moved down the face of his solitary being, on this small spec in the Milky Way, a solar system among billions in an infinite universe. Yet that small drop of water carried with it the beginnings of life. It had traveled billions of miles through eons of time. Maybe it was from rocks on another planet that had been released by some dynamic cataclysm. Possibly it had once been part of the Earth's oceans. *'Could it have been the same drop that had come from the eye of a child that had starved in Ethiopia or in New York? Could it have come from the spittle of a man congested from the burning air in London? Could it have run down the cheek of a mother in Asia watching her child die from a disease garnered from fouled and polluted water? Or could it have simply been a drop transpired from a plant on Earth?'* The one drop turned into many as Rad poured his heart onto the floor. His meditation was a difficult one as his mind traveled over the contents of the beautiful leather book.

The handwritten pages seemed to be endless. The book was small, but after absorbing one part, that section vanished and the next lesson began. This progression, Rad found, would not occur without the small sphere. Somehow, the connection of the sphere and the book brought about the words on the pages and allowed him to learn. He didn't understand the connection but was grateful for the knowledge.

It taught him of Earth's formation, the process of evolution and change, energy flow, cycles, biospheres and succession, the driving force of sex and reproduction, the beauty of life, the connectivity of all life, human history and cultures, world religions and other meditations, wild creatures, plants and places, soil, water, uncontrolled populations, energy, corporate greed, waste, pollution, toxicity, exploitation, nationalism, war, violence, bureaucracy, exploration and colonization, entropy, sadness, the dormancy of Earth, the small life-force that remained and a view of the human species since leaving earth. It covered so much and the beauty and power of the words consumed him. Rad pulsed with joy, anger, frustration, grief, hypocrisy and wonder.

Earth had been such an extraordinary, joyous ball of fire and diversity. *'What we had, and what we lost!'* He desperately needed rest. He slept.

***

Rad was awakened by the wind outside his survival dome; the fabric was talking to him as waves of air crossed the surface and small particles of dirt struck and danced away. He had placed the dome in a protected hollow surrounded by rocky crags. The wind was almost soothing, as he'd become used to these intermittent storms. He felt as if he were part of this world as it spoke to him, communicating its moods and feelings.

He gathered himself up, doing his best to clear his head for the day to come, and glanced out through the skyview that was built into the dome. The sun was rising, and the colors on the horizon were brightened and accentuated by the dust particles kicked up by the storm. Many diverse shades and hues of color were airbrushed upon the sky, painting a subtle texture across the horizon. Rad was happy here, but he wondered about his ancestral home. *'What would it have been like to wake to a storm there, walk outside and have it actually touch my skin?'*

As he had for many days, he spent his time reading and learning from the contents of the old leather book. He also used his compu-tablet to view maps of old Earth and pictures of areas that he had studied that day. In addition, he accessed articles and some videos from Earth's past. However, his studies were still incomplete. The old book concentrated mainly on the development of Earth's environment and civilization up to a certain point, indicating that something drastic had occurred without actually pinning down exactly what had happened and why. From the digital records that he'd downloaded from the lifeglobe's library, he knew that his ancestors from the Shelters had only been able to bring a percentage of Earth's recorded history with them. For some reason, there were very few records from the two hundred years before they had left Earth.

Rad took breaks to eat and glance outside at his surroundings, but it had been a day like many others. They had begun to blend together in his mind, and towards evening, as the night began to touch the planet, he sat and organized his thoughts from the day and laid out his tasks for the next. Before eating, he meditated, sitting quietly, his eyes closed, listening to soft, healing music and to the sounds of the oncoming night. But during his meditation, there was another sound, one that didn't fit. It was distracting, out of place and foreign. Rad opened his eyes. He had heard a thud followed by scraping and shuffling. It grew louder and more distinct as it pressed against his consciousness. He stood and glanced out the skyview, but the night blocked his vision. Inside the survival station, the small nightshines had begun to glow, further hindering his view outside. The vibrations persisted as Rad sensed a primordial adrenaline rush. His senses were becoming acute – his fear quickened. He turned his head, needing to focus on the location and intent of the sounds, and as he did, they vanished.

Rad didn't understand. It had been so clear, so close by. He took several deep breaths and blew out some carbon dioxide, cleansing his body and loosening his muscles. He settled back down, sighed and shook his head. *'Had this simply been foolishness?'* It was probably just his mind playing tricks on him. After all, he'd just been meditating, and he had been alone for quite a while now.

He relaxed, glanced again towards the skyview and lowered the light inside the dome. His tension eased still more as he could now see the stars that dotted the dark, silken sky. Each flickering light soothed him, along with the realization that other humans, like himself, were scattered across the same fabric of space. He felt less alone and wondered if any of his fellow humans had found another Earth-like planet. He hoped that they had, and that thought brought forth in him again his ancient need to breathe fresh, pure air and his dream of being able to lie down unencumbered on the surface of a planet and look up at an open, star-ridden sky.

\*\*\*

Fawn smiled at what she had seen in the small sphere within her upturned palm. Rad was adapting, changing. He was consumed. He was learning. He was becoming. The book had nourished him. His meditations calmed him. The next level of the Room would make it real. He was ready.

\*\*\*

The storm had abated and the strange sounds were gone. Rad lay back, gazing through the pages of the small book one last time before he slept. He thought of the time when Zeer had given him the book. 'Where had it come from? Where had she gotten it, and why had she given it to him?' Her eyes and the look of her were as fresh in his mind as the book in his hands. Zeer was such a beautiful mystery.

He put the book aside and turned off the small lights inside the dome. He was exhausted and ready to rest. Closing his eyes, he quickly fell asleep. It seemed that his dreams came sooner than usual that night. He dreamed of waking inside his shelter. He crawled to the door, unsnapped the layers covering the opening, crawled through the outer entry and left his small home. He gazed outside and marveled at the feeling. He seemed to know that it was a dream, but he loved it. He walked a few steps and looked back at his small home. At that moment, he heard the sounds again – the sounds that had caused him such anguish. He was caught outside, in the open this time, though, with nothing to protect himself. He panicked and quickly awoke from the dream and sat upright; his heart was racing and pounding. Realizing again that it was simply a dream, he was quickly relieved until he heard the sounds again. They were real.

His senses peaked, and his inner voice said, 'Not again!' The undulations did not hesitate this time but became more and more distinct. As far as he could tell, something or someone was directly outside the survival dome. He reached for the oxygen cup that was attached to the exchange unit and noticed movement in the outer entry of the dome. The scuffling continued as he stared at the entrance. The material moved, and a large, harry hand reached in and spread the partition. Rad pushed himself back. "Wait a minute! Who the hell are you?"

# 11
## Shawn O'Reilly III

Glancing up at Rad was a man with a very sheepish grin. He had a strong smell about him that almost knocked Rad over. His long beard, tattered clothes, dirty teeth and old crusted life-support suit, along with his friendly demeanor, nestled into Rad's home with ease and freedom as if he belonged there. "Would you feel better if I took my clothes off too?"

Rad glanced down and reminded himself that he was naked and had been that way most of the time for nearly a month. He laughed a little. "No, you're... you're fine the way you are." He collected himself and asked again, "Now, I'll say it again, who the hell are you?"

The man laughed. "I know I'm quite a sight. My name is Shawn O'Reilly the Third. I prefer being called Brit."

"Okay... Where did you come from, Brit?"

He looked Rad over one more time, smiled and continued. "I haven't been back in the lifeglobe for a year now, except to drop by and steal a little food now and then. You're the first person that I've seen leave and come out into the desert. Are you some type of weirdo?"

Rad laughed a little and asked, "Me? What about you? Are you okay? I mean...can I trust you?

"Trust me? I don't know...trust me to do or be what?"

"Trust you to not rip my survival station open, take my food, oxygen and supplies and leave me to die?"

Brit guffawed uncontrollably, slapped his leg, looked at Rad again and continued laughing.

Rad couldn't help it. When someone laughed that hard, it was difficult not to join in. He pointed at Brit's foot, which was rudely sticking out of his sock and lost it completely. Rad rolled on the floor out of control. He got next to Brit. One of Brit's loud horselaughs was right in Rad's face. It was too much. His breath was so bad that Rad's face contorted and oozed with disgust. This was so ridiculous that it set them both off again. It lasted for another few minutes.

"Now, Mr. O'Reilly."

"What...my name's Brit?" They were both still out of breath.

"Okay, Brit, you've been out here for a year. What the hell do you think you're doing?"

"I could ask you the same, but I know about you."

"You know about me. What do you mean?"

"Well, you're slightly famous. From what I can gather, you were an extremely talented Room's player who went off the deep end. There is some Room that you wanted to play so badly that you went nuts over it. You were missing, so I thought you might be somewhere out here. Besides, I know a sweet young lady named Shee."

"Shee wasn't supposed to say anything about me to anyone except a couple of my friends." Rad was upset at this. He thought he had known Shee well enough to trust her.

"To tell you the truth, your friends and Shee were worried about you, and Shee knew that a strange outsider like myself would not be much of a threat to your secret, so they wanted me to try find you to see how you were doing. It's been about a month since they'd heard from you. But besides being a little paranoid, and a lot naked, I think I can tell them you're alright."

Rad smiled. "You still haven't told me about yourself."

"Not much to tell actually. I hate lifeglobes. A very distant grandfather of mine was one of the first pioneers in space. He was one of the first to set foot on Earth's moon...'One giant step for mankind,' and all that. I figured that if he was able to go out there with as little protection as he did and take the chances that he did, I should be able to do a little trekking on my own. Besides, the dam lifeglobes give me claustrophobia."

Rad sat listening. This was one strange guy, but Rad liked him. He seemed straightforward and honest, and it didn't look like he was going to rip open his survival shelter. "Here I thought I was out here being so brave. You've been out here for a year? How've you done it?"

"My direct grandfather was a life-support bioengineer and so was my father. I've never gone through any schooling for it, but

I was able to learn a lot by just watching and working with them. Would you like me to take you to where I live?"

"Sure...can I get some clothes on?"

"I'd appreciate it."

***

They must have been traveling for about three hours. It wasn't a walk. It was a torturous climb through the Sharp Mountains. Rad was beginning to wonder if this was wise. He hadn't had much exercise during his stay in the dome. His muscles ached. Brit on the other hand moved like a mountain goat. He was obviously used to it. Rad kept his eyes on the back of Brit. This conscious effort seemed to help him, as if he were drafting behind someone on a speedcycle. He continued forward, but not without some pain in every part of his body, and not without his life-suit becoming more and more cumbersome. He had to stop. He yelled at Brit via the com-system between the suits and between heavy breaths. They stopped, but only for a second, Brit pointed to an area in front of them.

They moved on and came to a narrow tunnel, entered it, and began to descend. They passed through two sheathed barriers and came to a halt. Brit took off his helmet and suit, breathed deeply, and ran his fingers through his long beard and hair as if to say, 'Well, come on.' Rad hesitated then took his helmet off as well. The air was unbelievably fresh. There was something, something that he didn't recognize in the air that he was breathing. He watched and followed along as Brit moved further down the corridor towards a dim light. As they drew nearer, the light became somewhat brighter.

"Brit?"

"Just come on, I'll explain in a minute."

They reached a domed, cave-like room. It was warm and just large enough to be comfortable. Upon entering, Brit laid his outer clothing, shoes and survival items down. Rad took the rest of his suit off and did the same. There was a supple and extravagant covering on the floor. Rad's bare feet reveled in the texture. Brit spoke softly, and the lights in the room glowed brighter, warming the room and exposing more of it. Directly in front of them, covering and enshrouding the ceiling and walls was something green. To Rad's disbelief, he was looking at plants, thousands of plants. Some were similar to those that were in the lifeglobe, but many of them were completely unique and different. They were gloriously beautiful, thick and vivacious. Rad now knew what was different about the air. It was the moisture, sweet soft moisture, as well as the scent of plants permeating the air in the cave.

"Do you have a few questions?" Brit smiled. Rad stared ahead.

Brit explained that he had tapped an underground source of water on R-131. Evidently, during its birth, water had formed and rain had appeared for a period of time. Some of that water had been trapped under the surface of the planet in an aquifer. He had found a deep cave where the moisture seeped in. His bioengineering skills had then come into play as he developed some plants that could survive in this setting. The plants oxygenated the air, and he had created his own exchange unit to balance the gases in the chamber to sustain life.

"It's brilliant, Brit."

"Really can't take the credit, Rad. I just did some fiddling here and there. Got most of my ideas from my sires, you know." They laughed. "Sit down. Can I get you something? I can hear your stomach rumbling from over here."

"Thanks."

As Brit moved across the room, Rad's attention was drawn to the one wall where the water was seeping through the fissures of rock. It was as if the planet was giving its life-blood to feed the new life in the cave. This was hard to believe. R-131 was supposedly a dead and lifeless planet. 'What else didn't we know about this planet and others that were inhabited by humans from Earth?'

The cool, clear air filled his lungs. The plants sparkled under the beautiful glow of soft lights within the room. Rad then recognized the round, glowing spheres. They looked exactly the same as his. They seemed to emanate waves of brightness that were not just light, not just heat, but energy in its purest form. An energy that you could sense was strong, powerful and yet comforting. This incredible coincidence couldn't be ignored.

He was about to ask Brit about the spheres when he placed an earthen bowl in front of Rad. In it, a multi-colored liquid swirled with an almost mesmerizing affect. "What is this?"

"It's my specialty. I use some of the water here, a dash of almost anything edible that I could steal from the lifeglobe and some of the plants that I've grown. You'll love it. Think of it as an old Irish concoction." Brit noticed Rad's puzzled look and added, "You know, Irish, as in Ireland, an old nation that existed on Earth. I also threw in a bit a' whisky."

"Whisky?"

"You betcha. Great stuff. It'll put some hair on that chest of yours. Drink up!"

Rad picked up the bowl and tasted the liquid.

"What d'ya think?"

"It tastes delicious!"

Rad drank the liquid down, and Brit smiled at him in the easy way that he had. Rad had been famished. He felt better almost immediately, drained the last drops from the bowl and was about to ask Brit about the spheres again when Brit asked, "Feel better?"

Rad beamed and said, "Definitely!" As he spoke, he noticed Brit's hand reaching toward the small leather book that was on the floor next to him. Rad placed his hand on the book and put it into his pocket along with his sphere.

Brit looked at Rad and asked, "Important is it?"

"Yes."

At that moment, events seemed to happen almost simultaneously. Rad's mind reeled. He was bewildered, shocked and completely out of control. He glanced up. Across the room he noticed someone walking toward him. It was Shee. 'What?' Her motion was subtle and surreal. Rad then glanced back toward Brit. Brit's eyes were intent, not on Shee, but on him. In those eyes, Rad could see a fire. Baffled and off balance, he stumbled and fell backward. He felt as if he were falling into the deepest meditation he had ever experienced, further into himself than ever, more at peace, more in tune. He floated, it seemed. He lost sight - lost any cognizant, connective feel for the concrete physical world around him. "Brit...Mr. O'Reilly...Shee..." He breathed softly, let go and accepted. He soared.

# 12
## The Room: Level 2
## Old Earth

Rad's eyes opened slowly, cautiously. He was lying on some flat rocks with a wide, blue ocean sprawled out in front of him. Waves were licking the souls of his bare feet as he pushed up to his elbows and breathed in. The air was crisp and cool, edging its way into his lungs. He was alone, alone and free in the open air on a planet full and beautiful.

The sun was shining. His eyes could barely accept the stark, bright light glancing off the surf and the rocks. Above were the sounds of birds incessantly squawking, yawing and screeching. They soared magnificently with their lazy, luscious wings spread out, gliding on the ocean breezes. The swish of the water, the aromas of the plants and herbs nearby and the sounds of life were all around. A world such as he had never known, except from the pages of the small leather book and from his own dreams, lay stretched out across his vision.

As he rose up to a sitting position, his wide eyes filled with liquid from the bright sun and the wonder of what he saw. This was beyond comprehension. His thoughts were still hazy - his senses still somewhat suppressed and exposed at the same time. The coldness of the rocks and the raw openness of his body to the elements chilled him deeply. He realized that he needed to find shelter.

He climbed the rocks near the ocean in the hope of being able to see inland. The climb ended abruptly, and he stood peering across a landscape of lush evergreen forests, mountains, valleys, rock outcroppings and glaciers in the distant high mountains. From the remaining light of the sun, the crystalline views and the gold leaves dangling from the shrubs and trees in the vicinity, Rad felt that it must be autumn. He laughed at his use of the term, *autumn*, realizing how much he had learned from his recent studies. His time in the survival dome with the leather book was allowing him to view and understand this new place in ways that would never have been possible otherwise. He could see even more now what a gift the old leather book had been.

He wondered, '*Could I actually be on Earth or some other Earth-like planet? How did I get here?*' He was nowhere near R-131. '*What had happened?*' As these questions rolled around in his mind, the ethereal feelings of excitement that he'd had when he first woke up on the rocks began to ebb and change to a sense of fear and apprehension.

"Hey! Hello! Hello! Help me! Help me! Hello!" Silence.

He looked back out at the water. Its vastness and the overpowering landscape behind him felt heavy now - the weight almost oppressive. He was slightly dizzy and might be going into shock. He glanced around and found an area where there was a small grove of trees. The ground underneath them was dry and grassy. Nearby, he picked handfuls of taller dry grass for cover. He sat within the group of trees, leaning against one of them and covered himself with the long grass, using it as a blanket. The makeshift shelter gave him some warmth and a bit of protection from the elements.

As he settled in, he noticed that dusk was upon him. It would soon be night, and this good-bad dream, whether it was real or not, felt *absolutely* real to him. He curled up with his thoughts and slept.

In his sleep, he had one of those dreams that felt as if it was actually happening. It was extremely clear, crisp and colorful. A woman's face came to him. It was the old one from the Room. She was looking into his eyes, burning her face into his mind. He felt her strong presence. She spoke words that were precise and understandable. "Observe life and survive. The Room is constant yet changing. Be aware."

***

It was morning, and Rad was awake. He felt the hardness of the earth beneath him, the tall grasses brushing up against his skin and his body aching from the long night on the ground. He swept his grass blanket aside and sized up the frosty autumn morning. At that moment, the words that the old one had spoken came back to him. "Observe life and survive. The Room is constant yet changing. Be aware."

Now it was obvious. Rad realized that he was again part of the Room. He was on the second level. He had wanted this so much, and now, for better or worse, he'd made it.

He felt alone and exposed, sore, elated and somewhat puzzled. His stomach growled with little concern for his plight. He suddenly felt empty and hungry. He didn't know how long he would be here. It could be a moment more or an eternity. This Room was so life-like that anything could happen, including starvation. Other players who had been in less sophisticated Rooms had suffered quite real and serious injury. He couldn't take any chances.

He first emptied his bladder from the night and then realized that he needed to get some water back into his system. He could do without food for a while but not water. He stood quietly for a moment and could hear the sound of running water nearby. A short distance away, he found it. It was rushing through the meadow near where he'd slept, rolling over rocks and glistening from the sun's morning rays. It was a small stream. Cupping the liquid into his hands, he raised the water to his lips and drank. Its clear, cool softness oozed down his throat. He smiled, and for just a moment, felt safe. He drank more and then decided to clean himself. He felt itchy from being under the grass, and he also felt that the cold water would help diminish some of his aches. He removed his clothing and washed his face and body from head to foot. He was now more used to the water's temperature so he sat down in a slow moving pool. It felt especially good, somehow, to let the liquid run against the skin of his legs. He felt a part of it – raw and alive. Rad couldn't help but laugh at his thoughts and feelings; a huge smile crossed his face. He was naked again, but this time in a stream in an amazing place, taking a bath outside. He spoke aloud to himself, "God, I can't believe this!"

He'd finally had enough of the cold and stood up. The water streamed from his limbs, and he shook the excess from his hair. Reaching down, he picked up his clothes and shook them as well. He thought that maybe he would clean them in the water, too, but decided against it for now. He had more important things to do. Putting his clothes back on felt wonderful after his brisk bath. He thought he might even survive all this.

At that moment, Rad thought again about his empty stomach and wondered how he could gather food. He remembered putting the leather book and sphere in his pocket when he was in the cave and that there was a passage in the book that discussed how you could find food in the wild. He was glad that he had the book and wished that he'd remembered it earlier. He reached into his pocket, but both the book and the sphere were gone. He panicked for a second and then realized that he'd probably either lost them on his walk from the ocean or they had slipped out of his pocket during the night. He knew they'd be extremely useful so he began to retrace his steps. He needed to find them, but something stopped him dead in his tracks. It was the sound of snapping limbs coming from some trees nearby. There was something alive in there.

Rad stared. The sun was at an angle now where the light was just beginning to enter the forest. Something flashed directly in front of him. His gaze intensified, and he saw two eyes glaring back at him. He froze. He could barely see its outline, but from what he could see, it was probably a small sized animal, its head barely reaching his hip. It was aware and skittish. Ready to run, yet curious. He dared not move, but he wanted to see it more clearly so he creased his forehead, squinted his eyes and moved just a little to gain a better view. He succeeded and could clearly see it. He was ecstatic. It was a living, breathing animal in the wild, and he tried to remember what it was called. The name came to him as if released from a trap. 'Could it be?' He knelt slowly, trying to see its legs under the bushes. 'Four...? Yes four legs - slender, bony and strong.' It was definitely a small deer. He rose up again, and it bounded away into the meadow.

Rad couldn't help himself. He chased after the creature. He ran as if possessed by it. He jumped logs, brushed against sharp tree spines, stepped on twigs and still he ran on. The animal had far outdistanced him when he came to a second meadow and noticed it had stopped and was standing completely still. Rad stopped, too, and watched intently. It was so beautiful. He wondered why it was just was standing there. It looked to be gazing intently at something. Its head and eyes were frozen in place - its nose twitching.

All of a sudden, Rad could hear other animals growling and moving through the brush nearby. It was obvious that the deer had been aware of them before he had. Its limbs jerked abruptly, propelling it in a panic away from the sounds. The other creatures in the meadow suddenly appeared and outnumbered the deer ten to one. They attacked, moving swiftly in on the young animal, working together and surrounding her until she was down. The kill was quick and sure. He could see the life leave the deer as the creatures tore and yanked at its flesh. Their muzzles were stained red as they fed voraciously and left little in the grass to mention what had happened there.

Rad was stunned. He waited until the last predator had left and then walked over to where the deer lay. Looking down, he recalled how free and vibrant the animal had been. He had loved to watch it move and was amazed at its strength and the power of its limbs. Now, all that remained was its blood, some bones, bits of tissue and small pieces of flesh and hair lying there on the ground. The predators had left as abruptly as they had come, and Rad was thankful that they hadn't noticed his presence.

Kneeling down, he placed his hand onto the still-warm carcass. He touched the red liquid, the same liquid that sustained his own life. He wasn't angry at the animals that had killed to eat. He could still feel his own pangs of hunger that drove and pushed *his* particular need. He felt a loss, though. The remains of the stunning creature that lay beneath him was the first real land animal that he had ever seen. The book had explained and helped him understand the balance in an ecosystem and the need for life and death. However, witnessing it, being there at that very moment, was something else entirely.

It was almost too much. '*How am I to play this game, this Room?*' He was alone, sweating and cold, hungry and most likely in danger. '*Could I actually survive this?*'

Rad then remembered the book and the sphere. He was about to turn and leave again when a massive roar echoed through the air and slammed into his body with unbelievable force. His every muscle, every sinew, peeked with adrenaline. His head swung back toward the sound with furious urgency, and he set himself against what he saw. A huge creature with wild piercing eyes and strength beyond understanding was staring down at him only meters away. It drooled with anger and hunger and was poised to overtake him. He froze. Complete and utter terror moved through his veins. He knew that his time had come, just as the deer's had only moments earlier. All he could do was stand his ground – running was senseless.

As he stared back at the creature, he sensed a tugging at his limbs and a crunching sound that had begun emanating from within his body. He didn't take his eyes off his assailant until he was yanked again, this time more violently, as he was thrown to the ground. He couldn't believe what was happening. He was literally losing his form, morphing in seconds. He gained hair - coarse brownish hair. All of his limbs shortened and narrowed, especially his legs. His back flattened. His neck elongated, and his face and head stretched. It happened in the blink of an eye, yet Rad saw it in slow motion while pain of his transformation coursed through his body. The huge creature was confused for just a few seconds, but that was long enough. Rad's change was complete. He felt an uncontrollable urge to run. He bounded off. He moved on all fours. He ran for his life.

***

The leaves were lush, green and flavorful. The water cool and clear as Rad spent his time moving through the forest, living the life of the animal that had died in the meadow. A new deer now graced the many species of this land. It had been several days since his experience with the huge creature. He had outrun it and felt the uncontrollable joy of simply being alive. He was confused and uncertain about this Room. He wondered where it would take him, but he also was elated at being able to live in this stunning land, wild and free. Life! Serious, joyous, complex, simple, overwhelming life lay all around him, and he was part of it.

# 13
## The Room: Level 2
## Transformations

Transformation upon transformation. Shape upon shape. Life upon life. One-celled and many-celled creatures. Plankton. Small fish. Larger fish. Sea mammals: whales, dolphins, seals, penguins. Amphibians. Reptiles. Land mammals: monkeys, giraffes, horses, bears. Birds. Insects. Spiders. Prey. Predators. Scavengers. So many forms. So many points of view. Rad was each and every one. The variety was exquisite, the complexity profound. What he learned about evolutionary and ecological progression and balance were beyond description. Life in this place was beauty personified in its creatures, plants, geological forms, chemical makeup and the mixture of all this in a dynamic, living biosphere. Rad's next form unfolded.

The height was extreme - the view exquisite. He floated and moved effortlessly. The lush forest below seemed perfect and real as it rushed by with speed and beauty. Flight was an awesome feeling, and Rad had become accustomed to it in a very short time. Having feathers, a beak and talons were another matter. Everything seemed to fit, though. Everything seemed to matter - so simple, yet so right. Gliding down to the ocean's edge, the oil in his eyes filtered out the glare and allowed him to see beneath the water. He noticed a school of herring darting about as if they were one creature. Wings back, talons exposed, he dropped and plucked a single fish from the water. He soared back to his perch in a nearby tree, ripped the flesh and consumed the energy.

'What a world!' he thought. The air was moist with a freshness and purity that he was only able to imagine before now. Within this level of the Room, Rad existed in an altered state of reality, which he was beginning to accept. He had morphed over and over into various life forms and was fully aware in each of them, while learning, understanding and living their lives. He had come to love and feel a kinship for every one of them.

He thought back to his first transformation as the deer. It

had been a life and death experience that he had relived many times since then. Somehow, he had survived them all and was now sitting here, perched above the world, feeling the power and majesty of another wondrous day. And even after all of the lives he'd lived, he knew that being this particular creature was one of the most unique. It gave him such a special view of the world, and he knew that this memory would remain with him long after he was no longer in this form. The way it mated, soared and existed high above this world was unforgettable.

Hearing her cry, he looked up. Far above him she soared. It was time. The urge rose deep within his soul. He flew to meet her, to fly with her, to mate with her. They coupled in a dive of love - the earth rushed up to meet them. She pushed away. They glided with the warmth and knowledge of life continuing.

As Rad and his mate began searching for food, he noticed something moving below him. It walked upright. Its awkward movements seemed out of place in this natural jigsaw. He let himself glide downward in curiosity until the creature was crisp in his vision. *'It was human!'* Two-legged, slightly bent and balanced on those bipedal limbs. *'A young boy?'* He questioned his vision. It had been so long since he'd seen a human. He was torn. His original form was, of course, human, but since his transformations his allegiances had become multifaceted. He now felt that every creature was on equal footing with this...this human. He dove lower. The boy raised a forearm in defense. He clipped him slightly with his talons. There was a cry of pain and blood oozed from the wounds. The boy ran for cover under the nearest tree. Rad smiled inside. *'What a strange turn. What an unusual feeling.'*

As Rad pivoted in the air and flew to rejoin his mate, he felt himself begin to reel and descend. No amount of strength or will could change the pull of gravity on him. Looking down, he saw the earth flying towards him at a dizzying rate. His eyes locked onto the young boy's, as he catapulted downward.

\*\*\*

In the darkness, Rad could feel the warmth of hands

caressing him. He was being fed comforting liquids, oozing with steam and fragrance as they flowed into him. He could hear words, unusual words, and sounds all around. He tucked his body into a fetal position and concentrated on the dark. A voice summoned him, "Aronk. Aronk cods. Aronk." He shook his head and opened his eyes. Shapes danced across the ceiling above and firelight bounced off figures standing in front of him. He stretched, although it didn't seem that his limbs were as responsive as they should be.

It had been a woman who had spoken to him with those unusual words that sounded cut off and simple, yet full of emotion. She was so different. She moved with the purpose of getting him up and giving him nourishment. He hesitated, and at that moment, noticed that his body had changed again. He was very similar to the woman's humanoid type and build, but he was a young boy. His jaw felt different. His limbs were not quite the configuration that he was used to. She glanced in his direction and motioned at him to continue eating. He did, but he also started taking in the rest of his surroundings. The smells were odd. He had been, for some time, used to the smells of outdoor creatures. He had not been in a confined space with members of his own species at all since the beginning of his transformations. The odors were strong and pungent. The cave was lit with dim light from outside and from the fires within. Men and women alike were moving about, mingling and performing their duties with a definite, but understated, curiosity that he knew was directed at him. The men were bringing in meat that had obviously been gathered from a recent hunt; the women and children were preparing the food, working on what looked like garments of some type and the youngest children were running in and out of the cave playing together.

Steam and heat rose to the top of the cave while the light from the fires danced on the walls. Rad then also noticed an old man working on some paintings. He glanced over at Rad with a calm yet busy look. He continued his work. Rad watched with intent. The stain from hewed out bowls of colored liquid were placed on the wall with a stick that had been chewed and frayed at one end. He could see shapes of large and small creatures and of men and women hunting prey and gathering food. The walls seemed to be filled with stories.

Rad turned his head as a hand was placed on his shoulder. A young girl said some words and motioned for him to come with her. He rose up slowly and moved awkwardly with her to the opening of the cave. He glanced out. A stream flowed nearby. Trees and shrubs of many unusual types graced the area. The other children in the cave snuck glances at them as the young girl took Rad by the hand and walked with him past the entrance.

She seemed to have some purpose. She came to a cliff. It was evening, but they could both still see over a vast, flat plain that seemed to go on forever. They stood together in silence, gazing out over the expanse. Rad turned his head and looked back at the warm light from the cave and again out toward the plain; he recognized that he was viewing the early beginnings of the human race. The young girl then reached over, touched his arm and smiled in her own fashion. He glanced at her and then back down at his arm where he saw some scratches. At that moment, he remembered what had happened at the end of his last incarnation. His talons, when he had been the bird, had dug into the boys arm – his arm. Rad's eyes jumped upward as he heard the scream of a lone bird of prey crisscrossing the ever-darkening sky overhead. She again took his hand, and they returned to the shelter and the security of the cave for the night.

***

Rad woke with a belly hanging over him and four inquisitive eyes looking into his. A pregnant woman and the old man who had been painting the wall the day before were looking at the barely-healed scars on his arm. The old man was laying his fingers over them and then touching the stomach of the woman. Rad lay still, not knowing what to make of these gestures.

The old man and the pregnant woman then moved away as the woman who had given Rad food the day before returned to look at his wounds. She placed some type of herbal solution on them. He nodded his head, acknowledging a thank you for what she was doing and the help she'd given. She did not look directly into his eyes. This gesture created a flashback. During the time of his many transformations, he'd noticed other mammals using this same technique. It seemed that they had used it to maintain their space or their identity without causing any problems with other members of their group. Even the faces and eyes of these humans were not so unlike other mammals. The old painter reminded him of a big-eyed marmot - the pregnant woman, a soft young deer - his friend from the night before, a small burrowing mammal. They bore their young and fed them the milk of their breasts. All life was connected.

From the other side of the room, a loud cry echoed off the walls. Many of the women moved toward the sound, and the old painter joined them quickly. Rad stood and looked. The woman with the large belly had begun hollering in pain. She was obviously in labor. Rad had never seen a birth. Most of the births on the lifeglobes took place in a sterile laboratory.

Her pain had eased a little now. Rad could sense the eyes of everyone on him as the painter walked over to him again. He touched the scratches on Rad's arm and then went back to the woman and placed his hand on her stomach just as before. Rad sat down nearby. The old man seemed to want him there. The woman's ordeal continued for some time. At one point, water gushed from her vagina. Rad thought that the baby would come with the water, but it didn't. He watched, and every once in a while, the old man came over to touch him and then her.

There were no other men close to the woman other than the old painter and a few other young children. Rad assumed the old man must be some type of healer or religious leader, and he allowed Rad to stay because he was young.

The birth seemed so long, so painful, with moments of rest tucked in between. He wondered if she would be able to have the child. Finally, he could see some expansion of the vaginal area. There were nods of approval and words spoken. The old painter seemed to moan almost continually. The young children nearby became bored and moved on to other things. Her cries had almost become commonplace when Rad began to see what he thought was a head. She had been pushing harder and harder recently. The beginning had been so slow, and the time seemed almost frozen as Rad watched the birth of a living creature. The last push dropped the baby human onto some soft rugs of fur along with more blood and a cord that attached the baby to the mother. Rad was struck with the momentous nature of the event - the reproduction of life, with all of its helter-skelter choosing of size, color, shape and texture. Eons upon eons of evolution had occurred this way. But this was not happening over time. This was a minute link in that chain. He was there. He had experienced it.

Rad was caught up in his thoughts, then heard a shuffling and glanced up. The old painter held the child, and it was wrapped in a small blanket of fur. The mother was being washed and given nourishment. She glanced towards Rad as the painter held the child out toward him. On the child's forehead was a small painting of what resembled a bird in flight. Rad took the child and touched its forehead. He then shifted his glance back toward the old man and smiled.

***

After viewing the birth of the child, Rad lay in his sleeping area watching the fire and looking into the embers. He thought about the origins of the human race, about the lifeglobes throughout the galaxy and his ancestor's journey across space. They had been gone from Earth for hundreds of years, but he wondered, 'Where had they actually traveled? What had the human race truly accomplished?'

In this body, this prehistoric human shape, he stared at the rock walls, the fire and the people. He thought about the wondrous land where these humans lived. The smells, the seasons and the air were all such a huge part of their daily lives. Now the human race lived in lifeglobes on stark man-made structures that protected and gave them security and safety, but at what cost? They were totally separated from their environment – completely cut off from their world.

Rad let his eyes wander as he was consumed with these thoughts and many more. His eyes naturally drifted over to the fire burning nearby. He gazed deeply into its embers, and as he did so, the cave disappeared from his sight; nothing remained except the colors, the warmth of the fire and the glowing coals. He felt sleep coming on. With the embers still burning in his mind, slumber surrounded and consumed him.

# 14
## Rest

His eyes were only slits with layered tears acting like prisms moving and changing the shadowy light. He was slowly becoming more aware again – slowly succumbing to another change in his reality. He moved slightly and sensed his fingers resting on a smooth surface; a puff of air rustled across his face. The tears dried a little and his eyelids opened just a bit. His surroundings were still partially unfocused.

Rad closed and opened his eyes once more, doing his best to come out of the daze. The excess moisture from his deep sleep moved down his cheek, and he thought of the scene that he had just witnessed - the baby human being born. In conjunction with that thought, his body involuntarily stretched and he attempted to breathe more deeply. He was trying to wake up. He rose up on one elbow, but it was obvious that he needed more rest. He lay back down again and allowed himself some time. As he did so, his hand brushed up against the leather book and the sphere lying on the floor nearby. In his memory, he thought of the moment, so long ago, when he had realized that both had been missing, but here they were. Knowing they weren't lost helped Rad let go, giving in to his need for rest. He closed his eyes again and drifted off.

\*\*\*

There was a gentle nudging. Rad felt someone tenderly grasp one of his feet. He wasn't alone. He was aware of someone speaking softly and laughing.

Rad's eyes opened this time and focused more quickly on two large figures in front of him in the vestibule of his survival shelter. As he came to his senses, he was again aware of his nudity, his surroundings and the presence of Tal and Simon. He was obviously back on R-131. A slow smile crossed his lips. It was so good to see his friends. It was good to be home.

"You worried us, again. You've been gone for weeks. Shee

didn't know anything either, so she helped us get some survival suits so we could look for you. We located your tent from a satellite image and traveled out to check on you. Are you okay?" Simon was, as usual, open and right there.

"I'm alright. I'm just tired and hungry. Thanks for coming out to check." Rad was actually very grateful to see them and have the company.

"Here's something to drink and a bit of food we brought with us. Careful, drink slowly. The way you're eating you must be starved." Tal was extremely concerned.

They all sat, ate and talked about the survival shelter, the weather that day and other simple things until Simon finally asked, "What's been going on, Rad? What have you been doing out here?"

How could Rad begin to explain? He simply said, "I think I've just played the second level."

Both Tal and Simon's eyes grew large as they glanced at each other and knew that they'd better get Rad back into the lifeglobe so that he could recover. He'd have time to tell them more later. Simon couldn't keep his mind off the statement that Rad had made, though. 'The second level, my god, what could it have been?' By looking at Rad, he knew that it must have been very difficult. He had to find out.

***

Upon their return, Rad again slept for hours and awoke to the soft humming sound so familiar from his sleeping area and from the oxygen systems on the lifeglobe. Tal and Simon had left quite a while ago. They knew that he needed to be alone and quiet. They had spoken very little on the return trip.

He glanced out the circular window near his bed and caught sight of one of R-131's moons popping up over the horizon. He had been out there – outside. He had been in a cave without a survival suit. He had felt moisture and wind and had experienced a Room beyond any other. He had learned so much about life. Next to his bed, he again noticed the leather book. He held it but didn't open it, too much had happened. He again needed to pull back for a time and absorb what had been experienced.

Rad stood up slowly and walked into the living area of his apartment. It had been his home now for a long time. He then stared through his other outview toward the Center of the lifeglobe. It was busy with people. They were animated with excitement, as they were many nights. He remembered how it felt to be excited, to meet friends, talk, play the latest Room and simply enjoy himself. But although he could relate to how they felt, he had absolutely no desire to join them tonight, no need to walk from one sheltered enclosure to another. Too much had happened. He walked over, picked out his favorite meditative music, sat back and simply stayed in the moment thinking about the deer, the bird, the baby and feeling once again the wonder of it all.

***

Because of his long rest, Rad was able to wake up quickly the next morning and get out fairly early. He'd eaten, slipped some clothes on and decided that he wanted to talk to some of his friends in the governing council about Brit and Shee. He wanted to learn more about them. *'Where had they come from? How long had they been on R-131?'*

As Rad neared the offices of the council, some people saw him and recognized him from his earlier escapades. They edged their way closer to him, and a leader of the group began to speak, "Sorry to bother you, but are you Rad?

"Yes."

"We're players, and we heard that you played the second level of the old one's Room. Is it true?"

It was obvious that Simon had already begun sharing what had happened with his friends and other Room players. The rumors were spreading fast. He knew that many people had either heard about it or knew someone who'd played the Room. Interest and curiosity in it had obviously spread.

"I have, but I'm just recovering." That statement, he hoped, would gain him some time and some freedom from questions right now. It was such a personal experience that Rad simply didn't want, or need, to share it with a lot of people.

"We understand, but could we talk to you later about what happened? Simon's our friend, and he said you might not mind."

Rad laughed. Simon was so spontaneous, but Rad wished he could have kept this quiet for a while longer. "I'll let Simon know when I feel like talking about what happened. Check with him in a few days."

"Thanks."

Rad proceeded more cautiously now to the council building. After going inside, he went to the records department and asked to talk to Lowry. She was a friend of his, and he thought she would give him access to some of the personnel records, even though he wasn't a member of the council any longer.

"Lowry. Hi."

Lowry turned and recognized her old friend. "Rad, where have you been? Rumors have been spreading like crazy about you. We've been wondering where you were?"

"I've been outside the lifeglobe. I wanted to spend some time reading and experiencing the actual weather on the outside."

"It's so dangerous! I don't think I could ever stay out there very long at all. You never know!"

"It wasn't so bad. Uh…Lowry, I was wondering if you could help me?"

"Sure. What's up?"

"Recently I met two people that I've been curious about. One's name is Shawn O'Reilly III and the other, well, I never knew her last name, but she worked in maintenance for the council. Her name is Shee, spelled 'Shee.' Could you look them up and tell me where they came from?"

"Rad, I shouldn't, but come with me to the back of the office. We'll do it quickly."

It took about twenty minutes. Lowry checked and rechecked the records. There had never been an individual by the name of Shawn O'Reilly III located on R-131. She had found Shee's name, though. Her last name was Holloway. She had worked on R-131 for a while but was now on permanent leave.

With Brit, Rad could completely understand why Lowry couldn't find him in the records. He had been living under the radar and outside the lifeglobe for quite a while. He wondered why Shee had taken a leave of absence just now but set it aside and thanked Lowry for her help.

"You're welcome, Rad. Could we get together sometime now that you're back? It would be great to spend some time with you."

"Sure. I need to spend time with friends. I had quite an adventure outside. I'll get in touch with you soon."

"I'm looking forward to it!" she said.

As Rad walked out the door, he thanked her again and left the office to walk and think for a while. On his walk, he passed many people who looked his way and seemed to talk quietly to each other, but it really didn't affect him as it would have before the Room. He had been in a world that no one here could relate to, and he'd felt and lived things that seemed to transmute his soul to another plain of awareness. He walked into the Center and proceeded to have a drink of ale at a small pub.

He kept going over everything in his mind. He couldn't believe it all had happened, and yet he knew it had. He thought of everything, especially the old woman's eyes. It was eerie that, as he thought of her, he also remembered Zeer. He felt some kind of connection existed between everything that had happened to him, the old one, and Zeer. There had to be. After all, Zeer had given him the leather book, and it was shortly after that when she'd disappeared. He wondered.

The ale finally began to take over. Rad relaxed and quietly contemplated what he might do next.

***

He spent several days recovering, thinking and finally talking to Tal and Simon about what had happened during his time outside. They both were incredulous, but Simon, as Rad and Tal had expected, was wide-eyed and so taken in by what he'd heard that his questions were seemingly endless. Rad answered most of them until Tal finally put his hand on Simon's shoulder and said that he thought that Rad was probably ready to stop answering questions. Simon stopped, but he could have gone on.

Tal had one question, though. He wondered, "What are you going to do now, Rad?"

"I really don't know. I think I would just like to live normally for a while. Spend time with you two and some other people that I've promised and think about all of this for a while."

"That sounds like a great idea," Tal threw in.

Rad was quick to add, "Simon, I was wondering if you could keep this to yourself for a little while. Please don't tell anyone else, okay. People have been treating me like some strange phenomenon. I don't mind sharing all this with both of you, but really, I just want to have some time."

"It won't be easy, but sure. I'll keep it to myself for a few days, but you have to realize, Rad, that others want to know. This has become quite an event here on R-131."

"Thanks, I understand." Rad knew that Simon would try, but it probably wouldn't be long before he'd begin spreading the word again. It was hard to keep something like this to yourself on a lifeglobe.

# 15
## Questions

The natural rhythm of Loon moved towards daylight. Soft rays began to spread through the forest just touching the window. Zeer could hear the rolling sounds of Sholar in the distance. She had been on Loon long enough to feel very comfortable and was consumed by a sense of home. She rose up on one elbow and looked out. The whole front of her living quarters was transparent. It was like waking outdoors, yet she was warm, comfortable and secure.

A backlight towards the rear of her sleeping area began to glow as if in unison with the sun. Transcendent, radiant music with touches of ocean rhythms, forest winds, soaring birds and evening dot-bugs eased her awake and brought a smile to her lips. It was music that had been written by one of the great composers of Loon.

As she listened, she was thinking about how happy she had been here with the Learning Cluster. This had been her first home on Loon. It's where she'd met so many of her new friends, and it was also where she had gained much of her knowledge and understanding about Loon and its people. However, she now needed to decide which Cluster she would join and how she would give back to the culture that had brought her here and had so enriched her life. It was time to make that decision, but some other questions had been gnawing at her. She had to find a way to answer those questions first.

***

The meeting took place in the spiritual center of the Learning Cluster. Fawn, Landree, Brit, Dominie and Shee were there, among other members of the Circle. They were very excited about what had been accomplished. It was a great step for the people of Loon. It was something that had been discussed for many years, but bringing Zeer here was the first step in the process – the beginning.

"She is integrating in a way that we could not have imagined," said Landree with a proud excitement that he had never shown Zeer during her cycling. "I could feel her abilities, our common ancestry, and such curiosity that at times I was overwhelmed. She was filled, almost immediately, with a love of our world that I didn't think anyone could have unless they'd been raised here. Zeer has proven that we might be able to bring others to Loon and give them homes."

"All that you've said is true, Landree. It looks very promising, but don't forget that Zeer was very carefully chosen and represented the best of all of the individuals that we researched. Also, she is a woman, and women, we know, have more of a maternal, caring instinct built into them. The next task will be to bring a man here? That could prove more difficult because of several factors. As you know, I'm working with one right now. He's doing well, but I'm not completely sure yet." Fawn was much more cautious than the others in the Circle. It was her responsibility to make the final decision, along with their help. She was the one, though, who had been trained by Shar and had been given this duty.

Dominie then spoke, "By joining with Zeer, I have a unique perspective which I'd like to share. She represents the strain of the human race that left earth and moved into the galaxy. She demonstrated to me, during our sharing, the same love and connection to our mother that we all possess. She lacks some of the years of development and training that we have, but it is in her, and I believe that it is in many of the others that left earth as well. She can't be the only one."

Brit spoke with more caution in his voice, "We've settled on this planet and have a tremendous responsibility to our civilization and to the human race as a whole. No matter how much Zeer has proven herself, we must proceed with prudence. I met Rad, saw his dedication, and I like him, but we must remember what happened on Earth. We can't forget the destruction, the devastation or the cruelty. It is something that could happen again."

Even though Fawn was being cautious, she also needed to

97

consider every side of the argument and said, "And if it does? Remember we can't control everything. Chaos is a part of how our universe was created. The happenstances, the unique, the unexplained will always occur. We can't prevent it, but we *can* work very hard to move the human spirit in an ever-upward spiral of evolutionary growth towards an enlightening that will go even beyond the people of Loon." Fawn was now taking charge. This was a critical juncture in the Circle.

Shee had waited to speak. She'd been listening and thinking. "Everything that has been said is important, but I believe that we're now on this path, and we need to continue. As you all know, I've also met the man from Zeer's lifeglobe, and I feel that he has tremendous potential. I think we need to allow him to show us if he can fulfill that potential or not. Let's give him that chance. He needs to move into the third level of the Room."

"So, what's next?" Landree questioned. "Do we proceed? Do we halt the project for a time and do more study? Do we continue our search for a different male counterpart to Zeer, or do we keep working with our current prospect? Or...should we stop this altogether?"

Fawn paused and thought. "I will call you all together again in three sun-cycles. I want you to talk, think and come back. We will all share our ideas again and make a decision when it's time. I do want you to remember, though, that diversity is essential to a healthy species and a healthy planet. We all know this from what Loon has taught us. We will see."

The Circle concluded with more questions than answers, but with the hope that they would know how to proceed soon.

\*\*\*

It was late afternoon, and Zeer was coming back from a journey that she had taken to Sholar during the day to be with the Scree. She loved to return and converse with them, especially with her friend, Calna. They had bonded, and she had learned more from her than almost anyone on Loon. Whenever she visited the Scree, it always cleared her mind, especially when she was confused or had questions about something.

Since she had arrived, she was still in the dark about exactly how she had come to Loon. She didn't understand the technology that could bring her so many light years from her previous home. She also continued to wonder why she was here. She knew she was the first person that had been born somewhere other than Loon, but what was it all about? She thought back to all of the levels of the game, which she had played before arriving. There were points along the way where she had believed that she wouldn't survive; yet, here she was. *'What was the meaning, the plan, behind all of this?'* It was time to find some answers.

***

Zeer walked into the commons area in the Learning Cluster and looked for Dominie. He was sitting in a chair near a large window. She walked over and asked him, "Dominie, could we talk?"

"Of course."

She sat down next to him, looked outside for a moment, turned and spoke. "I want you to know that I feel very lucky to be here. I love the people, the planet, the environment and your culture's accomplishments. I feel so at home, and I'm looking forward to making a decision soon about which Cluster I'll be joining. But before I can make that decision, I have some questions that I'd like to have answered."

"If I can help, I will. What were you wondering about?"

"The memories that I have of my trip here are more dreamlike than real. I don't really remember much at all about how I got here. Why was I chosen? Why am I here? I am so far away from my old lifeglobe that I simply can't understand how this happened."

"I think I can help you with some of your questions. Others will have to wait awhile, though. The Circle has some decisions to make before you'll be able to understand everything, and you also have more to learn."

"That's fine. Help me with what you can."

Dominie proceeded the only way he knew how. He had Zeer take out her energy sphere, and he grabbed his from inside his clothing. They cupped their hands around their spheres and gazed into the light. The energy from both grew and surrounded the two. He explained, "Zeer, I'm going to take you back in time to when you had just returned from completing the final level of the Room. Of course, Fawn will be there, and you will see and hear what happened." Zeer acknowledged her understanding.

The light from the spheres changed, and she immediately saw herself sitting in front of Fawn in the darkened room on R-131. It was as if she were actually back in that place and time, watching herself and Fawn.

***

Zeer looked across at Fawn and gave a weak smile. She was exhausted. Fawn returned the smile and looked Zeer over very carefully.

"Zeer, it doesn't look like you have any injuries."

Zeer remembered her last moments of the Room and said, "I'm glad. I wasn't sure after what happened there my last day."

Fawn continued, "I want you to know that I'm very proud of you." She then handed Zeer her leather book and her sphere. "Here, keep these close."

Zeer simply said, "I will. Thank you."

Fawn then added, "Because of everything that you have learned and experienced. I know you're ready."

Zeer was still a bit foggy, but she responded, "Ready? Ready for what?"

"You and I are going to travel together to a place where you can rest and recover. We're going to my home."

At that moment, the energy sphere in Zeer's hand began to increase in intensity and meld with the glow from Fawn's. This combined bubble of energy surrounded them both. Fawn moved toward Zeer, placed her arms around her, and Zeer laid her tired head on Fawn's shoulder. She obviously felt comforted and peaceful; her body resonated slightly from the heightened energy all around. The brilliant light shimmered and intensified, and then they simply disappeared.

***

Zeer, after watching herself and Fawn vanish, started to ask Dominie what had happened but then noticed that the two of them were no longer seeing the room with the wooden door on R-131. They were now looking at the opening in front of the cave on Loon where she had awakened. In this vision of her past, a bright light exploded in front of the cave; the energy bubble appeared again, floating above the ground. Inside it, she could see herself in Fawn's arms. They glided into the cave, and the light around them began to dissipate. Zeer's eyes were wide as she watched. They touched the ground. Fawn continued to hold Zeer carefully. She took the sphere from Zeer's hand and gently laid her on some blankets.

At that point, the energy around Dominie and Zeer changed again. They were now back where they had started in the commons area of the Learning Cluster. Zeer sat quietly.

Again, as with so many times in her recent past, Zeer had seen something that challenged all that she had known. She now understood that she had traveled in the arms of Fawn from the lifeglobe on R-131 to Loon in a few moments in a bubble of pure energy. Of course, she had traveled with Landree around Loon during her cycle, but this...this was beyond belief. The people of Loon had somehow harnessed energy portals, which could transport them anywhere at any time in almost the blink of an eye. She now understood more about her experiences during the levels of the Room as well. This could completely change the way the human race lived. These energy spheres were a quantum leap into the future, and she could only imagine what else they could be used for with more training and understanding.

"My god!"

Dominie expected this reaction, but still he was taken by the look of astonishment on Zeer's face. "Our Technology Cluster developed the spheres over one hundred years ago, and we've learned more about them since. They are based on the very essence of matter and energy and the science of quantum physics that helps us finally understand matter from the largest of solar systems to the smallest parts of an atom. Laser research, Diamond Quantum theory and nanotechnology were also involved in their creation. We are still discovering uses for them and unlocking their potential. This discovery, though, has brought us to a moment of decision – a decision that we're struggling with right now. It does have to do with your other question, but I can't say any more. Hopefully, we'll all know more soon."

Zeer thought about what Dominie had said. She looked at the sphere in her hand with reverence and more understanding about the tremendous power that was there. She knew that she would learn more as time passed, but realizing that she had so little control over it made her feel very humble.

She glanced again at Dominie and formulated one more question. "Dominie, there is one other thing that I've thought a lot about and wanted to ask, but haven't until now."

"What's that?"

"When I first arrived, you and I were very intimate. I was awakening on Loon for the first time. The experience was warm, welcoming and seemed to go way beyond sexual intimacy. I know that every culture has its own ways, and you briefly described those to me when I first arrived here, but it seemed, though, that through our closeness I was actually experiencing and learning about your culture and you through our connection. I didn't feel violated. I felt, well, the only way I can describe it is, almost deep into myself, into you, and into Loon. What happened?"

"Since you've asked, I know it's time to explain it to you in more detail. Did you notice the sphere near us at the time?"

"Yes, afterwards."

"The energy from the sphere is, as you might have guessed, used for more than travel through time and space. It has the ability to match our energy vibrations. It pulsates and can complement our own personal energy, even at the cellular level if directed properly. You and I – all of us – we are energy at our core. The sphere's energy surrounded you and I, and through the act of being intimate, we've discovered that it heightens understanding and empathy. We can learn much about each other and our cultures – the very foundation of our knowledge is shared at some level. We have adapted it and use it whenever we get close to anyone and whenever we have a need to know more about one another. The Circle felt that if we followed our own customs from the beginning of your first cycle that it would help you integrate more easily and adapt more quickly to Loon."

Zeer thought for a moment and said, "It was incredibly special, and yes, it helped me grasp things much sooner than I would have otherwise. It was wonderful to share with you, Dominie. I feel very close to you and everyone here. It's funny, though. I don't really feel as if you're the one that I'd want to be my mate. Is that lost with the use of the sphere?"

Dominie laughed, "No, actually it helps you sense even more which person is right for you. You touched me deeply, but mating is definitely a one-person event here on Loon. We take it very seriously, but we also understand and value the importance of loving and experiencing others. When you do make love to the person who will be your partner, you will know. There is a oneness, a joyous wellspring of laughter and happiness that comes from that experience. Then it only gets better. I'll be excited for you when you have that experience."

"One last thing."

Dominie smiled. "Yes?"

"I know you said that you couldn't tell me some things, but I have to ask again?"

"Yes."

"So why am I here? Why me?"

Dominie put his arm around Zeer and spoke. "Because you were the right person; the person we needed here on Loon; the person that we knew could love our world and our ways as we do. That's really all I can say right now."

Zeer walked back to her apartment contemplating all that she had seen and learned that day. Once inside, she gazed again at her new world, and Loon gazed back at her and comforted her with its natural energy. It always had a very special effect on her.

She was home. She took off her clothes and lay on her sleeping mat with the sphere beside her. It had a subdued inner glow that could barely be seen, but it was there. She melted into quiet dreams.

# 16
## The History Cluster

For the next several moon-cycles, Zeer spent her time deciding which Cluster she was going to live and work in. She traveled across Loon and visited all of the major Clusters. Each of them was located in a very unique and beautiful environment, and just like the Learning Cluster, they were all virtually undetectable until you were within about a hundred meters of them. They were scattered across the planet in order to keep the impact of each settlement down to a minimum, and even though there were many of them, they still worked closely together for the betterment of their civilization and for the safety and continued existence of Loon.

Zeer held this approach in high regard. After what she had experienced in the Room with Fawn, she knew that the environmental underpinnings of this society were essential to the people's happiness and continued existence for many generations to come.

As she had come to understand through her travels, Loon's population had neither grown nor decreased in many cycles. They treasured their home, their lifestyles and their children's futures and having a stable, sustainable population was one of the greatest contributors to the human and environmental balance on Loon. They were a happy and healthy people. They valued the arts, humor, communication, their families and their future. They knew exactly what had happened to their ancestral home, and they were determined to not let that happen here.

The economic strength of Loon was not based on money as the currency for a good life. It was based on the understanding that every member of their world was extremely important and that everyone should be allowed to discover their own interests, pursue them, be allowed to change when needed and work for the good of their planet and each other. Improving life on Loon and being a healthy, grounded and productive member of their society were very important. No one was allowed to go hungry or be without a good home, health, education or companionship.

Everyone was responsible for the wellbeing of Loon and each other, and yet they also knew that they needed to strive and achieve as individuals in order for their society to continue to be strong and vibrant.

Zeer had learned and observed all of these things, and in her search, she had visited the Fine Arts Cluster near the Cliffs of Orn, the Environ-techno Cluster beside Sholar, the Healing Cluster, the Spiritual Cluster, the History Cluster, the Caretaker Cluster and the Culinary Cluster. There were many others, and Zeer visited most of them, reading and gathering information for her decision.

After great thought, she felt deeply drawn to the History Cluster. It was centered within the Mountains of Wonder but not too far away from Sholar. One of the main reasons that she felt so close to this Cluster was that it delved so deeply into, not only the history of Loon, but into the history of her ancestors on Earth as well. In addition, this Cluster continued to monitor Earth's current condition after the apocalypse, and after her experiences in the Room, she could never forget her old home and what it meant to her.

***

Preparing to leave for the History Cluster was exciting and sad. Zeer gathered together her belongings and the many memories from the last two full cycles. There was the leather book that had brought her so much knowledge about Earth, some clothes and some other items, including her own sphere. It was strange how such a small, light, luminous object could do so much. She, along with everyone on Loon, felt a deep connection to her own personal sphere. She glanced back at her apartment one last time, turned, and left for her new home.

Dominie and Landree were waiting for her outside. Zeer had chosen to travel with Landree in his bubble-chair to the History Cluster. It was such a wonderful way to cross Loon. She was extremely excited and a little nervous. The actual location of her new Cluster was along a high cliff in one of the tallest mountains in the area. She had been able to visit her new home recently, and the views were extraordinarily vast and breathtaking. She could see immense stretches of landscape as well as the edge of Sholar. It would be an astonishing place to live and work. She was looking forward to what she might be able to add to the historical perspective of the people of Loon.

Zeer gave Dominie a goodbye hug and then looked over at Landree. What a wonderful, giving man he was. They had shared so much when she first came to Loon. He'd been her teacher and her friend. His eyes twinkled back as they both sat in the bubble-chair and flew off toward the History Cluster and her new home.

"Landree?"

"Yes."

"I'm really looking forward to becoming part of the History Cluster, but I'm also sad to leave you and everyone in the Learning Cluster. Today, I've got a lot of emotions in me, and I can't help but think back to where it all began. I think a lot about my home on R-131, the people that I knew and cared for there and the experience of coming here. It makes me feel so small."

"That's to be expected, young one. You are still so new here. There's still so much to learn. As Loonites, we have spent centuries progressing, learning and becoming who we are. You're now part of us in a way that no one ever has. You came here from the outside. You weren't born from the original reproductive material that had been sent from Earth, but you are still our sister none the less."

"I know, but part of me would like to be able to help the other humans who have left Earth as well. What about them? They've all been on a great search for another planet like Earth. I know that they've been out in the galaxy for so long that the reason for their search has been diluted and almost forgotten, but it's still there. We all know how important it is for the human race to find its new home. Loon seems to be that home. I understand the delicate balance that exists here between the people and Loon. I would never want to destroy that, but what about the others?" Then Zeer had to ask, again, her burning question, "And...why was I chosen? I still don't completely understand."

Landree didn't speak except to say, "Don't worry, you'll learn in time." He then banked the bubble-chair towards Sholar, and Zeer watched with excitement as Landree set it down next to the water in a place where she knew that the Scree often visited.

"It might be a while before you're out here again. Speak to the Scree. Ask them your question."

Zeer moved forward, placed her sphere in the water and quietly thought of the Scree. A phenomenally large head moved out of the water towards her. It was Calna again. Zeer looked into her eyes.

"I know, young Zeer. You have a question."

"Yes," Zeer could feel Calna's concern.

Calna knew immediately what question Zeer had. Landree and Calna seemed to glance at each other knowingly and then back at Zeer. "You must work hard in your new Cluster, learn about our history and become even more a part of this planet." Zeer was startled at how Calna seemed to know everything that had been happening, even about her decision to become part of the History Cluster.

"You will understand more in time, Zeer. But, don't worry, the people of Loon love all of the human family and are working for them. Remember, diversity is essential to the health of all. You will understand more in time."

Calna began moving back into the water. The meeting was short, but somehow Zeer felt better and ready to move on. She walked out of the water, stepped back inside the bubble-chair and moved off towards her new home.

As the two of them glided towards the History Cluster, they were being watched by a large gathering of her old friends from inside the great hall of the Learning Cluster. The group was standing in a circle, each of them holding their sphere in the air, creating a large projected image. The image gave them a crystal clear view of their new friend, Zeer, and of Landree. They shared in this moment, and Zeer seemed to be able to feel the care and love from all of them. As everyone looked on, Loon's daylight dimmed, and the planet lay bathed in moonlight. She and Landree passed along the edge of Sholar on their journey. The water glittered as if diamonds dotted its surface - the night, a sweeping canvas of hope stretching out as far as they could see.

Standing next to the plastisheild covering of the lifeglobe on R-131, Rad gazed outward, watching and longing to be beyond the transparent wall. The surface winds blew, and the light was harsh with stark shadows and contrasts, the mountains rising in the distance. Rad's memory was fresh and hot with his recent experiences. But even though he yearned to be free again, it had also felt wonderful recently to just live and contemplate what he'd gone through for a while. Thinking back, it all seemed such a fantasy, but he knew it was real. Real experiences. Real people. Real places. Real living things.

Sweat from his brow slid down his forehead. He'd been resting for a moment; his speedcycle lay next to him against the plastisheild wall. He glanced up. The structure was impressive. The engineers had outdone themselves building it. He could see in all directions with a minimum of obstructions. The workers from the terrarium had planted extravagant varieties of trees, shrubs and flowering plants wherever they could. It was a very pleasant place to live. However, Rad still felt claustrophobic. His yearning had grown. *He* had grown, and his view of life had expanded.

He had read so much in the leather bound book about Earth. Its environment at one time had been so vibrant. He looked out again and saw R-131, but his mind's eye visualized Earth from the pages of that wonderful book and from the phenomenal experiences of the second level of the Room. He saw humans as they should be – vulnerable, free and in the natural world.

Rad had spent the last months enjoying Tal, Simon and Vella, a young woman who had recently moved to R-131 from a lunar settlement nearby. She and Rad enjoyed each other, laughed and had spent a lot of time talking about the life they were living. She was a great friend and companion, and she enjoyed Tal and Simon as well. They had all become very close. However, Rad's memories and his subconscious were beginning to take hold again. His thoughts wandered, even when they were all together. Tal, Simon, and especially Vella, had noticed the change in him. They were all aware that he seemed to be starting to focus on the Room again. It worried them, but Rad could no more control his thoughts than he could forget what had happened.

He climbed back onto his cycle and flew off. It brought him out of his obsessive remembering and relaxed him. He pulled up to the building where he lived, hopped off, folded the speedcycle and bounded up the stairs to his living quarters. He always felt the best there. His living area was filled with things that meant a great deal to him: pictures of his family and friends, places he'd been, music, art, decorations that reminded him of significant times in his life and items that brought beauty to his home. Two items were especially important to him – the sphere and the book. They lay next to his bed, and as always, he felt drawn to open the book and read. Tonight, though, he decided against it and glanced out at the Center of the lifeglobe. He would contact his friends and go out again. He simply needed their companionship and a good time.

\*\*\*

Vella saw Rad first and snuck up behind him. She poked him in the ribs, causing him to flinch and laugh. She always seemed to bring a smile when Rad saw her.

"You're a pain, Vella!"

"Yeah, I know. You love it, though, don't you."

"Sure."

They both laughed and noticed Tal and Simon coming down the walkway toward them. When they all met, they hugged and started ambling off together. They knew which room they were going to play tonight.

Simon summarized all of their thoughts by saying, "This is going to be fantastic!" Everyone agreed. The rooms on R-131 had continued to evolve and change more and more as high-level players were drawn there.

\*\*\*

They stood together just outside the entrance – a touch of

apprehension passed between them. Looking at the exterior of this Room, it seemed that there was absolutely nothing special about it. It was the newest game on R-131 and was just on the far side of what was considered the Center.

Vella's hand brushed Rad's as all four of the companions shared glances and obviously questioned what was soon to happen. Passing through the doors of any Room, especially on R-131, brought up feelings of nervousness and insecurity as well as excitement. One never knew for sure what would happen, who would be chosen or what would be seen or felt. It was, simply put, always a very powerful experience. And this Room, in the short time that it had been in operation, was already known as one of the most hypnotic and was the one that everyone was talking about, especially at The Club. It had a very simple name. It was called "*One.*" Anyone who had experienced it had left exhausted because of the physical and mental energy that had been required, but they'd also been exhilarated by the depth and quality of the experience.

The four were ready. They stepped up to the simple door. There was no light or vid to view them, no automated system to let them in. They'd heard that the door simply locked when the optimum number of participants was inside. Tal placed his hand on the handle and turned the knob. The door opened. Simon glanced back and noticed others coming to participate. The door shut quickly as they entered a small room. They read a sign that asked them to take off their shoes and place them under a bench. Another sign was attached to a door at the far end of the room. It said, 'Please come in.'

Simon led the way. They had wanted to enter the room early so that they could get the best seats around the viewing area. They glanced into the dimly lit enclosure and noticed that there were no seats. However, a comfortable floor covering caressed their feet. It made them all smile nervously and look at each other. Their eyes began to adjust to the low light. They could now see small candles that looked as if they were floating near the center of the room. They sat near the candles on the floor. Meditative music played in the background; the melody embraced and surrounded them, creating a quietly energetic, expectant atmosphere. They waited. No one spoke.

Others arrived. The room filled. The tension was building. No one knew what to expect. No one knew how it would begin. The music flowed on, adding to the nervous anxiety being fostered and created by the rising and falling within the melodic line and rhythm of the music.

Then the volume lessened, and everyone could then distinguish soft murmurings around the room. The music finally faded completely, and even the murmurings stopped. Everyone felt a mild, cool breeze as the candles were noiselessly extinguished and darkness fell.

Nothing happened for what seemed a long, drawn out, uncomfortable period of time - the amount of time that produces questions in a person's mind. It was awkward. And then...the tiniest point of light pricked the darkness, almost unnoticeably. It was several meters off of the floor in the center of their vision, and even though it was infinitesimal in size, everyone's eyes were drawn to it. They stared at the small light, and at the same time, the floor, the air, their bodies and the room began to vibrate from a single deep note - one note, prolonged as if by the constant bowing of a symphony of cellos in absolute unity – a note that encompassed and penetrated the souls of the gathered. It focused and delivered them into the moment.

Sitting on the soft material that covered the floor, Rad looked into Vella's eyes. Everyone had begun to feel a shift - a shift in time, space, and reality. The note continued. The players lost touch with their bodies. The room seemed to melt away. They were now in space. The lifeglobe was far below them – stars spread out above. They were floating as a group. They could see each other clearly. Surprised, quick glances moved between the players. They gasped; every person there had been chosen.

It was unsettling, mesmerizing, frightening, and completely overwhelming at the same time. It had happened in the blink of their collective eyes.

The longer they were there Rad and the others began noticing a slight glimmer, a sparkle, and a curved shield, which surrounded them. Everyone tried to breathe normally and remain calm, but what they were experiencing seemed impossible. They should all be gasping for air in this weightless vacuum and feeling the utter coldness of space. They didn't. Physically, they were comfortable. The experience was mind altering.

Communally, the group was still in a circle, still in their original positions. With the passing of each second, however, each one of them became more and more tense and nervous as they floated in this weightless environment of space, transfixed by the realization of the distance between where they hovered and R-131.

The sphere of glimmering energy that surrounded them was slightly more evident now. Vella also noticed the tiny ball of light in the center of their vision and pointed in that direction for her friends to see. They looked, and as they did, they suddenly burst towards the surface of R-131. They couldn't actually feel the movement, but they could see what was happening as if they were being propelled from a tremendous height directly towards the planet - naked, open, and fragile. The surface flew towards them. They all knew that this was the end.

But in the very moment that they and their bubble were about to crash into the lifeglobe on R-131, they changed direction and jetted across the surface at a height that allowed them to consciously observe the planet's topographic variation - its sad, raw beauty. Skipping across R-131's surface, they could see its moons on the horizon becoming larger as they rushed forward.

Covering almost the entire planet at lightning speed, crisscrossing its surface and passing over their lifeglobe several times, gave the exultant passengers, for the first time, a perspective on their planet that was beyond words. As suddenly as they had plunged toward the planet, they now were again above it, sitting calmly observing the stars. That lasted only a moment. Then they took off again towards R-131's moons and experienced the craters, the icefalls, the deep canyons and the many features of each of the white lunar orbs near their world.

Slowing and settling down lightly, the players landed on R-131's outer moon, B, and in the distance they could see their home hovering in the dark blanket of space. Rad merely shook his head in wonder, and Simon finally spoke what they all felt, "I can't believe this." It was said plainly, but all of them agreed.

Vella grabbed Rad and Simon's hands and saw the questions in Tal's eyes. They were sitting hundreds of thousands of kilometers from home on a moon of stark and marvelous splendor. They breathed deeply and sighed almost jointly as the moments passed.

In the middle of the gathering, voices began to come out of the small bright light. It was almost a chanted chorus, calling to each of them. Listening more intently, they noticed the voices gaining strength and power while continuing to emanate from the small bauble. As this happened, a surreal vision of a human being appeared in the middle of their circle. The person was caught inside a smaller translucent bubble. Watching carefully, they could now see that it was a man fighting to get out, yelling silently. His eyes showed the strain of capture, of being held and desperately trying to free himself. Then Rad, Vella and Simon realized who the person was. It was Tal. They quickly looked over to where Tal had been. He was no longer beside them. They wanted to go to him – help him. They couldn't. They were held in place, unable to move towards him. He looked in their direction without actually recognizing that they were there and then unexpectedly, he stopped struggling, sat quietly for a moment longer and then vanished.

Everyone looked around the circle trying to understand and decipher what was happening. Then, another person in the group vanished and re-appeared in the center inside a bubble. Struggling again at first, then becoming subdued and again fading from view.

One by one, each individual that was there appeared in the structure at the center and vaporized and was gone. Finally, only Rad and Vella were left. They held each other. Then she was no longer in Rad's grasp. She was gone. He was alone.

He felt empty, worried, expectant... He was facing his home planet. The light was just beginning to crest the horizon; morning was touching its surface.

At the point where the small bright ball of light had been, Rad now noticed a dark point of emptiness. It grew. He felt the pull of it. It tugged at him physically. He was being wrenched towards it. It consumed him. He was thrown into it. He felt terror. The type of fear that consumes and controls every nerve. The darkness had a heaviness to it that was eating away at everything around him. In that moment, he looked back towards R-131 and reached out towards his home. Then, he was gone.

***

Back inside of *One*, the members of that night's gathering were together again, sitting in a circle, gazing at what was happening to Rad. Each of them had been on their own individual journey after leaving the moon, experiencing moments that belonged only to them. However, for some reason, they were all back now witnessing the last moments of Rad's experience. Tears, sighs and spoken thoughts of fear were shared, and then the room was quiet. The lit candles rematerialized, hovering in the air. The circular outline of *One* reasserted itself, and the luxurious covering on the floor again caressed their bodies. A silent understanding of completion passed through everyone. It was done.

As the players began to leave, they could still feel what had happened, but no one said a word. No one could put out of their mind what they had witnessed at the very end. They had seen Rad reach out and then watched as he had been yanked into an abyss. He was simply gone. It chilled them. Vella was the only one who finally gave voice to what everyone was thinking, "Where...where is he?" She couldn't believe and wouldn't admit that he was gone.

The last to leave the Room were Rad's three friends. They'd stayed behind in the hope that he would somehow reappear, but then they, too, left and walked into the night. The door closed behind them, and as it did, Tal reached back just to check. The door was locked.

# 18
## The Decision

The mineral-laden liquid moved and spread across the sand like shifting glass. It was a clear, warm evening on Loon with the sheets of liquid pulsing in and out, and the warm sun moving across the sky near the horizon. Its bright rays were glancing off the water-laden shore, sparkling in the eyes of the members of the Circle on the beach. It was an important meeting. It was time to decide.

The small group remained seated, meditating together, hands touching, sitting on the beach near Sholar. They had come to a decision. It was clear that they were ready to proceed. Dominie, Shee, Brit, Landree and Fawn had guided the other members of the Circle on this beautiful evening through a serious and thoughtful discussion. At the start, the views within the Circle were varied, and it was obvious that everyone there had come prepared, ready to discuss and back up their ideas with facts and research. However, in the end their opinions coalesced and all could feel the correctness and positive energy connected with the direction that the late afternoon's discussions had taken. The agreement was tangible - the pathway clear. They all had agreed that they could not act as if the human race outside of Loon did not exist or that they didn't deserve what the people of Loon had found. The cost could be high to open up their society to the humans outside of Loon, but because of their beliefs, they could not turn away. Tonight it had begun in earnest, but the exact course and outcome would only be clear in time. They would need to proceed carefully and slowly.

As they came out of the intense process, everyone realized what had been set in motion. Rad was now the key. He was their choice – the male counterpoint to Zeer – and Zeer was to be more deeply involved in the process. They would now have to watch, wait and observe.

Fawn, spoke to the assembly with these words, "If Rad is successful, we continue forward." Everyone agreed, and at that very moment, Fawn separated from the Circle, leaving to prepare for the final level of the Room.

***

Zeer was not aware of what had happened that day. She didn't know how her life would soon be altered. She had been immersed in learning, studying, researching and adding to the knowledge and records in the History Cluster. She had expanded her understanding of Loon's people, their culture, their story and the history of Earth that had brought them to Loon. There was so much to learn and record. What she had experienced on R-131 and the other colonies where she had lived had also been shared and added to the massive knowledge of the History Cluster.

She had been working that day looking for relationships between the civil wars of the early twenty-first century and the political and corporate decisions that had been made during that time. The ethnic and religious civil wars at that juncture were the beginning of what was the eventual decline of all life on Earth as well as the massive environmental degradation that would affect everyone on the planet. It was extremely sad and yet exceptionally important and captivating.

Zeer was just finishing her work when she noticed a group of her friends talking excitedly in the gathering area. She walked toward them and glanced out at the beautiful evening. Loon was spectacular tonight. The Mountains of Wonder were splashed with the paint from a red, orange and yellow palette as the sun's light passed through the liquid prism in the atmosphere. She smiled.

Nearing her friends, their voices became more coherent. She heard that someone, a male, had been chosen for the next all-important level of research. There was obvious interest and support for the plan that had been discussed for so long and was now going forward - a plan that would change life for everyone on Loon.

Zeer increased her pace and asked, "What's happening? I heard something about the plan going forward."

Everyone started talking at once. Then they all laughed and let Prime, the one who had brought them the news, continue the conversation, "He's been picked. A male has been chosen. If he succeeds, our plan for diversity and expansion will finally happen, and Zeer, you were the first. Now, this will tell us if it can really work."

Zeer felt awkward, yet excited. She knew that the plan that everyone was talking about also included her in some way. "I wonder who it is? Have you heard?"

"We haven't," Prime said, "but we've heard that he passed the second level. There has been a lot of discussion by our leaders in the Circle. They obviously decided to go forward. They'll keep us informed as things progress."

Zeer thought back to the dangerous experiences that she had gone through in the third level of the Room. She knew that there was a chance that, whoever he was, he might not succeed. He might not even survive. Choices. There had been so many of them.

"Thanks for letting me know. I'm going to try to talk to Dominie or Landree and see what I can learn from them."

She waved as she quickly walked off toward her living area. She was wondering about the man who had been chosen and how this would affect her life, her studies and the future of Loon. *'What would happen now?'*

\*\*\*

Zeer had been able to talk to Dominie and Landree but wasn't given any new information. She was told that she would meet with Fawn after her return.

Rumors raced around the planet. The population was so connected and close that everyone knew at least someone in every Cluster who knew something important, some piece of information about the project. The excitement was growing. Zeer was becoming anxious as she waited to be contacted. She couldn't help but listen to the rumors and come up with scenarios of her own.

She finally received a message one evening asking her to return to the Learning Cluster. Fawn would be there, and she wanted to see Zeer as soon as she could. Zeer was relieved and yet very apprehensive. She would finally get some answers.

*\*\**

The time arrived. Zeer stood outside Fawn's living area. It was in a remote corner of the Learning Cluster. It was very quiet there. She could see a light under the door to Fawn's quarters. She walked tepidly up to it. It opened. Zeer glanced inside. The lights within were dim. It took her eyes some time to adjust, but she finally noticed Fawn standing near her circular outview gazing out at Loon.

Fawn had returned from R-131 about an hour before and had changed into some relaxed and comfortable clothes. Her hair was hanging down towards the lower part of her back, and she continued facing outward as she uttered, "Zeer, thank you for coming."

Zeer responded, "It's always an honor to spend time with you, Fawn. I'm glad to finally be here and glad you're home." They embraced and turned together to gaze outside, their eyes soaking in the glorious morning on Loon.

# 19
## The Room: Level 3
## War

There are those times when we rest and the quiet solitude of sleep with its dark cover pulled over our eyes goes beyond a night's deepest moments. Yet it does not frighten or harm us; we grow from it; we energize because of it. It teaches us, enhances creativity and brings us joy. It adds to our lives.

But there are also those sleeps when we lay uneasy and unsettled in the night. The kind that we wake from, shaky, unbalanced, wondering or confused. Sleeps from which we seemingly barely survive.

***

Coming to, very slowly, from a long and arduous night, Rad's eyelids worked their way open, closed and open again. He lay on a hard surface covered by a thin, rough blanket, and as his awareness increased and the radius of his pupils adapted, he noticed mild rays of light entering from the upper portion of an archway. He could smell spices and other odors that at first seemed completely alien to him. They were tantalizingly pungent, but the longer he sniffed and took in their aromas, the more he recalled being exposed to them before. It had been on a lifeglobe - one that he had lived on before R-131.

Beyond the aromas and the light shafting onto his face, he heard voices. They were speaking in a tongue that he didn't recognize. The words were quick and strung together. They were male and female, and it almost sounded like an argument. He wasn't sure.

He sat up quietly in the darkened room, stood slowly and moved toward the wall with his hands outstretched in order to avoid making any inadvertent noise. His fingers touched a rough, prickly, surface. His eyes strained to gain some understanding of where he was and what was happening around him.

The voices moved closer and then a curtain of some kind

121

opened in the archway, flooding the room with light. He threw his arm up against the sudden brightness and a hand grasped his elbow. He was surprised but quickly relaxed because of the gentle touch. His nerves were on edge. He was trying to understand as his experience changed second by second. The voice behind the hand said, "It's alright. Come with me."

Rad moved into the light and walked into a bright, sparsely furnished room. There was a cooking oven at one end with strong odors emanating from it.

"We found you laying outside our house," the man said. His eyes were dark along with his hair and his features sharp; his skin was leathery and tanned. A strong-featured woman was standing beside him. She had an exceptional smile that extended to her eyes. Rad assumed this was the man's wife.

Rad didn't quite know what to say for a moment but then decided to keep it simple. "I'm really not sure how I got here." He noticed a look that crossed between the man and the woman. He thought he understood.

"Everyone has those nights. Don't worry. My name is Fadil, and this is my wife Ahd. Come sit down and eat. I'm sure you could use the nourishment."

"My name is Rad, and I'd love some food. I'm famished." Rad could tell that they probably believed that he was a tourist. He assumed that they thought he'd probably been out the night before drinking and had just ended up on their doorstep. He would go ahead and foster that impression.

They all sat down together and enjoyed a morning meal and some very strong coffee. Rad felt much better and was beginning to understand more about where he was. From his studies of Earth, it seemed as if he might be in the Middle East somewhere. Fadil and Ahd seemed very kind and well educated. He was lucky they'd found him.

During the meal, they'd talked politely, and Rad had asked about the food and the city. They had wanted to know where Rad had come from. He thought quickly and told them that he'd come from Boston. It was the first place that came to his mind. As they conversed, though, Rad was trying to come to grips with what had happened. He was again astounded with the reality of where he was. He had somehow left R-131 at the end of the game, *One*, and now he was on Earth again but at a much later time in history. This had to be the next level of the Room. *'Why did the old one bring me here?'*

"You speak English so well. I was wondering how you learned to speak my language?" Rad asked.

Fadil spoke for both of them and said, "We've traveled a lot, and we went to school in England. That's where we met, and we learned English there."

"I see... Thank you for the meal and for giving me a place to stay last night. It was really nice of you to help a stranger in need, but I won't stay. I'd better be going."

Fadil asked, "Where are you staying while you're here?"

Rad stuttered and said, "I...I really don't have a place yet. I just arrived."

"You can stay with us until you find a place," Ahd commented.

"Thank you, but I couldn't impose."

"It's okay, you can stay with us," Ahd said, as Fadil seemed to agree but with obvious reservation in his eyes.

"Okay. I really appreciate it. Thank you." Rad knew that he actually didn't have any other choice. He was still very disoriented and needed some time to figure out this level of the Room, so he accepted.

After the meal, he decided to go out and explore and get a better feeling for the city and try to understand why he might possibly be here. He was in the city of Riyadh. The streets were busy. As he walked, he noticed people talking, cars passing and storefronts with people lingering outside or going in to buy whatever was on hand. He walked through a marketplace and immediately connected the smell of spices, vegetables and cooked meats to those from Ahd and Fadil's home. It was an active, busy city, and he was again walking outside unencumbered and free. The sky was wonderful and the air very hot and dry. It was so different from anything he had ever known. He passed by men smoking and cars puffing out fumes and clouds of exhaust. The smells were not all healthy, he could tell. Some even made him cough and wish that he was still in the filtered air of a lifeglobe, but altogether, it was a precarious, chaotic and exciting place to be.

As he moved amongst the throngs of people, he passed by two younger men. They were speaking in English. One was obviously of western descent, but both were dressed in the local style. "Do you think the Americans will do it?" one wondered.

"Most of us don't really believe they will, but our leaders are taking it seriously. You've noticed all the military activity. This is a dangerous time."

"Do you know what you're going to do?"

"I have a friend who lives outside the city. I'm going there. What about you?"

"I'm staying here with my family. We don't live near any palace, government building or military complex so we should be fine. And even if the Americans do fire their missiles, they're accurate, but I still don't believe they'll do it."

Rad walked on wondering what they had been talking about, and as he moved away, he noticed that both of them were looking at him with suspicion. He simply ignored the look, but the longer he was out, he couldn't help but observe many others on the streets looking at him the same way – some even with anger in their eyes. Rad felt on edge and vulnerable; he didn't feel safe here.

He spent the rest of his day watching and trying to learn as much about where he was as he could. He, too, began to notice a substantial amount of what he assumed was military activity. As he walked, he observed men in uniforms with guns and other equipment that looked like weapons. Rad thought that he remembered this era from his studies about the wars and problems on the Earth during its history. He racked his brain to recall more about what he'd read.

The day was quickly coming to a close. He was making his way back to Fadil and Ahd's house and finally reached their home about dark. He knocked. The door opened. Ahd welcomed him in, but he could tell the mood in the house was different as they sat down to eat.

As they were eating, Rad brought up the subject of what he'd heard the two men talking about earlier in the day. Fadil's face reddened and Ahd's demeanor became serious as well. "Yes, we're all afraid of what might happen. You might not have heard, since you've been traveling, but within the last week there have been a string of attacks within the United States. The American government says that it believes that a Muslim extremist group that hated the U. S. caused these attacks. The bombs that went off in several cities across America caused a great deal of damage, and thousands of people lost their lives. The American government believes that those responsible came from our country. Our government is preparing for the worst, and all of us are afraid of what might happen."

"What exactly might happen?"

Both Fadil and Ahd looked at Rad in a way that showed their surprise at his question. Fadil said angrily, "What do you think will happen?

"I don't know for sure. I really don't," Rad said apologetically.

"Their forces are in our ocean and in the air around Riyadh. They're an angry nation…"

In the middle of Fadil's words, explosions racked the area outside the apartment. Doors and windows burst inwards. Both Fadil and Ahd took the brunt of one of the powerful blasts. They fell forward, and Rad could see the glass and mortar that had penetrated their backs. They both lay there motionless and bleeding on the floor.

The blasts continued. Rad had been thrown back and was on the floor as well. He looked down at himself. He was stunned and in shock but wasn't injured. He got up and checked both Fadil and Ahd, but neither was breathing, and he couldn't find a heartbeat. Outside people were screaming and running. Rad could see them through the large, jagged opening in the wall. He didn't know what to do except to run and get out of the building.

People were lying everywhere. Dirt and clouds of gas floated in the air with craters puncturing the pavement where streets, cars and people had been just moments before.

As he went outside, another bomb exploded. He ducked down behind a car as it hit and destroyed a large building. Soldiers were filling the streets, moving quickly in unison towards the outskirts of the city. They were pouring out of buildings from every direction, and as they passed him, some couldn't help but notice his skin color and demeanor. Hatred filled their eyes, but they kept moving, hurrying to their destination.

Chaos, death and destruction spread in every direction. Non-discriminate bomb blasts continued. Husbands, wives, children, soldiers, older people, people just going about their daily work – all of them lay dying and maimed. Most of the injured and dead were simply citizens living their lives. *'They were not an army going off to war! What was this?'*

Rad ran for cover. He ran wherever he thought it might be safer, but where would that be for a foreigner in a country under attack? It was getting darker outside, but he saw a temple a short distance away and headed in that direction. He reached the doors just as another large explosion hit the back of the mosque. Several men ran out shouldering past him, running for their lives. Two of the men, however, stopped directly in front of him, looked at him with pure hatred, grabbed him and drug him on the ground as they moved away down the street.

They yanked him into a large warehouse where Rad had noticed soldiers coming from just moments earlier. It was dark inside except for a few small overhead lights. They threw him on the floor and spoke in angry tones to each other. Rad couldn't understand what they were saying, but he knew he was in danger. Both men had bloody patches on their clothing. They'd been injured in one of the blasts, but the wounds didn't seem serious. He also noticed that they had similar armbands with Arabic lettering on them. One pulled out a gun. He was swinging it around as they yelled at each other.

Rad looked around. Fear and adrenaline rushed through his system. *'How could this be the Room?'* His life was in danger here. These were real people in the middle of a real war in a real world. He remembered his fright and flight response during the second level of the Room when his life was in danger. He'd made it through all that. It grounded him. He breathed and began to look for a way out of this. He wondered if he would have to kill to survive.

Rad spoke as firmly as he could, although he knew his voice shook slightly. "Do either of you speak English?"

They both looked at him, one with a sneer on his lips, spittle coming out of his mouth from the force of yelling. They ignored Rad and continued their angry tirade.

Rad then noticed a small vehicle located a short distance away along with some other pieces of machinery that he might be able to hide behind. A little further in the distance he could also see a small crack of light entering the building. It might be a door.

He was deciding what to do when another huge, thundering detonation rattled and shook the ground. The two men grabbed on to each other as they lost their balance for a moment. This was Rad's chance. He sprang to his feet, ran to the car and slid behind it. Shots rang out. He'd made it, but the two men were on their way towards him. He moved as fast as he had ever moved and ran to the next piece of equipment, looked around for some type of weapon and found a large iron bar on the ground. With the bar in hand, he cautiously glanced around the barrier at the men moving his way. They didn't know that he had a weapon, so they moved toward him with abandon. His fingers wrapped tightly around the long bar, and he focused his attention on the one with the gun. Once the men were near enough, Rad jumped out and swung the bar downward as hard as he could. The bar cracked against the man's hands. He yelled in pain and dropped the gun. The other paused for just a moment, which gave Rad the chance to jump for the gun and grab it. He pointed it at the men. Their eyes changed from hatred to fright as Rad moved them back towards a door to his right. He pushed the handle to open the door and saw a room inside with no other exit. He signaled the men inside, shoved a heavy piece of equipment in front of the door and placed the bar behind the handle to lock them in.

For the moment, he was safe, but outside this building, the destruction continued. Nowhere was safe. He ran toward the crack of light that he'd noticed. It was an exit – a street lamp lit the night outside the door. He glanced out, opened the door and sprinted towards what he thought was a park in the distance.

He stopped, frozen in his tracks. Just as he had started to run through the hazy and rancid smoke from the bombs, an emotional shock hit him. All around him lay thousands of people, parts of people, blood, cries of agony, total bedlam. *'What caused this hell?'*

A small, young girl was running, calling out, crazed and afraid. Rad ran towards her. Her clothes were torn and shredded. She was alive, but where was her family? He caught her and held her. Her body shook as she cried and cried and screamed in his arms, and inside, he too screamed, *'My god this is sick! A moment ago all of these people were just living their lives. Now this!'*

He held the young girl close - her shaking sobs echoed inside his body as terror rained down on the city in the dark.

# 20
## The Room: Level 3
## AmeriCorp

Rad awoke with a rush of emotion. He couldn't help a barely audible shout. "Where the hell am I now?" He was sitting against a wall in an alley of what seemed to be a much different city. Someone had just been checking his pockets and moved away quickly as he awoke. People were walking by, staring. He glanced down at his lap, where only a moment before, he had held the young child in the middle of a war zone.

He blinked, and as he did, the sounds and smells of the alley assaulted his senses. He retched from the sour stench, just barely holding down what he had in his stomach. He got up and walked quickly out toward a street. He saw large, architecturally benign buildings - all with a similar structure and look. People were passing by dressed in simple clothes, walking, riding bicycles and traveling on small three-wheeled vehicles with engines that spewed out noxious fumes. Some were eating at food stands that seemed to be everywhere along the street; others were rushing to get to their destinations, and many were going in and out of the buildings.

Rad's clothes had somehow been altered since his last experience. He now wore a very simple pair of pants and a shirt, very much like the people around him. As before, he had no idea where he was, but it seemed to be an exceptionally busy, sterile and sad existence. Not a single person was laughing or smiling, and very few were even talking.

In the distance, he saw a rack with bicycles in various stages of disrepair. Some people seemed to be grabbing them, hopping on and riding. He thought, '*Why not?*' and walked over and chose one of the better ones that he could find and started riding. He recalled reading about and seeing images of these types of bicycles. They were nothing like his speedcycle, but they would allow him to look around and cover more distance.

It took him a little while to get used to the old bicycle, but as he did he traveled outside the city and noticed many extremely small huts. They seemed to go on forever as he watched the same type of people that he'd noticed earlier going in or out of them. It looked as if they might be going to or from work. The homes were incredibly close together, and he saw clothing that hung between many of them, drying in the acrid air.

As he continued on, he came to a few green areas where very large and shiny buildings were situated. He noticed that the people entering and leaving those buildings carried themselves much differently and were clean and well dressed. The difference between them and the people dressed like him was extreme in almost every way. These people were even using a different means of transporting themselves. They were coming and going in small flying vehicles. Rad watched and followed some as they flew back into the city. He couldn't keep up, but he followed in their general direction. They were flying towards the buildings where the others seemed to be working.

He gazed up and saw some of the flying machines landing on the roofs of the non-descript buildings. At that point, he couldn't help but observe that the top floors of each of those buildings had more windows and looked more livable.

It all brought questions to Rad's mind that he couldn't answer, so he road back to where he had regained consciousness and stopped to look more carefully. It seemed that there was a deeply engrained class structure in this world. Down the alleyways, he looked at the people that he had seen when he first arrived. These people didn't go in or out of the buildings and had dirty rags on for clothes. They huddled in the many side streets and alleys, and their only transportation, as far as he could see, were their own two feet. They seemed to be settled into the heart of the city – not moving out to where most of the others lived in the small huts.

He walked hesitantly back down the alley where he had arrived and found a young woman who looked to be about twenty years old huddled in a brown, ragged box with her young daughter. They were sitting on top of a tattered cushion. He moved closer, and her eyes focused nervously on him. She scooted back into the box even further, although it didn't seem that she did it as much out of fear as out of caution. Her eyes and demeanor were brave and strong. She grabbed a piece of wood that lay on the ground nearby and waited to see what Rad would do.

He raised his hands in a gesture of appeasement and tried his best to seem non-threatening and then spoke to her, "Don't worry. I...I just want to talk. I have some questions that you might be able to answer. I won't come too close. I promise." He smiled at them, and the daughter smiled back. The mother remained cautious – her gaze unwavering as she watched Rad's every move.

"What kind of questions? Who are you, and why did you walk into our alley?" she asked in a strong, mocking way.

Rad could tell from the way she spoke and carried herself that she was educated. It was confusing. "You speak well, like you've had an education, yet you're living here in a box with your daughter. How could that be?"

"I *am* well educated! Don't you know anything?"

"I'm new to your city and trying to understand what's going on?

"New? What do you mean *new*? People don't travel in or out of any city in AmeriCorp."

"I'm sorry, but I don't know about your home, this AmeriCorp, and I did just get here. I came in from outside the city. I've always lived a lonely life and thought I'd come in to see what was going on." It was a guess on Rad's part about how he might not know about her home. He didn't know if it would work, but he'd see.

"I've heard about people like you who live in the mountains west of here. I never believed it, but now I'm thinking that maybe there's something to it. Your name is Rad?"

'*Whew*,' Rad thought to himself giving a silent sigh inside. "Yes. Could you tell me more about what's going on here? What's your name?"

She avoided the name question for now and said, "Okay, we'll talk, but we'll have to be careful and watch for the tiny eyes."

"What do you mean?"

"You don't know about those either? They're tiny mechanical devices that continually move about the city by the thousands. They monitor us. They are the eyes and ears of the AmeriCorp Government and the "PoliceCorp." If you see me move my little finger like this, we'll need to change the subject and talk about something benign. Just follow my lead. Also, I think you should take off that shirt and put this on. You won't look like you're a Worker then."

"Okay." Rad couldn't believe what he was hearing. *'Their government was continually spying on their own people?'*

The woman must have changed her mind about giving Rad her name. She told him as she spoke. "My name is Jana. I've been an Outcast for about three years now. My husband stayed on in the Worker's group. I haven't seen him for a long time."

"Jana, do you mean that you chose this life instead of working in the buildings and living outside the city in the huts?"

"Yes." Jana's daughter snuggled closer to her and seemed to be listening intently to the conversation.

"Why would you do that?"

"Well..." Jana stopped talking and raised her little finger. Rad didn't look around, and they started talking about how warm it was last night. He noticed a small hum coming from above his head and felt extremely strange knowing that every word and movement were being recorded. The tiny device hovered for a few moments, moved down in front of Rad's face and then flew off.

Rad exclaimed, "Shit! That felt gross!"

Jana commented, "You get used to it, but I always feel somewhat violated. Anyway, we all live in AmeriCorp – a country that is basically one big corporation. Everything, and I mean everything, is about money and business. Human rights have gone by the wayside as well as freedom. I believe that the Outcasts have the most freedom. That's who we are, but we have to be very careful about not creating any problems for the government."

She continued, "There are basically three levels to our society, and every city in the huge country of AmeriCorp is designed in the same way. There are the Elite, the Workers and the Outcasts. The Elite are in the corporate government and at the head of all the smaller business corporations. They are, to varying degrees, extremely wealthy and will do anything in their power to stay that way and remain in the Elite. The Workers are just what you would think. They work for the corporations. Their wages are just enough to allow them to live and purchase goods that they need from the corporate businesses, but they're not wealthy by any means, and their lives are heavily controlled and sadly very short. They work long hours, and their freedoms are limited. There are some other groups such as the PoliceCorp and the MilitaryCorp that work with the Elite to help maintain control over everyone. Then there are the Outcasts. The Elite would like to see us disappear, but they put up with us as long as we stay out of their way and don't cause trouble. If we're seen mixing with the workers or out of our hideaways during the day, we're picked up and never seen again. The Outcasts are people who have made the decision to not be part of the corporate society. As I said, in some ways, I think we have the most freedom, but it's a dangerous existence and very difficult."

Rad sat listening. He remembered reading something about this time in his book, but living it and talking to Jana made his stomach turn. This was Earth, and this seemed to be what was once called America. He remembered from his studies that this country used to tout its freedoms and its people's spirit. *'What in the hell happened?'* His first guess was greed and power – two very corrupting influences.

"This is making me sick, but could you tell me more about the Outcasts?"

"Of course, the Outcasts are made up of the leaders and thinkers that disagree with the corporate government. In our history, many of us tried to change the path that this country was traveling down but were unsuccessful. However, now there are many of us and also many sympathizers who won't, or can't, speak out. We even have a few supporters within the Elite." She hesitated a moment as if deciding what she should say next. "There's more that I could tell you about what is going on now in our movement, but you have to know that I'm putting myself, the movement and you in great danger. I trust you to a certain extent, because I've never met anyone quite like you, but I don't trust you completely."

"I understand. I'd feel the same. One more thing I'd like to ask is if I could get some food. I'm starved. I road all around the city today on one of the bicycles that I found, and I've been awake for a long time."

"I think I can help."

***

Daveed was in the PoliceCorp control room as his tech device beeped at him, showing him a video of Rad and Jana. He could hear them talking, and he knew their location. They seemed to just be chatting about the weather, but the computer's database didn't know who Rad was. He was classified as an "unknown." This had never happened to Daveed before. He notified his supervisor, and they immediately sent a PoliceCorp vehicle out with three officers to find Rad and bring him in.

# 21
## The Room: Level 3
## Escape

Rad had left the alley on his bicycle and was eating in a small park nearby. The food was simple but would sustain him. He was grateful, and his energy was returning. He couldn't help but wonder about all that Jana had told him. This country was a place where its people suffered in silence, were worked to the bone and whose lives were incredibly difficult. The wealthy and powerful controlled their lives and lived with very little concern for either the Workers or the Outcasts. *'How could they not care about everyone?'*

At that moment, Rad looked up from his food. He first noticed one of the tiny eyes hovering above him and then saw a flying vehicle about twenty-five meters from where he sat. On the outside, he read the word, *PoliceCorp.*

He simply reacted. He reached up, grabbed the buzzing eye and crushed it beneath his foot. Then he quickly jumped onto the bicycle and headed down a narrow path in the park as fast as he could go. He heard the thump and felt a gust of wind as the vehicle landed. As he pounded the pedals, he also heard shouts and saw laser beams hitting trees above his head. Limbs flew in all directions. He had to get away from here.

Glancing ahead, the path diverged. One way seemed to descend further into the park. The other looked as if it went out of the park and into the busy city. Rad chose the second, left the park and shot down another alley. He zigzagged in and out through several back ways, jumped off his bike, hid it behind some trash and hurried through an open door into a dark building. It was deserted; at least, it seemed to be. He ran up some stairs, continually on the lookout for the small eyes of the PoliceCorp. It was dark except for a few shafts of light guiding his steps. He ran and ran upward, finally reaching a room where he could look down on the alley below and back into the park where he'd begun his escape.

He could now see and hear the flying machine moving

135

around the park. He knew the officers inside were searching for him, but at this point, they didn't seem to have any idea of his exact location. Another PoliceCorp vehicle flew into the area and started searching the alleyways, and he also now heard the humming of many tiny eyes pulsing through the air around the park and nearby sections of the city – the sun glinting off each of them as they, too, sought him out, edging their way into any crevice where he might be hiding. The pursuit still seemed random, though, with nothing indicating any specific interest in his location. He seemed safe enough for now, but he'd have to stay alert.

***

Night set in, but Rad knew from the continued sound of the flying vehicles and the constant hum of the eyes that the search was continuing. They hadn't found him yet, but he knew that it would only be a matter of time.

The good thing was that the search seemed to have widened and was even less focused near his hideaway. Maybe he could get at least a little rest.

He lay back in a dark corner as far away from the room's window as he could get. He covered himself with some scraps of cloth that he'd found on the floor. He tried not to sleep, but he did need to rest. He jerked his head up several times as his body's need for sleep was trying to overcome his desire to protect himself. Finally, he lost the battle; his eyelids closed, and he slept.

## 22
## Interlude

Fawn took Zeer's hand and walked over near the warm fire and sat with her. She smiled and said, "Zeer, it's time to speak with you about what's happening with our culture and about our plan for the future. First, though, we want you to know that we have found another person that we've chosen to possibly join us here on Loon. It's a man that you knew from when you were on R-131. His name is Rad."

Even though she didn't know Rad that well, he had made an impression on her, and of course she remembered the times they'd spoken. She'd thought a few times that it might be him, but wasn't sure. Her life had been consumed for a long time now with the Room and now Loon. She really hadn't thought much about him since she'd last seen him.

"Yes, I remember him. He seemed intense, and I remember he loved to ride his Speedcycle. He was also the one that you had me give the book to."

Fawn nodded and continued, "Rad has shown great promise. He is definitely intelligent and a learner. He wants more from his life and has an uncontrollable urge to be outside the confines of the lifeglobes. He is not a habituate as you were, but he loves to be in his body and feel strong. The Speedcycle suited his needs in that way, and he's progressed through our Room well. Though I have to say that he's a bit more reckless than you were. He's completed levels one and two and is now in the final level. You know how difficult and dangerous that level is, and you also know that his life is at stake. Every decision he makes is extremely important."

"In the levels of the Room, has Rad experienced the same times and places that I did, or are they different?"

"Zeer, we decided a long time ago that the man and woman that we chose for the Room would have experiences that related specifically to them. Of course, what you went through is similar, but other aspects are very different. The most important thing is that whoever passed and became part of our culture needed to have the same knowledge and understanding that we do of the importance of the individual and his or her relationship to the environment and to society in general. Balance in all things, Zeer, as you now know and understand."

"Yes, I understand. So what am I to do?"

"To begin with, you and I will observe Rad's progress together. First, we'll see what he has done so far and then we will watch as he enters the most difficult and final level. If he survives, there will be a point where you will enter the game with him, just as I did with you. We believe that since you have experienced the Room as Rad did and because he knows you, you can have a very good influence on the outcome of the final level of the Room for him."

Zeer wondered, "And what will I do?"

"We won't know that until it happens. Let's get started."

Fawn took out her energy sphere, and the light surrounded them both. They then began traveling through Rad's experiences, watching, listening and discussing his progress.

## 23
## The Room: Level 3
## Jana

Rad opened his eyes and uncurled his body. It hadn't been an easy night. He was a bit stiff from the hard floor but glad for the pieces of cloth that had provided some warmth and comfort. He sat up. It was morning. He watched as rays of light filtered through clouds and polluted haze and entered his broken window several stories above the city.

He shook his head to wake up and jerked with surprise. Directly across from him, he could see a person sitting against the opposite wall. Startled, his breath left him, and he stifled a scream. He looked more closely and could see now that it was Jana.

"Jesus! You scared the shit out of me Jana!"

"Sorry, we've been looking for you most of the night. We found out what happened to you, and I've been hiding as well. I can't let the PoliceCorp find me now that they've seen us talking. They'll probably kill both of us if we're found."

She continued, "What are you really doing here? I've thought more about it, and there's something pretty strange about your story. We've never met anyone from the mountain area. It's a rough trek from there to here. Are you sure you want to stick with that story?"

Rad thought for a moment and decided that he would simply tell her the truth. He had nothing to lose. "You're right Jana. I'm not from the mountains. I'm going to tell you the truth and explain why I'm here. Well, as much as I know anyway. It's going to be difficult to believe, I know. I hope I can trust you. So here goes..."

Rad and Jana talked most of the day and into the early evening. He was right about it being difficult for Jana to believe, but she listened, asked questions and did her best to trust Rad's story. He also trusted her more and more as he let his story out.

She noted, "I can't quite believe that anyone could make up anything so wild, so I'm going to give you the benefit of the doubt. But what you've told me is way too crazy for me to buy completely. Anyway, whether it's all true or not, you're on the same side as the Outcasts now, and you're in trouble with the PoliceCorp. What are you going to do?"

"I don't know Jana. I seem to be safe for the moment, and I know I'm here to learn about Earth during this time period. I appreciate all that you've shared with me. It's horrible how much this world has changed. At least in this country."

Jana then gave Rad more information, "From what we can gather and from the information that we've stolen, the corporations all over the world seem to have taken over. They are huge, and the governments, what are left of them, no longer exist to help people. For the most part, the governments *are* the corporations. They provide their workers with as much money and education as is needed to sustain profitability, and they want the workers to have children to be able to maintain the needed pool of employees and consumers for a stable economic environment, but that's all. People all over the world are living very short lives and are suffering, whether they are fighting against the control of the corporations or working for them. Environmental and social degradation are on the rise, and money and greed have become the main forces that push our world ahead. As I alluded to before, many of the Workers, most of the Outcasts and a few of the Elite want to change things, but that means going up against the power and might of the corporations, which realistically will only cause the deaths of many of those who try. Most of the rich at the top of the social and economic ladder don't want any drastic changes. A huge change through revolution is definitely something we're debating and considering, though. We can't live like this much longer, and we're getting to the point where the needed change outweighs the huge risks."

"I can see what you're saying. I couldn't live this way either. I think I need some time to consider everything you've told me and see what I can do to help while I'm here. I'll stay up in this room for one more night and then get in touch with you tomorrow. How can I do that?"

Jana thought for a moment and then said, "Just stay here. We'll get back to you in the late afternoon when the workers are going home. Thanks for caring and for talking with me, Rad."

"Thank *you* for teaching me and showing me what your world is like. It's not an easy place to survive is it?"

Jana nodded and slipped out the door into the night.

Rad looked out the window over the city. Shacks and shanties, small streets, smoke, and sterile buildings carpeted the landscape as far as he could see. Small lights could barely be seen through the miasma of dust and pollution, and the smell of the city wafted in through the window - its odor rancid, stale and sour from overcrowding, sickness and decay. He thought to himself, *'What they had done to this beautiful place? The people who ran the corporations were destroying the Earth, destroying each other, and destroying life on what was once a magnificent planet.'*

Staring and thinking, Rad was extremely sad and bewildered at what he was learning about Earth's history as it unfolded before his eyes. He felt numb. He shook his head and sighed in despair and held his head in his hands.

He was about to get up and move away from the window. He needed to rest. Just as he stood, though, a small glow appeared next his hand on the broken windowsill. Noticing the sphere of light frightened him. It must be another PoliceCorp device; he'd been discovered. He began to slide back into the darkness as quickly as he could. "Damn you! You're not going to do this!" he hissed. The glow from the sphere grew, though, and surrounded him. It lifted him off the floor. He fought back, hitting at its surface, with little consequence. It picked him up and moved him through the skeletal window frame and outside the building. He gasped, as he looked straight down several stories to the alley below. There was nothing beneath him to keep him from falling to his death except the translucent sphere that surrounded him. He was completely exposed, and he knew that he was in serious trouble. However, just then, at his most vulnerable moment, the sphere, with him inside, shot into the sky and away from Earth. He was thrown backwards from the acceleration and suddenly realized that this had nothing to do with the PoliceCorp. It was the Room – the old one. He was still frightened and nauseated from the speed and height of his ascent, but he now understood that he was not going to visit the PoliceCorp, at least not tonight!

## 24
## The Room: Level 3
## Above Earth

Above Earth, within the clear bubble, Rad was experiencing a dizzying view. He noticed some satellites passing by, and somehow this, plus his rapid accent, had given him a feeling of vertigo. He closed his eyes for a moment. The feeling subsided.

He carefully opened his eyes again and could see darkness and starlight curved around the Earth to the horizons for as far as he could see. The only other large objects in the sky were the sun and the moon, which were both radiating their beauty into the dark void beyond. His heart was still pounding from the experience, so he tried to breathe and slow his pulse. He needed to think more clearly and concentrate on the moment. As he relaxed, a memory surfaced of the last Room that he'd played on R-131 with Tal, Simon and Vella. This experience was comparable to that but much more dynamic and incredibly more real and frightening.

Shifting his eyes downward again toward the gigantic globe hanging in the dark night, he also remembered the first time that he'd seen it in the first level of the game. At that time, the Earth was blue and green and white with many other colors patchworked across its surface. Now, some colors could still be seen, but they were muted and grayed as if he was looking through a dirty lens. He could see huge, floating islands of white and brown lying upon the ocean's surface, obviously unnatural and man-made. A semi-opaque haze of brown suffused the atmosphere, where magnificent white clouds of moisture had once existed. And where he'd seen vast forests of green and mountains covered with lush foliage, he now saw areas with scars of abuse and reckless destruction. The devastation was vast.

Rad then shifted his gaze toward an area that seemed to be the city from which he'd just made his escape. As he did so, the sphere suddenly began to move in that direction. It was traveling too fast for him to maintain his concentration, though, and the sphere again responded to his thoughts, decelerated and allowed him to relax. It seemed that he was learning to steer this amazing flying orb with his mind.

Realizing this, he again thought about the city, and within moments he hovered above it, seeing that it covered many square kilometers and sprawled into the distance. Being in a position to make out more detail, though, he observed that this was not where he had been only a short time ago. This was not where he had met Jana. This city was far more broken, much further along history's path. This city was falling apart and sat in a gaseous soup that lay thick and harsh well beyond what he'd seen only yesterday. He could also distinguish people in rags walking awkwardly and milling around – thousands and thousands of them obviously ill, thin and malnourished - their bodies in different stages of entropy.

He transported himself outside the city and could see sections of land in various stages of environmental degradation. There were pit mines and dry drainages where rivers or creeks had flowed at one time as well as hillsides of brown or black where trees and shrubbery had once existed. Devastation, maltreatment and ruin lay everywhere, containing only small, sickly pockets of green vegetation barely holding fast to the land.

He journeyed out again to get a larger picture and moved more quickly around the globe. He could hardly see a part of the Earth that had not been affected. Even large mountains had sections of rocks and minerals ripped out of them with raw sores left behind. Some of the oceans of the Earth had a shiny, black film covering them, and the floating mats that he'd viewed earlier from space were actually large masses of trash, oozing with rot and decay.

Rad's stomach turned. He felt an overwhelming grief and depression for what the human race had done to their home. He retched from the sickness of seeing thousands of carcasses of both humans and animals where they had just seemed to lay down and die.

When he did see rivers, they were filled with dirt, raw sewage and trash. Ice covered areas had sections where it looked as if the ice had simply been scooped up and taken away. And finally, he could also see thousands of factories billowing heavy brown and black soot into the air.

Rad climbed higher again, trying to look for any area that might still be green and healthy. At first, he only saw those small, random patches that were clinging to life. There didn't seem to be a single place where the Earth was still pure and untouched by this madness. Continent after continent, ocean after ocean, river after river, desert after desert, mountain range after mountain range and biome after biome ruined beyond belief. The Earth was dying or dead.

Then as he passed over South America, he noticed a large section of green lying near the equator - an ecologically verdant area that covered many square kilometers. He remembered from his studies that the rain forests along the equator were, at one time, one of the more diverse and fertile places on Earth.

He moved closer then and became aware of structures within the green almost hidden from view. He continued downward to get as good a look as he could.

Getting closer allowed him to see that the area was not as healthy as he had first thought. Yes, the trees were green but a green that looked ill and off color. There were skillfully built structures and people working on various tasks and going in and out of buildings in the center of this secluded green oasis. Very near the buildings, he also noticed what looked to be a spaceport or launching area where many ships were being built. 'What was this?' The chasm was hideous and huge between this place and the rest of the world.

It also hit Rad that this area's people looked stronger and healthier, wore better clothes and looked as if they were busily working toward something. He knew it must have something to do with this spaceport. This place was, as far as he could see, the only part of the Earth that was somewhat unharmed.

Rather than look more closely for now, Rad decided to journey further to see if he could find any other places like the one he'd just discovered. He crisscrossed the Earth many times. He found another settlement on an island north of what used to be

Australia and another on the continent of Africa; both were also near the equatorial regions of the Earth. The only settlement that wasn't near the equator was located at the center of the North American continent below a huge range of mountains close to a befouled city in ruins. There could be others, but it was obvious that most of the Earth was in decay with only a few pockets where the human race was hanging on just trying to survive. He gazed down on this world that he had dreamed of, a world whose existence had changed from an exquisite gem to a rotting piece of garbage dangling in space, putrefying and moving ever closer to its absolute destruction.

Rad sat in utter shock. The sobs began to come, rivers of tears gathered momentum, soaking his clothes and consuming his body. He could not believe what he was witnessing and experiencing. He continued to stare through his tears at the Earth, his breath coming in short gasps, his heart pounding and his hands holding his face in absolute disbelief and anger.

He lay down in the sphere, no longer being affected by vertigo, and stared out past the Earth towards the moon and sun and in the direction of where the human race would later migrate and live. He felt totally ashamed of what had happened here, of what humans had done to each other and to their home. He couldn't cry any longer. Only dry sobs ushered from his chest. He simply closed his eyes and gave in to the sadness.

\*\*\*

On Loon, Zeer and Fawn sat together and watched everything that Rad had seen. They saw him lying in his sphere sobbing and giving in to exhaustion. They too had tears on their cheeks from the experience and felt again the total shock and devastation of what had happened to Earth's environment, to the animals, the plants and to the people.

Zeer spoke softly, "God, I could never look at that and not feel ashamed and torn apart inside. I know Rad was absolutely overwhelmed. I worry about him."

Fawn comforted her, "He needs to rest now, and I think

you do as well. We'll talk more after you rest."

"Okay, I'm exhausted. I'll just lay here."

Fawn then stood, glanced down at Zeer and picked up her energy sphere. She walked into her sleeping quarters and knew that it was important for Rad to come down from the intensity of what he'd seen and felt. He needed to experience some hope again. He needed some time to recover. She closed the door to her room.

Meanwhile, Zeer sat up and watched Fawn go into her room. She saw the door close and then noticed a bright glow edging out from underneath it. She understood that Fawn was doing everything she could for Rad, so she lay back down and closed her eyes to rest.

# 25
## The Room: Level 3
## Reprise

The young girl's hand carefully brushed across his face as he lay resting quietly on the forest floor. The bird songs were especially beautiful today - a variety of multi-colored species gazed down on the seen below. Frogs were croaking, and small monkeys were gliding through the trees yelling and communicating to each other.

His eyes seemed to be opening slightly, and the girl stepped back a moment to look at this strange person curled up on the ground near her village. Sunlight etched a beautiful pattern on his face, small bugs crawled across his body and flying insects buzzed near his ears. He swatted at one as he came to, stretching and waking up.

Rad shook his head and slowly opened his sleep-laden eyes and yawned. He was confused and obviously didn't know where he was...again. However, moving from one reality to another had almost become something that he'd come to expect. It felt almost commonplace. In his hand, he sensed warmth and looked to see the small, glowing sphere resting on his palm. He kept it there, glanced up and noticed the young girl. She smiled at him, which brought a grin to Rad's face. He thought immediately of the young girl in his arms earlier in the Room, but this one was healthy and alive. Her look warmed him inside, although his previous memories were fresh and still painful. He didn't say anything immediately but looked around and began to observe the magnificent, rich and fertile life all around. After what he'd just gone through, this reality was a welcome sight.

She said something to him that he didn't understand. She noticed that he didn't move, so she held out her hand. He put the sphere in his pocket, took her hand without thought, stood up and walked with her through the lush forest. He was still surprised to be here but so glad that he was.

They walked together to where the forest ended at the edge of a cliff. The young girl pointed and smiled as if to say, look at this incredible place. Rad turned, and his breath left his chest – a valley lay below. It was covered with waterfalls and birds, animals and green forests, plants and vines and numerous creatures that he didn't recognize. He could also see a small village; the huts were constructed of natural material, with cooking fires burning and people walking, sitting, working and just being alive and happy. The valley had vibrant sounds that were natural and everything seemed to just fit – fit in such a way that no one could have planned it, or painted it or created it. It was simply natural and the way it was meant to be. It was wondrous as it lay in juxtaposition to his last reality.

The young girl, in her innocence, laid her hand on Rad's arm and tried to get him to come with her. She pointed down to the small village, but for right now, Rad felt that he needed to stay at the cliff's edge. He needed to be alone. He gave her a big smile and gestured to let her know that he would remain here for now and try to come down later. She shook her head in understanding, let go of his arm and started to walk away. He waved goodbye to her but wasn't sure she would know what that gesture meant. She imitated the movement, seeming to comprehend, and started running quickly down the path towards the valley floor. He watched her leave.

***

The young girl had been gone a while, and Rad decided that he wanted to get a better view of the Earth at this stage of its evolution. He knew what he could do. He took the sphere from his pocket, and again it responded to his thoughts. It encapsulated him, and he soared upwards and along the curvature of the Earth.

He observed massive, dense forests, which spread across the equatorial regions and beyond. He saw deserts with crystalline oases dotting moisture-laden low-lying areas. Continuing on, he became aware of mountainous areas that were engulfed by evergreen forests and capped by pure white glaciers. And beyond the land, were the surfaces of blue and green oceans covered by white-capped waves and the movement of large creatures. He could see huge plains of grass with undulating herds of animals, graceful flocks of birds and small human settlements, which dotted the landscape. This was a time when the Earth was a living, healthy organism that nurtured all life with its bounty as well as with its sometimes harsh but glorious beauty.

His heart felt calm for the moment, as he existed in the here and now of this part of the Room. He thought about the young girl and guided the sphere back down to the edge of her valley. He placed it back inside his pocket and spent several days with her people. He could smile again.

Late one evening, he walked back up the trail overlooking her village. The scene there was breathtaking. He looked up into the sky and took the sphere out of his pocket. He was considering gliding up into the twilight to look at the heavens and view the immensity of space and the distant stars. He was at peace here. But just as he felt that peace, thoughts about Earth's future intruded. He remembered the direction that life on this beautiful planet would take – evolving to a place of death and degradation. *'How could it happen?'*

No sooner had the question popped into his mind than suddenly the sphere in his hands glowed and enveloped him. It jerked into hyper-speed. He could no longer control it. He was thrown against the sides of the sphere and felt strong vibrations as he was hurled around the Earth at super-light speeds. His mind and body were not equipped for such a journey. The heavy weight of momentum pressed against him, and blood rushed to his extremities. The last thing he remembered was multi-colored lights flashing along the surface of the sphere.

# 26
## The Room: Level 3
## Sparks

Even before his consciousness returned, he knew that he was no longer above the Earth and no longer in that time when the Earth was blossoming into such a breathtaking paradise. The Room had again altered his reality.

Lying on the ground, he decided that for a moment he didn't even wish to open his eyes. He let his other senses take over. He didn't want the shock of seeing where he was until he was completely awake.

He thought back to when he had met Jana and the condition of the Earth and the people at that time. This felt similar, but the stench of ammonia and decay, the foul air and the sounds of pain and suffering were magnified a hundredfold. He could hardly breathe and had already begun to cough, his lungs were trying to get rid of the dangerous toxins that he was taking in with every breath. The moans of suffering, the sounds of shuffling feet, the diseased coughs and the agonized cries of pain surrounded him. His fingers touched the ground near where he lay and a sticky liquid covered the ground. The feel and texture disgusted him. He could smell its fetid odor as it rose to his nostrils. He couldn't imagine what he would see when he opened his eyes.

But open them he did. The first thing that hit him was scores of human beings who were barely recognizable as such. Many had oozing pustules covering parts of their bodies. Their faces were swollen, limbs hung and moved at irregular angles, with obvious abnormalities and mutations showing up on some. Their eyes looked through narrow slits of sorrow at the world, as they barely walked along or sat or laid or crawled - moaning, coughing, crying or silent and withdrawn. A few of them almost looked normal, but all of them had soiled cloths covering their noses and mouths in an attempt to keep out the rank and polluted air that surrounded them wherever they went. Some of the healthier ones that Rad had noticed seemed to be trying to help others less fortunate, but the scene was devastatingly heartbreaking.

The paths where they walked were filled with all types of trash and rotten garbage; trickles of rancid water flowed into stagnant pools on the ground, while feces and urine were spread at intervals along the paths, thus accounting for the odor of ammonia and a portion of the bacterial decay that spread everywhere.

Food in varying stages of viability looked as if it had been brought into the area with vegetables and some fruit lying haphazardly on carts along the paths and streets. People seemed to be checking each cart for anything that looked edible and nearby each cart was a pipe sticking out of the ground where people were getting water for consumption or cleaning. It was noticeably clouded and brown, but it was obvious that the people needed liquid badly and readily consumed it, no matter the quality.

This was truly a hell on Earth that Rad could never have imagined. He was barely able to keep from retching and adding to the stench that surrounded him.

He had to look away for a time to gather himself, so he began to look towards the buildings and structures in the area. He had no idea where he was, and there was little that he could recognize to give him a clue. All of the structures that he could see were either demolished or broken down to the degree that they were unrecognizable. He looked more carefully and saw people inhabiting any nook or hideaway that they could - any place that could give them a bit of cover.

As he gazed at the depressing scene, Rad suddenly felt a hand on his shoulder. He turned around and looked up into the healthy brown eyes of a man whom he didn't know. He seemed to be in his thirties, was dressed in a special suit of some kind, and was carrying a brown bag over one shoulder. He smiled at Rad. He said, "Where did you come from?"

Rad couldn't believe what he saw but managed to reply without thought, "I...I'm here...I'm here from the future, from a time and place a long way from here." After seeing all this, there was no way that he could make something up. The truth just came out of him.

The man gave Rad a quizzical look and asked, "Oh…and what's your name?"

"Rad."

"Well, Rad, my name is Sparks. Wherever you're from, I think you need to come with me before you get into trouble out here."

Rad didn't disagree and followed Sparks into a small building that he hadn't noticed before. The building didn't seem to fit into the surroundings. It was made from materials that were different than any of the buildings nearby. It was very modern looking with a few windows and a metal-gray exterior. As they neared the structure, Sparks unlocked the small hut by using something from his pocket. They went inside. Sparks turned on a light, which was followed by a humming sound. As Rad glanced around, he could see lab equipment, what looked like medications in bottles, a chair, a table and some utensils. Rad didn't understand what was going on. "What's all this for? You don't look like everyone else. You're not diseased and miserable. I don't understand. How can you be healthy and in such good shape when this place is so completely polluted and the people in such horrible condition!" Rad was becoming angry.

"I know it seems strange, but for some reason I was born with an amazing immune system. I've never been sick or caught any disease, and my body seems to cope with the pollution, viruses and various bacteria without any problem. I don't know why. I guess I'm a bit of a freak. I do get some small rashes, and that's the reason for my suit, but other than that, I'm fine. Because of that, I've spent most of my adult life learning as much as I could about why my body is this way, and I'm out here to see if I can help. Maybe by understanding my genes and by trying to find ways to mimic what's going on in *my* body, I can somehow alleviate some of the suffering and pain in the world."

Rad looked at Sparks, glanced carefully around his medical hut again and then outside at the horrific scene. "I admire what you're trying to do, but I have a question. Is this the only place on Earth where this is happening, or is the whole world a festering pool of pollution and disease? And one more thing, it doesn't look like you live here. Do you?"

Sparks' face turned very serious as he looked at Rad. "It seems pretty far fetched, but maybe you do come from a different place and time. Your questions are pretty strange. Anyone who lives here would know the answers to those questions." He thought some more and added, "I know my story must sound pretty wild, too." Rad smiled and agreed.

Sparks smiled back and then answered one of his questions. "The whole Earth is almost completely ruined."

Rad then simply asked, "How?"

It was difficult for Sparks to believe that Rad didn't know, but he explained anyway. "For hundreds of years, the number of wars and local skirmishes increased in number and severity all over the world. Many cities and whole countries were completely wiped off the map, but there were groups of businesses that actually benefited financially and grew incredibly because of these wars. These corporations became so strong and powerful that they were able to seize control of the governments and the people, subjugating and manipulating them for prophet and greed. At first, the people were glad because the wars began to abate and the countries became more stable, but by then the corporations were beyond anyone's control. Their own self-interests did not include the health and well being of the people or the planet, and this gave rise to the massive air and water pollution that you see now. And yes, it's on a global scale, along with massive changes in climate and weather patterns and colossal increases in the number and types of viruses and diseases that simply have no cures. The human population is dwindling, and what's left of the animal and plant populations is going fast."

"But I saw food on some carts in the streets."

"That's genetically grown food, bioengineered and radiated to help it last a little longer. It's grown in massive hydroponic labs from seeds hidden away and now being used at rates that ensure the supply of food won't last long."

"Who is doing the work to grow this food, make the clothing, work in the hospitals, educate the children and feed everyone? Who brings out the carts with food? Who keeps the water flowing in the pipes? Who...?"

"Okay, this is a very long story, and if you want to know more, we'll need to go to the Shelter for the night and talk. Come with me."

Rad had no idea what the "Shelter" was or where they were going, but he knew that he needed to learn more, so he left with Sparks, moving along the paths away from this landscape of horror towards a huge wall in the distance.

***

Sparks and Rad walked up to a wall that seemed to be covered with a substance that looked much like the material that was used to build Sparks' hut. It was about five meters tall and continued on far into the distance to the right and the left. Rad couldn't see the end in either direction. The wall looked as if it had a bend to it, although, Rad couldn't tell for sure. Above the wall were very substantial support girders that curved up and out of sight. He could see a girder about every fifty meters. On top of the girders was a layered substance of some kind that covered the structure and was transparent. It hit Rad in a flash! A lifeglobe! It looked incredibly similar to the lifeglobes that were designed to house people at each of the settlements across the galaxy in his own time.

"My God! I've seen this before!"

Sparks obviously didn't know what to make of that, so he just kept walking up to the wall, pulled a small, black object out of his pocket and pushed a red button on it. They heard a whooshing sound as a door opened.

"Come on Rad. We need to decontaminate before going inside the Shelter."

Rad hesitated.

Sparks urged him forward, "Come on. Let's go!"

Rad went inside.

***

After decontamination, Sparks took Rad on a short tour of the Shelter before taking him to his apartment. Rad was surprised at how much at home he felt. The Shelter's layout and technology were very familiar to him. He couldn't believe what he was seeing. As he'd thought before, the Shelter was dramatically similar to a lifeglobe. Not exactly, but the basic structure and technology that were being used in all of the lifeglobes that Rad had lived in had obviously been derived from the same fundamental plan as this Shelter, and here it was right in front of his eyes. There was the hydroponics lab for gas exchange and food production, the water collection that came from a deep well and a recirculation unit. The architecture was similar, and the entire facility had a self-sustaining, closed environment, completely separate from what was outside, very much like the lifeglobes. The strong translucent shield covering it all and allowing what sunlight was still available to pass into the Shelter was also recognizable along with the energy producing facilities. Seeing the Shelter was like viewing an ancient link that connected this time and place directly to his own.

They had just finished the tour, and Sparks took Rad to his apartment. They ate and then sat down to talk. Rad had many questions, but first he explained the similarities to Sparks between the Shelter and the lifeglobes located across the galaxy. It made sense to Sparks. If Rad had come from the future, then those settlements throughout the galaxy had not yet been created, but they would be, and, he knew something that Rad didn't. He knew about a plan for everyone in the Shelter that was very close to going forward.

"I think I'm beginning to believe your story more and more, Rad. You know more about how this Shelter works than I do. What did you say you did on your lifeglobe?"

"I was part of the governing council that helped run each of the them that I lived on. We encountered scientific challenges, social problems, and had to work within the environment and on different types of planets. Each lifeglobe had it's own specific and unique problems that constantly needed attending. It was important work for the lifeglobe, but it always left me feeling like I needed something more. That's why I started playing the Rooms. As I've already told you, what's happening to me now is part of one of those Rooms, but this one is like no other. It is phenomenally real and is being played out on a huge scale of time and space. It seems like a test, and I feel as if each decision I make influences the outcome. I don't really understand what's going on, and I don't know what the eventual outcome will be. I'm in the middle of it, though, and I know that it has a lot to do with Earth, and I think this time period is crucial."

Rad then looked directly at Sparks and asked for his help. "Sparks, I need to know some things from you. I need to know as much as you can tell me about what's going on here in the Shelter, why it's so isolated from the poor people outside and anything you can share with me about the people who live inside the Shelter. What are their plans, and how did all this come to be? What's going on here?"

It took Sparks a long time to explain, but as he did, Rad was able to see what was happening and had an idea about how the settlements across the galaxy had started. "The wealthy people of Earth had, for quite some time, isolated themselves from most of Earth's population. The wealthy came from the big corporations and businesses that had taken over most of the governments around the world. Their main purpose, of course, was to maintain and increase their wealth and power, and they had accomplished this at the expense of the other people on Earth, its resources and the environment; all of which were in a state of complete collapse."

Sparks continued, "The wealthy over time then sequestered the smartest and best doctors, scientists, architects, engineers and military leaders to build Shelters for them and protect them from the many environmental, social and weather-related hazards that were sprouting up randomly across the globe. These dangers, which they were largely responsible for creating, ranged from severe environmental pollution, to crime and devastation that had become the norm, to innumerable viral and bacterial diseases as well as natural hazards associated with global changes in climate and temperature. These Shelters, which are now located around the world, are for the wealthy only. The leaders of these Shelters communicate with each other, share information and have created a plan for their future survival. At this point, they care very little about anyone or anything, except themselves. They know that the Earth is no longer a viable place to live and that all the life on the Earth is dying. For these reasons, they have decided that they will have to leave the Earth."

Rad shook his head and thought about the Earth's long and sad history. "So what's the rest of their plan?" Rad asked with disdain.

Sparks hesitated a moment, again wondering if he should share what he knew and then continued, "The Plan? Well, it's, of course, only known by the people in the Shelter, and not completely by any of us, except our leaders, but this much I do know. In a few months, all of the people living in each of the Shelters around the world will be leaving Earth to populate the galaxy. The ships have been designed to travel at close to light speed, but it will take time for them to reach any viable planets, asteroids or moons. The reason that they aren't using our own moon and mars is because those have already been settled; their resources have been tapped, and the inhabitants have started suffering from many of the same problems that have been created here on Earth. The goal of the Shelters will be to create settlements away from the disease and horrible environmental conditions that exist here, and in their travels, try to find another Earth-like planet to populate again."

"You mean populate and *use*, right?"

"I'm sure that's what many of the Chosen want, but who knows, maybe they've learned something. At least, I know some of them have."

"The Chosen?"

"Yes, the Chosen is the name of the people who live in the Shelter. They feel that they have been *chosen* to be wealthy, powerful and more human than the other people on the Earth."

"A name they've obviously assigned to themselves, right? I'm sure if the people outside could name them, it would be quite different."

"I'm sure you're right."

"What about the people who will be left on the Earth? What about their lives? What about the Earth itself? Are they planning to do anything for the people left behind?"

"All of the people outside the Shelters call themselves Terrans, which is a very old name for Earth. The Chosen are doing less and less for them, especially as they get closer to the day of their departure. The Chosen have always maintained a large stockpile of resources for themselves. I can't see them changing at this point, and I'm sure they will leave behind as little as possible when they depart. It looks like Earth and most of its people are going to be abandoned."

"My god! What are *you* doing? What's *your* plan? You've been outside trying to find cures and help people. Are you just planning on leaving?"

"Well, actually, with the help of a small group of healthy friends outside the Shelter and with the help of a few scientists and engineers within, we've begun to make some gains. I don't think the leaders and most of the Chosen know much about it, but we've even begun to establish a healthier, safe area in the mountains outside the main part of the city where we are treating people, feeding them and building a small community. It's a very slow process, and the numbers are still very small, but we have hope. I plan on staying here and continuing to do what I can. I can't see leaving Earth."

Rad thought about this for a moment and asked, "Do you have any records of what Earth used to be like when it was a functioning biosphere? If you stay, what are your plans for the planet?"

Sparks answered, "Yes, the records indicate to us that our home was once a magnificent world, so part of what all of us that are working so hard want is to somehow help Earth heal as well. I know it's an almost impossible task, but with new ideas and a new philosophy about living, we can make it happen. Of course, we can't be successful in one generation, but we'll do what we can."

Rad, after hearing everything, felt drained and helpless. He thought about what Sparks had told him and about the Terrans and the Chosen. He thought about the Room and wondered why *he* had been selected to be here and what this was all about. Part of him just wanted to get out of here and go back home, but he also felt the gravity of Earth's demise pulling at him and crying out for help. He knew that he only had one thing left to ask. "What can I do to help?"

## 27

The Room: Level 3
Visionaries


The meeting had just concluded. Members of the Shelter's Visionary Council were getting up from their chairs and walking towards the exit. The final touches had been put into place for the plan. The Visionary Councils from all of the Shelters around the world had been together during this final meeting via a live laser feed, and the screen had just gone black for the final time. No more meetings would be held. They were moving forward.

Each of the councils felt their plan had taken in every conceivable problematic situation. The scientific community had the ships and sleep-modem tubes ready for habitation and travel, and every ship could be broken down into pieces to help create the initial shelters for habitation and exploration. The ships' computers could help find suitable planets, asteroids or moons where the humans could mine materials that would be needed to survive and create the larger Shelters where they would live. Only a minimal amount of food and water was necessary for the trips because every person was going to be in sleep-modem tubes and fed via a drip system during flight. They would only land on planetoids that had some source of water. Once the plan took effect, no person would be in control. The computers and robots on each ship would be coordinating it all.

They understood that it would probably take many, many generations to find another Earth-like planet to inhabit, but they also knew that they could no longer live here. Earth was dying, and the Chosen must survive, even if it did mean puddle jumping from one planetoid to another until they found a real home.

Along with the many ships that would carry the people into space to find new homes, one very unique experimental ship was being built to travel beyond light-speed. It would be populated by the most sophisticated computers and robots ever developed on Earth, along with the DNA of the greatest humans who had ever lived. Over the last thirty years, a project had been implemented to collect DNA from all of the most renowned thinkers, scientists, leaders, corporate heads, and philosophers from Earth's current and past history. The computers on the ship were specifically designed to look for another Earth-like planet - a planet, whose environment was untouched and healthy, possessed many resources and could sustain human life.

They knew this was a long shot, but if it succeeded, the robots and computers on the ship could create humans from the DNA that had been collected, teach them about what had happened on Earth, raise them to the point where they could inhabit the new Earth-like planet and also teach them what they would need to know to survive.

It was the hope of all the Visionaries that if this succeeded, the humans from this experiment would then find and bring all of the Chosen from the various settlements around the galaxy to their new home. The Visionaries weren't sure that their new ship would perform as planned, but they had to try. The success of this venture could provide humanity with a new viable home to live on more quickly than jumping from one rock to another ever could.

***

Harlequin, the head of the Visionaries, stayed in her chair as she watched all of the other council members leave the chamber. When they were gone, she pressed one button to lock the door to the room and another, which again activated the satellite screen on the wall. It brightened, but this time only the leaders of each council could be seen. Then had dismissed the rest of their members, just as Harlequin had done.

Harlequin spoke in measured and serious tones. "As you know, there is one more part of our plan that our scientists have worked tirelessly on."

The heads on the screen nodded.

She continued, "We have discussed this for many, many years now and have agreed that there is one more decision that needs to be completed before we're done."

She paused. Everything had been thrashed out and readied for this moment, but the faces on the screen ranged from determined to ashen, some with their jaws set, while others were wiping tears from their eyes. Some nodded with agreement; others held their hands up to their mouths and shook their heads in disbelief at what was about to be decided.

Harlequin continued, "If everyone agrees, after we leave the Earth, the final part of our plan will be enacted." No one uttered a word. Harlequin waited.

"So, we agree that Earth's reset will occur one month after we leave. Drones flying across the entire surface of the Earth will release the toxin. All human life will be extinguished, and the toxin used for this will quickly degrade. Of course, some animals will die as well, but most of the plants, animals, insects, sea life, bacteria and viruses that are still alive will be left untouched. This will, hopefully, allow the Earth to reset itself over the millennia, and become again the productive, healthy planet that it once was. The Pariah must die. They are weak, diseased and are really no longer human. They must be eliminated for the planet to heal if our ancestors are to ever return." Again she paused for a moment and then spoke this well-known phrase, "Earth must be cleansed for the Chosen to return."

The mouths on the screen repeated the phrase with little emotion, "Earth must be cleansed for the Chosen to return."

Harlequin touched the button again. The heads disappeared. She unlocked the door and walked away. The room fell silent.

***

Zeer sat beside Fawn watching the horrible and final level of the game, which she had already experienced once. Seeing again the pain and suffering and destruction of such a beautiful world, though, especially after living on Loon, was excruciating. The people Rad had met and the situations that he was experiencing were different from what Zeer had gone through, but the fundamental nature of what was happening was much the same. During her time on Earth, she had stayed and tried to help, but the degradation had been too severe, the chaos too complete, the diseases too pervasive. She had never known about Sparks and what he was trying to do. Her experience in that level had been at a completely different location.

Shortly before she had completed the game and been brought to Loon, she remembered watching the ships ascend into space with the Chosen inside. She thought back to that moment and could still see herself and the Terrans that were gathered around her staring skyward as ship after ship rose into the sky, burning brightly and then soaring out of sight. Zeer hadn't been told about the plan when she was in the final level of the game, but she did know about the Shelters and the stark division of wealth and power on Earth. She knew the Earth was dying and remembered clearly looking into the eyes of those that she had left behind.

Fawn looked over at Zeer and made a conscious decision *not* to show her about the Visionaries' last meeting and the final part of their plan, at least not yet. The way Zeer was feeling, if she were told, it could push her over the edge, and she might attempt to enter the game prematurely and try to stop what was happening. That history could not be changed, and altering events in the future or the past was a very dangerous thing to do.

Fawn saw the tears in Zeer's eyes, held her and felt her sobs of anger and frustration. This history was something that everyone living on Loon was taught and shown. It was part of their education growing up, and the people of Loon never wanted to repeat what had happened on Earth. It was important that they never forgot.

Zeer looked up at Fawn and whispered, "Rad and Sparks seem to be helping people and doing some good. I need to go there. I need to see if I can help this time."

"Soon Zeer. Soon…"

## 28

The Room: Level 3
Healing

Rad and Sparks wished that they could find out more about the plan that was being worked on by the leaders of the Shelter, but right now they couldn't worry that much about what they did or didn't know. They had an impossible task laid out in front of them, and they needed to stay focused. Besides, Sparks wasn't in on the planning; he only knew the information that had been shared with him and all of the other Chosen. In addition, he knew that he was someone that the leaders would never share too much information with because of the work that he was doing outside the Shelter. The only reason that he and his work were tolerated at all was because of his unique immune system. The doctors and other scientists in the Shelter were extremely interested in Sparks. He had become their guinea pig, as they poked and prodded and ran tests to determine what was behind his amazing immune system. They were hoping to find something that could help the Chosen, especially since they would soon be traveling throughout the galaxy and living in new and hostile environments. Sparks understood that they were using him, but it allowed him to do his work and help, so he just went along with it.

After leaving his apartment in the Shelter, Sparks continued to share more information with Rad about his work and the small community that he had been establishing west of the city in the mountains. The community was located in a part of the mountains that, even though it didn't completely protect its inhabitants, was much more livable than the city and a place where people could heal and recover with the right help and medications. The air, although not perfect, was better and the water, being closer to the source, was much cleaner.

Sparks had chosen certain Terrans from the city to bring to his mountain settlement whom he'd felt were treatable and well enough to make the journey. He transported them one at a time on the back of a motorized three-wheeled tri-bike that he'd taken out of the Shelter. He had started growing some food from seeds that he'd stolen from the Shelter's hydroponics lab, and he'd begun to give the people fresh vegetables, good water and a place to stay that was at least somewhat isolated from the dangerous disease ridden city. He'd also begun to treat them with drugs and ointments that he was developing on his own from herbs that could still be found in small pockets in the mountains as well as drugs that he could get from his friends in the medical wing of the Shelter. The number of people that he was able to help was miniscule at this point, but the results were significant, which gave him hope.

In order to get to the area where the huts were located, Rad and Sparks first had to travel through the city. They road on the tri-bike and passed hundreds of people that Rad knew could never be healed. They were either dying or too ill for intervention. However, he also noticed Terrans who were still strong enough to get better with the right treatment and care, but it would have to come soon. He looked at Sparks and knew that he had to help him.

As they traveled through the city, Rad and Sparks had needed to cover their mouths to at least minimally protect themselves from the vial air rushing past, but when they left the city and began the climb up into the mountains on some narrow dirt trails, the quality of the air seemed to improve somewhat as well as the health of the vegetation. They brushed past some shrubs and trees that almost looked normal, but they also noticed many that had succumbed and were shriveled, dead or sick mutations of what they once were. They continued on, and dust flew out behind their vehicle as they ascended higher into the hills.

Finally, they reached a cliff area that overlooked a valley. Rad couldn't help but think back to the last cliff that he'd seen with its vast, pristine views. This was different, though. Sparks pointed towards the valley floor, and Rad noticed four rounded huts made of branches which were used as supports and covered with a material that looked like a milky-colored cloth. The area still had some green growth in it, and to Rad's surprise, there was a small stream running in the bottom of the valley. It was a tiny oasis in the middle of a colossal environmental catastrophe. Glancing up to the head of the valley, he saw a large mountain soaring upward and disappearing into the hazy sky.

Sparks nodded toward the valley and told Rad to hang on. They traveled down a worn zigzag path that took them to the valley below.

Rad could hardly believe that anything like this still existed. "How did you find this?"

Sparks smiled and said, "A lot of looking. I thought that the mountains might harbor an area like this. It was a shot in the dark, but it worked out."

Rad wondered about the covering for the huts and asked, "Where did you get that material? What is it?"

"Well...I stole it. I got it from the Shelter with the help of some of my engineering friends. It's a non-flammable cloth that is bioengineered to resist bacteria and other disease-producing agents, and it also has the ability to hold in warmth and protect the people as they heal. I started this project with two people that were still relatively healthy, and now they are well enough to help others as I bring them here."

Rad noticed the small garden and what was probably a well for water. There were fires burning outside for cooking and warmth, and the four huts were all near each other. He also noticed lights shining inside the huts. "Lights?"

"Yeah, my friends from the Shelter again. They were able to give me some lights, heaters, small cots and bedding. Also, we have an energy turbine that is run by the moving water in the stream. I was able to get that up here on the back of my bike to help us run everything. It has the capacity to create more energy than we need, so we even have room to expand and take in more people. I wasn't able to get a cooking counter to make the meals, but the fires work fine for now. I'm sorry we have to create the smoke, but in time, I'm hoping to get a cleaner way to cook. Here, let me introduce you to some of my new friends."

Rad and Sparks walked to every hut and met six people. Rad stopped and spoke with each one and was surprised at how good they looked and how they smiled and even laughed. Their demeanor was completely different than the thousands of Terrans in the city. One of the men named Sam took Rad by the arm and spoke to him. "Do you know what Sparks has done for us? He's given us our lives back. I'm alone and don't have a family, and because of him, I'm hoping that when I'm well enough I can help many others come out of that dark hell."

Rad agreed with him and felt a sense of hope here that he knew didn't exist many other places in the world. He was thinking, though, that there must be other locations on the Earth where people could still live and heal. Pockets, possibly bigger and with even more resources than this.

After meeting the people in the huts, including Seamus and Mary who were the first people that Sparks had brought to the valley, Sparks took Rad into the hut where he lived and worked. There was a cot for Rad to sleep on. He smiled, as he thought about living and working here as well as going to the city to assist people there. It wasn't much, considering the monstrous problem, but it was something – one step at a time.

***

So Rad and Sparks began working and planning together. Sparks found Rad's help invaluable, mostly because he was an excellent organizer and planner - skills that he'd learned from living and working on the lifeglobes.

They were able to acquire one more tri-bike for hauling things and for carrying people. Not only did they bring people up to the huts to help them, but they also started delivering drugs to the Terrans in the city that had proven to be affective. They would notice that someone had a certain symptom or injury that they might be able to relieve with treatment and then they would approach them to see if they would be willing to take the medication. Their work was slow and plodding, but every day they accomplished a little more. They were even looking for spots in the city that they might be able to turn into treatment centers, using the same techniques they'd used in the valley – training healthier Terrans to be their helpers.

Rooms

***

One evening as Sparks and Rad were traveling back up into the mountains, Rad became dizzy and stopped to recover. Sparks halted and walked over to Rad's tri-bike and looked at his eyes and felt his forehead. "Are you okay?"

"I'm fine. I'm just tired."

"Well, if you start feeling worse, let me know."

They completed the trip into the valley. Rad looked around at what they had built. Now, instead of four huts, there were ten, and the area had turned into a small bustling village with people cooking, working in the garden, resting, recuperating and tending those who needed treatment. It was a community of healing. Rad and Sparks both felt good about what was happening, but it wasn't enough. They had to keep at it every day.

Inside their hut that night, they were discussing what they could do to move the project ahead at a quicker pace. They talked into the night and came up with several ideas.

Sparks yawned and thought about what they'd decided. "I think this is the only way we can help people on a larger scale. I need to go to the Shelter and talk to Harlequin about what we've accomplished here and demonstrate to her that with their help and the help of the other Shelters around the world that we could actually conquer these problems. The Chosen might even be convinced to stay. They don't have to leave the Earth. She must realize that leaving is a very risky venture, so why not stay and heal the Earth and it's people."

"I agree that it's worth trying, Sparks, but there's a good chance that she'll say no. You'll have to be ready to ask if we can use the Shelter after they leave. Having that huge facility at our disposal would allow us to do so much more than we can now."

"You're right. If she says no, I can't see why she wouldn't let us use the Shelter. They won't be using it anymore. Maybe I can even get some of the scientists, engineers and medical staff to stay and help us."

Rad yawned and said, "That sounds good. We'll talk more tomorrow. Time to sleep."

As Rad lay there getting settled, his leg slipped out from under his blanket. Sparks was just turning out the light when he noticed a large soar on Rad's leg. He hurried over and grabbed Rad's ankle. "How long have you had this?"

Rad just shrugged. He'd been hoping to keep this from Sparks. There was too much to do. "I guess a couple of weeks. It's not anything."

"Yes it is, and you know it. I'll get some salve and some pills to help with this."

"I need to keep working, Sparks."

"I think you'll be able to if you take these, put on the salve and rest for a few days. You need to heal this before it gets worse."

"Okay." But Rad knew that he couldn't afford the time. Sparks and the people in the city needed him. He'd seen the pills and salve work with others. He'd be okay.

## 29
### The Room: Level 3
### Zeer

Zeer had seen about all that she wanted to see. Fawn had mentioned that Zeer would leave soon to go to Rad and bring him back to Loon. She felt it was past time to finally get this done.

"I'm ready, Fawn. You promised that I would be going back to Earth soon. It's time to do it. Rad has experienced so much. He's ill and working incredibly hard with Sparks. I need to go there and be involved. I didn't have a chance like this when I was there, and they could use my help."

"I don't think you should go quite yet, Zeer."

"Please, I need to do this. The people are suffering so much, and the Earth is crumbling. You know that here on Loon we work closely together to solve problems. The more closely we work together, the better the outcome. It's no different on Earth. I know they could use my help. Please..."

Both Zeer and Fawn heard someone clear their throat. They turned to see Landree standing in the room.

Fawn was the first to speak. "Okay, Landree, you've been listening. You know what's going on, and you also know how delicate the situation is at this point. What do you feel we should do?"

His eyes seemed to bore into Zeer as he pondered the question. She didn't say any more at this point. She had great respect for both Fawn and Landree. She wanted to wait until he spoke.

"Zeer, it's obvious that Rad is ready to be part of Loon. He's learned much and would be a wonderful addition to our world. Everyone sees that. But if we send you too early, before he's completed the last level of the Room, something could happen to both of you. There's another thing as well. The situation there is so horrible, so dangerous, that I'm not sure it would be good for you to experience it a second time. You've just recovered from your previous experience with the Room. You made it through the first time, but you never know. We have great plans for both you and Rad, and those plans, along with bringing Rad back to Loon, are extremely important.

Zeer lowered her head gathering her thoughts and then looked back up into Landree's eyes. She smiled slightly, remembering all that he had done for her and all that he'd taught her. He meant so much to her. She spoke quietly but with determination. "I know the incredible gift that you and Fawn and all the people of Loon have given me. It's something that I can never repay. However, for days and days now, I've been looking at my ancestral home again, seeing how sad and desperate the people were and how sick the Earth had become. It's affected me even more deeply than before, not only because of what I went through, but because of Rad's experiences and what I've seen through *his* eyes. I can't turn my back. I know it's not my time, but it is my place. I can go there and possibly do some good. If nothing more, Rad will need help getting treatment. He won't stop working, and I could possibly take over some of his duties so that he could heal. Then we could come home to Loon. Please…"

Zeer glanced back and forth between Fawn and Landree, waiting for their answer. Fawn was the one that made the decision. "Zeer, it's near enough to the time when we need to bring Rad home. We will help you go there. We will give you some time to help Rad heal and do what you can for the people. Then we will bring you both home. You must be very cognizant, though, that you, Rad, Sparks and all the people of Earth are in terrible peril, and that you must never speak to anyone about Loon, your time here, or what you know about their future. You *must* know that time is a very delicate dimension; our movement through it and what we do when we're out of our own time is something that we need to be extremely cautious about. This must all happen without anyone knowing about us, or any assistance on our part. Do you understand?"

"Yes, I do. Thank you. Thank you so much. I'll be extremely careful, and when we're asked to return to Loon. I'll make sure we do."

"Okay," Landree said after allowing Zeer and Fawn to finish, "we have a lot of work to do to get you ready to go. You need to be briefed, and there are some additional things you need to learn."

Zeer sighed and said, "Thank you...both of you!"

***

Zeer was prepared for her passage through time and space back to the Earth. She would do this trip alone, but, of course, she would travel with the aid of her individual energy sphere. The sphere had been programmed for the journey and would maintain Zeer's bio-needs during the trip. All she would need to do was understand what was going to happen and depend on the sphere. Being calm and meditative would allow the orb to more easily interact with her and help keep her safe. Also, the sphere was never to be off of her person. She must keep it with her always, especially on a trip this dangerous.

The day came, and Zeer was as mentally and physically ready as she would ever be. The only possessions she was allowed on the trip were the energy sphere, some water, a bit of food and the clothes that she wore.

All of her friends from the different communities on Loon were there that day. She could see the worried looks on many of their faces, even though they did their best to smile and wish her well.

She told everyone goodbye and then walked over to where Dominie, Landree and Fawn were standing. It was very, very hard to leave Loon. She had some tears in her eyes, just as they did, but they were also showing her that they were confident in her return.

"Please be safe," Fawn said.

"I will, and I want to tell all of you again that my life has been immeasurably changed because of you. Please know that I'll return soon, and I *will* bring Rad home safely."

They all watched as Zeer held out her orb. Its energy shimmered around her. She sat down in a lotus position, ready to start her meditation. She smiled, breathed deeply and she was gone.

***

The sphere returned Zeer to consciousness directly above the Earth. She had just entered the atmosphere's toxic soup and was traveling at speeds that took her breath away. It had been some time since her previous experience with traveling in this fashion. It was still surreal and breathtaking. She doubted that it would ever feel any different.

It had also been quite a while since she had looked directly upon the Earth at this moment in history. Comparing it to Loon gave her an even greater perspective on the cruel and senseless destruction that lay below. It sickened her, but it also increased her determination to do what she could while she was here. The sphere set her down near the city where Rad and Sparks were located. Now she needed to find them.

***

Rad was working in a broken down building in the city. He was handing out medications and giving vaccines for various ailments. He and Sparks had become a good team. Rad was excellent at organizing and figuring out the logistics of accomplishing certain tasks, while Sparks was an amazing biochemist and healer. He was able to synthesize remedies by studying his own body's chemistry and using whatever natural herbs could still be found to produce cures and medications to help people feel more comfortable. He was also still getting some help with equipment and some medicine from his friends in the Shelter. He was surprised that the leaders there hadn't been trying to stop him yet, but he figured that they were too busy with their plans to leave the Earth. Ordinarily, the leaders in the Shelter were extremely rigid about hording their supplies, so Sparks was glad he was being left alone.

***

Zeer had been searching the city for about a week. At night, she slept outside with the people and gave what aid she could along the way. She had met many Terrans whose spirits were crushed – many with little hope - people of all ages who saw their lives as being unworthy and unimportant. They simply existed and waited to die.

Some Terrans had spoken to her about the one thing that all of the people outside the Shelter had in common. They hated the people who lived inside. They had seen enough to know that everyone inside the Shelter had all the food, water, medical attention, clothing and protection that anyone could ever want or need. They were even sheltered from the many viruses and diseases that afflicted the Terrans. It was obvious that they were much healthier and that they even breathed cleaner air. It was also known that everyone inside the Shelter, while referring to themselves as the Chosen, used a word for the Terrans that showed their complete disgust and hate for them. They called anyone outside, the Pariah.

As Zeer continued her search one morning, she noticed a line outside a broken down building. This struck her as very odd. She hadn't seen the people doing this anywhere else. Even when she'd seen them scavenge for the food and water that was available, she'd never seen them stand in a line. Life here seemed to always be disorganized and chaotic, but here was an actual queue where the people sat patiently waiting to move forward. Some of the Terrans were even helping to move the line along and guide others forward when it was their turn.

Zeer walked up to the door where everyone was to enter and looked inside. She saw a large room with windows broken and trash and dirt swept outward toward the walls. The center of the room, however, was cleaner with a table and several individuals talking to the people from the line that snaked inside. They were asking them questions, listening and then handing out supplies of some kind. She walked in toward the table. One of the helpers asked her to stop and get back in line, but she continued forward, gesturing that she didn't need to become part of the line.

Rad was giving a small child an injection. He finished,

threw the needle he'd used into a bucket to be cleaned and reused and wiped the sweat from his forehead. As he did, he noticed a woman in relatively clean clothes and a jacket standing and watching him. He looked again. She was familiar. *'Where is she from?'* He couldn't place her and needed to get back to helping people. The next person came forward. Rad just shook it off and went back to work.

Zeer saw that it was Rad, and even though she had been observing him for quite a while now with Fawn and had recognized him immediately, in person, he looked weaker and seemed to hobble more on the leg where the sore was located. She stood and watched him. The line of people waiting was still extremely long, but she saw that the medications and supplies had all but disappeared. Rad and his team would have to stop soon. She didn't want to bother him while he was helping people so she moved into the shadows and continued to watch.

Just then, Sparks walked through the door. Zeer saw him immediately. He went to the table and spoke to Rad and his aids. They had decided to stop working for the day. Sparks turned and told everyone to come back in five days. They would be able to help more of them at that time. The bit of hope that Zeer had seen on the people's faces seemed to melt away as they turned and walked back out into the city.

***

Zeer waited outside. It was almost dark as Rad and Sparks finally came out of the building with the remaining members of their team, and the very first thing she heard was Rad coughing. Sparks reached over and gave him something for his cough, then they loaded up the two tri-bikes with the remainder of the supplies and containers that they'd used that day. Sparks asked Rad and a member of his team to drive the vehicles back to the valley. It was obviously a subtle way to get Rad off his injured leg. He reluctantly agreed.

As Sparks and the remaining members of his team started walking towards home, Zeer followed and could see how weary they were. Their shoulders were drooping; their feet dragged the ground, and they were silent, absorbed in their own thoughts. Zeer continued to walk well behind them, wondering if she should make contact with Sparks and let him know who she was. Because of their weariness, though, she made up her mind to keep her distance, see where they were going and then show herself sometime later.

***

Zeer couldn't believe how far they had walked after working and spending so much time doing what they could for the people. She also stared wide-eyed at the valley, noticing fires burning, people milling around and the small huts that seemed to glow with light. Seeing it with Fawn was one thing but being there was even more impressive, especially as she considered how quickly all this had been done. She knew how much the Terrans had helped them, but the drive, the push and the ideas that had accomplished these tasks had come from Rad and Sparks. She was in awe and glad she was there to help.

She saw which hut Sparks had entered and noticed that someone had carried some plates of food inside as soon as he had arrived. When the person came back out of the hut, Zeer watched as they returned to the cooking fires.

When she felt that no one would notice, she skirted the area and found an obscure spot where she could sit and observe just at the edge of the firelight. She leaned up against a tree and felt her eyes getting heavy as she watched the people go about their jobs and then begin to move into their huts for the night. She couldn't fight it any longer. She had to rest.

Zeer fell asleep quickly, but just after doing so, she was awakened by a loud "snap." She looked up. There were three dark shadows backlit by the fires hovering over her.

"Who are you?" one of the shadows asked. He was holding something that was poking Zeer in the chest.

She froze and spoke slowly, "My name is Zeer. I'm a friend of Rad's."

"Rad didn't mention that any *friend* was coming. Why are you here? Are you from the Shelter?"

"I...I'm not from the Shelter, and, no...Rad didn't expect me. He'll know me, but he didn't know that I'd be here."

"How in the hell did you find our home?"

Zeer just told them the truth. "I saw Rad and his team working today and followed them here. I could tell that they were extremely tired so I thought I'd just rest here until the morning and then go to meet him."

"Well, you're going to meet him tonight!"

The three men helped Zeer up and took her to Rad's hut. The one who had spoken to Zeer went inside. Rad and Sparks stuck their heads out to look. Rad still didn't seem to recognize her.

"We found this woman near the camp. We don't know who she is. Is she from the Shelter?"

Sparks came forward and looked at her closely. "I've never seen this woman before. I don't recognize her from the Shelter or the city."

Rad just stared. Zeer thought that she noticed a slight twitch of recognition in his eyes and wondered if the hood that she was wearing might be keeping him from recognizing her. She pushed it back away from her face.

Rad asked, "What's your name?"

"My name is Zeer."

Rad hesitated for only a second more and then rushed over to look directly into her eyes. He grabbed her by the shoulders, examined her carefully and then the bright light of recognition beamed across his face.

"My god! It *is* you! It's you! I thought you were dead or somewhere where I'd never see you again. This is unbelievable! How...How did you get here? Where have you been? What...?"

Zeer laughed and everyone else just looked on, bewildered.

"Well, it's obvious that Rad's not going to sleep for a while, but I'm exhausted," Sparks was saying. "Let's leave them alone. The rest of us will find out more tomorrow what all this is. You two go get reacquainted."

Zeer accepted Rad's hand, and they moved over to one of the fires. They sat down and looked at each other as the crackling logs burned yellow, red and orange and created a flickering dance in their eyes. They couldn't stop smiling. Neither could believe what had happened, and Rad was having a difficult time comprehending that Zeer was actually there. They talked deep into the night and fell asleep near the fire, keeping each other warm.

***

During that night, Rad had had many questions. Zeer had done her best to answer them and yet be careful to follow Landree and Fawn's directions. She'd told Rad about being chosen by the old one who ran the Room and completing the first two levels. Then she'd led him to believe that she was still playing the Room on level three, just as he was. She'd explained that during the third level she had been on another part of the Earth but then had been brought here, for some reason, about a week ago, where she'd found Rad and Sparks.

As they'd continued talking, Rad told Zeer all of what he knew about the Shelters and Sparks and what they had been doing to help the Terrans. They had also both shared memories about their experiences on R-131 and their common drive to play the most elite Rooms wherever they'd lived. They'd discussed the old one, the levels of the Room, the energy spheres, the fact that both of them had met Brit and Shee and the learning that they had experienced from their leather books. They'd laughed and remembered the few times that they'd met, the ride that Zeer had taken on the speedcycle and when they had seen each other in the hallway outside their apartments.

It had been a night of remembering, reconnection and of surprising joy. It was also a night that neither of them had expected, nor would they soon forget.

***

Morning brought the warm glow of the reddish sun as it rose through the deep layer of smog over the valley and the mountains. The air was better here than in the city, but still not easy to live with. Rad and Zeer opened their eyes to this and the morning routines of the people living in the valley. The fires again had been lit. Food was being prepared for the morning meal. Others were just beginning to come out of their huts; stretching and yawning themselves awake from their night's rest.

Rad and Zeer sat up, noticing a blanket that someone had placed over them during the night. It was warm and comfortable. They were huddled together against the morning's chill, but the day had begun.

Zeer asked if there was any way that she could clean up a little, and Rad showed her where everyone bathed and cleaned themselves. It was a natural shower. People would stand in the stream under a very small waterfall that splashed down from a rock overhang. It was very cold, but Zeer decided that it would be a good thing to do after the long week she'd had. "I'll be back to eat after I do this," she said with some apprehension in her voice. Rad laughed.

Although the sore on his leg was not getting better, and he was still very tired, he felt more energetic and excited this morning than he had for a long time. He was astounded by the turn of events. It made him think about the Room again. He'd asked Zeer what she thought it was all about. She only shrugged and said that the old one had told her that they both would understand at some point.

Sparks walked out of his hut and glanced over at Rad. "Well, you two had quite a night. I woke up a couple of times to your laughter and your voices. Did you ever sleep?"

Rad answered, "We did, but only a couple of hours. It's okay. Seeing her has given me new strength."

"That's great, but now, tell me what's going on."

Rad proceeded, giving Sparks a shortened version of what he knew about Zeer's appearance here and who she was. Sparks just shook his head. "Both of you come from this Room you've told me about? Well, Zeer seems strong and healthy, and we could sure use her help right now. I'm glad she's with us."

Rad smiled, "So am I..."

\*\*\*

Zeer came back from her cold shower revitalized and awake. She joined Rad and Sparks for breakfast and met many of the people in the valley. You wouldn't say it was a joyous gathering, but it had some light-hearted moments and was a morning that everyone there would remember. They all felt more hope and more determination as they welcomed their newest member and discussed what they needed to do next.

\*\*\*

The following few weeks flew by as they created new medicines, met with each other, helped the people in the valley and continued to expand what they were doing in the city. The Terrans within the city were talking more and more about the people who were providing medicine and relief in ways they had never known.

The water and air were still severely polluted with toxins. The food was horrible at best, and people's lives were still on the line every day. They remained diseased, with many of them being deformed or crippled from horrific viruses or from the toxins in their environment, but at least more of them were getting some aid from these caregivers. Some people's lives were actually improving.

Rad, Zeer and Sparks, along with all of those who now were part of their team, were working better together and were more able to spread their aid to a larger segment of the population. Life in the city was slowly, ever so slowly, improving, but it was still too measured for many of them, and the people were still suffering terribly and dying every day.

\*\*\*

Zeer was now involved in most of the aspects of the work that was being done. She couldn't get over the dedication of everyone involved, but she was especially proud and more and more connected to Rad and Sparks. Sparks was a remarkable healer, and his body continued to be strong and healthy in the midst of everything. Rad was phenomenally dedicated, and he had channeled his abilities as a leader and his focus as a player to a cause that he believed in completely. He and Zeer would sit and have endless talks. They discussed what they had learned and experienced about the Earth when it was a pure and pristine wilderness – when it was a place whose beauty and immense diversity had given rise to the human race. They compared what they had learned about the wars and how the corporations had usurped the governments', as well as the people's, rights to survive and live on their planet, and they agreed that the wealthy's lust for money and power had been utterly insane and destructive.

In the evenings, though, the two sometimes just spent time together. They walked on trails and looked into the sky, wishing that they could see the stars, but happy for their time in the valley with everyone there and especially happy to be with each other.

*\*\**

One thing that was a great worry to Zeer was that Rad was not getting any better. The sore on his leg was getting larger, had started oozing puss and his cough had continued to worsen. It didn't slow him down a lot, but his illness was something that Zeer and Sparks spoke about often.

"We've been able to help so many. Why can't we heal Rad of this disease?" Zeer was worrying more every day.

"I think it's because Rad has not been on the Earth for very long. All of the toxins and diseases are so new to his body that his immune system is having a very difficult time dealing with them. My medications just aren't strong enough to bolster him and heal the disease, and it's probable that he has more than one virus attacking him."

Zeer sat with Sparks, listened and then had to share something. "Please don't mention this to Rad, but I need to let you know that I'm here to take him back to someone named Fawn. She's from our time, and she is the old one that Rad has mentioned to you from the Room that we are both involved with. She's told me that it's about time for this to be over. She's found out what she needs to know about Rad. I'm not exactly sure what that is, but I had to tell you. She will let me know when it's time, and I'll have to do what she says."

Sparks sat quietly for a moment. "I need both of you so much, but I also know that soon the people in the Shelter will be leaving Earth. Then I hope we can use their Shelter and many of their supplies for our purposes, and I have so many wonderful people to work with now, thanks to both you and Rad. I know he's not well so I agree that it's time to take him home, but first, I need your help with something."

"What's that? You know we'll do anything for you."

He thought a moment more before continuing. "First, I need to get some information. I need to find out precisely when the Chosen are leaving, and I need to know what they are taking with them and what they're leaving behind. I have to learn as much as possible in order to get ready for what will come after they're gone. I already have a plan for how I'm going to do that, but once I get the information, I'd like to have you and Rad help me figure out the best way to help as many people as possible. I know that I can count on some help from some of my friends inside the Shelter, but the more minds I have to work out the problems, the better chance there'll be for success. What do you say?"

"Of course we'll help. We can help you with the logistics, help you carry it out and also get ready for when Rad and I will have to leave. I'll talk to him."

"Zeer thanks. I understand that you'll need to leave. This is not your time or place, but your help... Thank you."

"I do have one question, though. You mentioned that you had a way to get the information that you need. How are you going to do that?"

"Well, I know it won't be easy, but I'm going to try to go directly to the head of the council, to Harlequin. I want to speak to her, tell her some of what we've accomplished and ask her my questions directly."

"Do you think she'll tell you?"

"I don't know, but maybe if she sees what we're doing out here and that we actually have a chance to turn things around – maybe, just maybe, she will give me the information. They're leaving, so it really shouldn't be difficult for her to tell me. At least that's what I'm hoping. We are all humans after all, not just the people in the Shelter. This is…was, their planet, too!"

"I hope you're right."

## 30
## The Room: Level 3
## The Meeting

The next week Sparks traveled to the Shelter and set up a meeting with Harlequin. It wasn't easy. He could tell that he wasn't very welcome, and it took a lot of talking to get the meeting, but he finally succeeded.

He walked into Harlequin's office. She looked up for a second, finished something she was working on, slid her glasses off and spoke to Sparks in a condescending tone. "I don't have a lot of time so tell me what you want."

It wasn't the best start to the conversation, but it was the attitude that Sparks had expected. "My name is Sparks."

"I know."

"I've come to talk to you about what we've been working on in the city. We've had some successes and things are changing for the people outside. I also have some questions that I'd like to ask."

She simply said, "Go ahead."

"As you know, the Terrans are suffering terribly. You also know, my immune system is quite rare. Your scientists have been studying me for some time now, and I've been studying myself for much longer. I've found ways to relieve suffering for these people, and in some cases, even begun to cure their illnesses. We've established a research and safe facility in the mountains and some help centers in a couple of the old broken down buildings in the city. We're using these to work with people and do what we can. The people that we've successfully treated have become our assistants. We're working hard every day, and we believe that we've started something worth continuing."

Harlequin spoke quietly, "I know what you've been doing. We've known since the beginning."

Sparks continued, "I'm glad, so you know that we've made some progress. It's not a lot compared to the problem, but we've proven that people can be helped. Things can get better."

"So, your question?"

185

Sparks swallowed and asked, "I want you to rethink leaving the Earth. With the combined knowledge of what we're doing and the wonderful resources that are at your fingertips, we could do great things and change the course of history here. It would take a huge commitment from all of the Shelters, and it would take a long time, but we could change the dynamics of what is happening to our world, if we only tried."

Harlequin narrowed her eyes and simply said, "We are not changing our plans. They are set in stone. The Visionary Councils of every Shelter have agreed. The answer to that question is very simple. No!"

Of course Sparks had prepared for this and kept pushing on. "I understand that there has been a massive amount of planning to leave the Earth. I thought that's what you'd probably say, but I had to try."

"If there's not anything else, I need to get back to work," her impatience and anger were bubbling up under the calm façade.

"I do have a couple more questions. Since you've decided to leave, could you tell me when that's happening?"

"I wouldn't tell you except that the announcement will be made today anyway. Everyone in all the Shelters on Earth will be leaving one month from today."

Sparks wasn't completely surprised, but it still was a sad thing to hear. "I'm sorry you won't rethink your position but thank you for telling me." He paused a moment and then continued, "My last question, for now, is this. Since you'll be leaving, I know that there are items that you won't be taking with you from the Shelter. Items that we could use to help the people left behind. Since you won't need these things and won't be using the Shelter after you go, I would ask if we could use it and whatever is inside for our work. It could help us immensely."

Harlequin burst out laughing sadistically. "I don't care what you do with the Shelter once we're gone. Do whatever you like. I understand from what you're saying that you won't be coming with us."

"No, I won't." Sparks wondered about her quick

acquiescence to his proposal but wasn't going to worry about it right now. He'd been able to get what he wanted. "I want to thank you for this. It will mean everything to all of us left behind."

"Don't thank me, Sparks. You're an idiot to stay here and work with the Pariah. They are dirty, filthy and stupid. They are the scum of this sick planet, worth no more than the dying world that they live on. You could leave and go forward to establish other colonies of life with real humans - talented, bright, unique people with genuine futures and intelligent plans for the human race. But no, you will all die here. You can only make an infinitesimal dent in the horrific problems of this planet. If you have any sense at all, you'll come with us in a month. Now, leave my sight. I hate stupid people."

Sparks stood for a moment. His own anger bursting inside, but he held his temper. He had what he wanted. He didn't care about this woman. She was sicker than anyone outside her precious Shelter. *She* was the Pariah.

He breathed deeply to calm himself somewhat and started analyzing what she'd said and the anger and hate behind it. He saw now that the Visionary Council not only wouldn't help anyone outside, but they seemed to abhor the Earth and everything on it. He turned and walked out the door, slamming it behind him.

***

Sparks was still fuming and thinking about the meeting as he walked into his apartment in the Shelter to pick up a few more pieces of clothing. He had many emotions inside after his confrontation with Harlequin but was extremely glad that they would have use of the Shelter and everything in it. That was a major boon for what they were trying to accomplish. He wondered, though, why that part was so easy to attain as he contrasted it with the vitriolic revulsion that she possessed toward the Terrans and to the Earth itself.

He picked up his clothes and was leaving when he looked up and saw someone standing in the doorway. It was Gwen, a scientist and doctor in the Shelter who had helped Sparks on several occasions. He greeted her. "Hi Gwen."

"Hi. I noticed you walking into your apartment. Can I talk to you for a moment?"

"Sure."

Gwen gathered her thoughts and said, "I like you, Sparks, and I respect what you're doing for everyone outside. Everything is in such a terrible mess. The world's falling apart."

"Tell me about it!" He smiled at her. Gwen was a good person.

She continued, "Did you hear that we're leaving Earth in a month?"

"I was just in a meeting with Harlequin. She told me."

"Are you planning on leaving with us or staying?"

"Gwen, you know how important this is to me and how much we've accomplished. I have to stay. I can't leave the Earth now. Not when we have a chance to do some good here. I know what we've done isn't a lot compared to the tragedy that people are living with everyday, but I have to try."

"Well..." Gwen hesitated and seemed to be searching for something that she wanted to say. "I...I figured that's what you were going to do. I just want you to think very carefully about your decision. There's a rumor... Now, understand that I don't know any of this for sure, and you know how rumors fly inside this place. It's probably nothing."

"*What* is probably nothing?"

"Okay...the rumor is that the council has something planned for Earth after we leave. No one except Harlequin and a few of her closest confidants on the council know exactly what it is, but we've heard that they plan on doing something serious once the evacuation has taken place – something big."

"What else do you know? That's not enough for us to go on."

"I'm sorry Sparks. It's all I know. But if it were *me*, I'd be on those rockets in a month. I wouldn't stay behind."

Sparks' head was reeling, wondering what they could possibly have planned. He had to know. "Is there anything else that you can tell me, Gwen?

"No. That's it. What are you going to do?

"I don't know, but I do know that I'm not leaving here. Please, please don't mention to anyone that you've told me about this. It's very important."

"I won't. I wish you would reconsider coming with us, but I know how hard you've worked. I'm sorry that I didn't know more."

Sparks reached out and squeezed his friend's hand and said, "Thanks Gwen. It's okay. I'd better get going. I need to talk with Rad and Zeer."

# 31
## The Room: Level 3
## Crossroads

The evening fires had been lit for cooking meals for everyone in the camp. Sparks looked into the valley with a feeling of gratitude and friendship as he watched everyone going about their chores – each person providing for the welfare of everyone else. He was very proud of the work that Rad, Zeer and he had done, and he was also incredibly glad that he had made so many friends with the Terrans. There was so much sorrow in the world at this time, and the Earth was so damaged that to be able to foster at least some optimism filled his heart with hope for the future.

He walked down the path in the darkness and continued mulling over in his mind what had happened with Harlequin and his conversation with Gwen. He was relieved and excited to know that they would be able to use the Shelter, but also very worried about what Gwen had intimated. If only he knew what the Visionaries had planned to do after they left. Being in the dark about something like that was intolerable. He had to know.

Rad and Zeer had just started eating some soup and greens when they noticed Sparks returning. They waved him over, and Zeer made a place for Sparks to sit down near their fire.

"We were getting really worried about you. What took so long? You must be starving. Rad went to get some food for you."

"Thanks. I'm exhausted, but I learned a lot today. Some of it good and some just created more confusion. I'm not sure what to think."

Rad walked back into the conversation and handed Sparks his food. "Glad you're back, Sparks. Let's all finish eating, then you can fill us in on what happened today."

All of them ate, but Sparks could tell that Zeer and Rad could hardly contain themselves. It was obvious that there was no way he was going to make it through his meal without telling them what had transpired with Harlequin.

"I can tell you two are doing your best to let me eat, but

you know you want to hear about what happened, so I'll tell you." He couldn't help but laugh a little. They had all worked so hard together, and he knew that they were anxious to hear the news. It was obvious that they cared deeply.

In between bites, Sparks began telling them about his day, highlighting his meeting with Harlequin and then his encounter with Gwen. He then sat back, finished his food and waited for Rad and Zeer to respond.

They felt exactly like Sparks – happy that they were going to have access to the Shelter after the Chosen had left but confused and worried about what Gwen had said.

"I can't imagine that they would do something more to the Earth and the people who remain here. What would they gain? I don't understand. And Gwen didn't know anything more?" Rad just didn't get it.

Sparks responded, "No. I asked her more than once. She's my friend. I know if she'd known more, she would have told me."

Zeer looked at both her friends and summed up what all of them were thinking. "We have to know what they're going to do. From what I've learned about the Visionary Council since I've been here, I know that all this is not just about their survival. They're also very concerned with maintaining their economic and social status as well as their hold on power, no matter the cost. And from what you've said about your meeting with Harlequin, they don't care at all about the Earth or its people. The combination of those things frightens me. We need to find a way to get to the central computers in the Shelter and find out what they're planning. I do not trust them."

Sparks nodded in agreement. "You're absolutely right, Zeer, but what could we do even if we did find out that the Visionaries were planning something horrible? We don't have any weapons, and we don't even have enough healthy people to break our way into the Shelter."

Rad had been listening and was ready to jump in, "Everything they do is controlled by the central computer system – everything. As they get ready to leave the Earth, the central computers will help plan and implement that exit. That will be one program. After that, everyone inside will be gone so the central computer system will likely have other programs designed to do things like lock up the Shelter, maintain surveillance and security and, finally, implement whatever they want done after they leave. I know she said that we could use the Shelter once they're gone, but I agree with Zeer. I don't trust them, and they'll want to keep us out for a while, anyway, even if it's just to make sure that their departure is protected."

Sparks and Zeer agreed and Rad continued, "I have a lot of training with computers. I've spent a great deal of time with the engineers on the lifeglobes where I worked, learning about the systems that were designed to maintain the environmental conditions and the general operations of each one. I think that, with your help, I can hack into this program in the central computers. We should then be able to determine what it's going to do and delete it, if we need to."

They all sat quietly for a moment. The background sounds of the camp were comforting. The fires had begun to burn down, and their Terran friends were slowly moving into their huts. Zoe, a woman that always seemed to be watching and caring for others, offered some tea to the three before she went to bed. They accepted gratefully, warming their hands around the containers and blowing across the hot liquid to cool it. They were all aware that they were at an extremely important crossroads. So much had been accomplished, but what did the Visionaries have planned? That was the question.

Sparks concluded their planning session with this thought. "Okay, I think we all agree we need to act, and we have the beginnings of a plan. The three of us will continue to work out the details, and since I'm the only one with access to the Shelter, I'll have to do some research, ask questions, call in some favors and see what I can do to figure out how and when we can go forward. We'll need to move quickly, though. A month isn't a lot of time." He finished his tea and knew he had to get some rest. These next weeks were going to be very difficult.

Rad and Zeer remained near their fire. They weren't talking now. They were just watching the last of their friends who were finishing up their chores for the night. Finally, only the two of them remained outside, huddled together by the fire. Neither of them seemed to want to go to their hut. There was a soft evening breeze blowing toward the city so the air was somewhat better tonight. The sky was murky, as usual, but it just felt good to be there together, sitting, being close.

"Can you believe everything that we've experienced, Zeer?"

"No I can't. I'm just glad I'm here to help. I'm glad I'm here with you and Sparks."

"And we're both glad you're here, too. Having you work with us and just having you around has made a big difference. Thank you."

Zeer looked into Rad's eyes, noticing that he seemed paler. She continued to worry about his health, but tonight she didn't mention it. She just smiled, gave him a gentle kiss on the cheek and snuggled up a bit closer. They held each other into the morning.

# 32
## The Room: Level 3
## The Plan

This game that had started on R-131 so long ago had been steered by Fawn. She had created it to help both Zeer and Rad understand the importance of their ancestral home, its history, and what could happen to a world and its society when the inhabitants of that world lived out of balance with nature. It was critical for them to gain this knowledge in a way that allowed it to become a part of them to the very core of their being. Their interaction with the Room had to be real beyond doubt and had to unfold according to their own actions, even if it meant putting them in danger. Fawn did have the ability to make some adjustments along the way, but her capacity to actually control the outcome was limited at best.

With Zeer, the Room had played out in a way where she had achieved the needed understanding without too much danger to herself. With Rad, however, his path had been much more chaotic and hazardous. Fawn had to intervene more often so that Rad could learn and yet make it out alive, and during a significant portion of the third and final level, the Room had been, for the most part, out of her control. She was thankful that the Room was nearing an end, but she was on edge and worried about the outcome. All that she could do at this point was to watch, listen and wait. The people of Loon were tense and worried, just as Fawn was, but they believed in their leaders and knew that they would intercede when they could.

Everyone was aware that this was a very dangerous moment in time. Fawn's energy sphere was her only link to Rad and Zeer as she and Landree sat watching and waiting. Because of her worry, Fawn was poised to return to Earth at any moment, but Landree reminded her of the free-will doctrine on Loon. If they jumped in now, they might save Rad and Zeer from harm but lose their hearts and minds. Rad and Zeer might never forgive them for intervening because of how much they cared and how important this was to them. Fawn agreed to wait, but in turn, she reminded him of their immense responsibility to bring the two home safely. Those competing thoughts tugged and pulled at them while they observed the plan moving forward. If successful, Zeer, Rad, and Sparks' actions had the potential to even change the history of Earth, but changing certain aspects of history could also be very dangerous.

They sat tense, watchful and very worried.

***

With the help of a few of the Chosen and many Terrans, Zeer, Rad and Sparks worked night and day to prepare; they were finally ready to execute their plan and enter the Shelter. Tomorrow was the day, and only three days were left until all of the rockets would leave the Earth. *'Would everything go as planned? Could they trust everyone involved to remain silent and do their part to help?'* These questions and many more were at the forefront of their thoughts as the time to act was almost upon them.

They spent the day double-checking every part of their plan and going over every detail. They all knew exactly what was expected of them and had spent the time needed to prepare.

Sparks was responsible for laying out the logistics of the plan. He had coordinated the participants, the time frame as well as what everyone would do. He'd also gathered materials that they might need. Zeer, having been trained as a habituate, knew how to stun a person and put him or her out of action if needed. Rad would be the one to override the controls on the central computer, hack into it and find the program. All of them would then look at what the Visionaries had planned, the time table for the event and determine what action they would need to take. If it put the Earth and its people in any further danger, they would, if possible, delete it. If it were benign, they would leave it in place.

Even with all of the days and weeks of planning, they knew that any plan, no matter how well thought out, would probably *not* go exactly as designed. But they were as mentally and physically ready as they could be, and each of them had experience with thinking on their feet and making quick decisions. The one person, who wasn't one hundred percent, was Rad. His illness had continued to worsen; the lesion on his leg was larger and festering. He had more discomfort and wasn't as agile as he would normally have been. Also, his cough was something that would need to be controlled. Before and after entering the Shelter, it was essential that they travel as noiselessly as possible so Sparks had been working on something that would, for a period of time, calm Rad's cough and numb the pain and soreness in his body. A few days earlier they had given Rad a small dose of the medication to test its efficacy. It had seemed to work well, but would it last long enough for them to get in and out of the Shelter? That was the question.

\*\*\*

The day had finally arrived. Rad, Zeer and Sparks worked as usual in the city and made sure they were in separate help centers. Recently they had been spending their days working independently in order to serve more people, and they had decided that it would be best to maintain that pattern just in case someone was watching them. They also hoped that security from the Shelter would be lax now because of the preparations for the impending departure from Earth. That looked to be the case, as Sparks had noticed earlier in the day that there was only one guard outside the entrance to the Shelter; normally there were more. It was a positive sign.

Dusk was upon them. They'd all worked with many people that day and normally would have been extremely tired. However, knowing that this was the day that they would enter the Shelter provided them with a significant amount of nervous energy. They were all keenly aware, eager to get started and somewhat frightened. They met at a predetermined spot in the woods outside of town. The coming darkness would be their cover.

They picked up a small backpack of supplies that they had stashed in the woods several days earlier. Inside were clothing and some other items that they would need that night. They took off the clothes that they had worn that day and changed into camouflaged outfits that were dark in color. They also covered their faces with black, soot-darkened oil. There had been a great deal of debate about how they should enter the Shelter, including a suggestion to simply walk up to the main entrance and nonchalantly enter using Sparks' keypad, but in the final analysis, they had decided to do it as quietly and unobtrusively as possible with the aid of a small diversion. They didn't want to take any chances. Next, they started on a path that would keep them as unexposed as possible. They walked slowly on soft-soled shoes, moving closer and closer to the outside wall of the Shelter.

Rad had already been given the full dose of the medication by Sparks. He felt a little light-headed, but other than that, it was doing its job, and he felt much better. He even moved better.

Sparks whispered, "Okay, we're close enough to the lights from the Shelter now to be spotted. Let's stop here and wait. We'll be able to get inside easily once Silas does his job. There he is, behind that rock." They all looked and saw a large boulder about twenty meters from the door. From their angle, they could see Silas kneeling behind it, waiting for the signal. Sparks crawled gingerly in Silas's direction, caught his attention and gave him a thumbs up sign.

Silas waited for a couple more minutes, watching for the guard to face his way. At that moment, he stood up behind the rock and started walking toward the guard. Silas made enough noise that the guard noticed him almost immediately. He was acting like he was trying to sneak up on the guard. The guard yelled, "Who are you? What the hell are you doing here, Pariah?"

Silas threw a rock, hitting the guard in the leg. "You stupid bastard, don't call me a Pariah!" The guard yanked his laser gun out of its case and fired, but Silas was already on the run. The shot missed him and glanced off the boulder. He was chosen for this task because of his agility, speed and the accuracy of his throwing arm. He zigzagged up a path back into the city; the guard hollered and ran after him, firing his weapon. Silas had a good start and looked like he'd be okay, but the three needing to get inside knew they didn't have much time. They couldn't depend on the guard being gone very long.

They ran toward the entrance in an oblique fashion, skirting the wall as closely as possible. A small whole in the wall, located about three meters up, was where they knew the surveillance camera was located. It was near the entrance. They stood below it. Sparks cradled Zeer's foot in his hands and helped her shinny up the wall. In her hand was a small container of the same dark oil that they had used on their faces. She was able to rub it on to the lens of the camera, not entirely blacking out the lens but making it darker and much more opaque. Sparks then helped Zeer down, and they walked carefully toward the entry door. Sparks pushed the button on his keypad; it beeped, and they entered the Shelter and made their way to one of Sparks' friend's apartments close to the entrance. This was Gwen's place. They'd spent time together often and had given each other entrance privileges. Sparks knew that Gwen wouldn't be home very early that evening so he'd chosen her apartment for their first stop.

Even though they were inside the apartment, Rad spoke quietly, "Well, we've made it this far. Let's check the backpack one more time to make sure we have what we need before we clean up and change."

They all agreed. Everything seemed to be there. They washed their faces and changed into the clothes that Sparks had hidden in Gwen's place earlier in the week. This would allow them to avoid drawing attention to themselves once they left her apartment.

Zeer looked up at how all of them were dressed and couldn't help but laugh a little as she said, "We all look a bit pretentious, don't you think?" They glanced at each other and started laughing. Rad had gold sparkles on his shirt and a gold chain on his bare chest. Sparks' clothes were obviously expensive, the rich colors bringing even more amusement as he strutted around the room. Zeer had on a short black dress, showing off her beautiful body, with jewels around her neck and in her hair. She had her hand on her hip and was modeling for the boys. It was a moment that they needed before leaving the apartment. Sparks and Rad looked at Zeer and commented at the same time. "Wow!"

"Won't these clothes bring more attention to us?" Rad asked.

Sparks spoke confidently, "You'd think so, wouldn't you, but no. You'll see when we walk out. We'll blend in fine. Hopefully we won't see very many people, though, because we'll be staying in the hallways, not out in the main areas where more people might be gathered. Also, it's early enough that not very many people will be walking back to their apartments yet. There's supposed to be a big meeting tonight in the main hall. It's about the departure in two days. That should help, too."

Next, they hid the few tools that they carried with them in their clothing, collectively took a deep breath and walked out into the corridor. The hall was not brightly lit. There were small lights glowing above each door. The floor was carpeted, and as they traveled along, Rad and Zeer realized how huge even this small part of the Shelter was. The hallways were like a maze with doors on each side. They were happy that they had Sparks to guide them because if it had been left up to them, they could have easily become disoriented and lost.

Sparks led the way, greeting the few people that they did encounter. Rad and Zeer watched and listened to Sparks carefully, emulating his mannerisms and his greetings. So far their journey to the central computer core was uneventful, which is the way they wanted to keep it.

As planned, they remained in the hallways, and at intervals, seemed to be spiraling down to lower and lower levels until they reached a locked door at the end of one of the corridors. Sparks tried the door. As he knew it would be, it was locked, but there was no guard. Often times, one was posted here, but not tonight. So far, all of the preparation was panning out. He pulled out a tool from his pocket, flicked it on, and shined the light on the panel by the door. They saw the panel flicker and could hear small clicks. The door opened slightly. Sparks seemed relieved as he tilted his head and blew out a small amount of air. He held his index finger perpendicular to his lips for silence and opened the door a little more, glancing through the crack into the room beyond.

At that moment, they all heard footsteps. The sound was coming from the other side of the door. Sparks, as swiftly and quietly as he could, partially closed the door. They all stood motionless, breathing in soft quick breathes, their hearts pounding. Sparks waited and then opened the door a crack again and looked inside. He nodded them forward and opened it a bit more and mouthed, "He's gone."

They slid through the opening onto a platform with a railing. The platform edged about three quarters of the big room. They had to be careful. The platform's surface was made of metal grating with small one-inch holes. Looking through these, you could view the floor of the room below. The room they were in was circular, with the center area being well lit. The floor was concrete, and the walls were made of cold, grey metal. Zeer took off her shoes in order to be able to walk more easily on the platform without making noise or catching a heel. They could see the man who'd passed by. He was walking away from them along the curved platform and had come to a staircase. He walked down the steps to the large room below. His footsteps were echoing off the hard surfaces, and they could hear him talking to someone. They were obviously guards. Again, thankfully, Sparks had been correct about there being less security. He glanced down where they stood and held up two fingers and gave a small smile to Rad and Zeer. They understood.

They didn't dare go to the railing and look down. The light was brighter there and overlooked the heart of the room below. They needed to move very slowly and cautiously along the dimly lit wall of the platform away from the light and away from the two guards below them. From this point on, it became very tricky to keep from being detected. All the guards had to do was look up and notice movement in the shadows. They were very exposed.

Standing near the wall, Sparks spoke almost inaudibly and pointed. "We need to get to that door. That one," and he pointed toward the far end of the platform.

Rad and Zeer followed Sparks, plastering themselves against the wall and moving as noiselessly and cautiously as possible. They were getting close to the door when Rad felt a cough tickling his lungs. He held his breath. Held the cough inside. He did everything he could to fight it, but he couldn't stop himself. It wasn't loud and was muffled by his body fighting against it, his hands held over his mouth, but it could be heard. They all froze. Silence. They moved on.

Reaching the next door, Sparks simply opened it bit by bit, hoping it wouldn't creak. It wasn't locked, and it opened without a sound. One thing about the shelter was that every part of it was well maintained at a level that verged on the obsessive. That was a good thing right now.

They walked through the door and down a stairway that was made of the same metal grating that had been used on the platform that they had just left. They were thankful to be in a different room than the guards now. At the bottom of the stairway was a smaller oval shaped room with boxes stored on shelves next to its walls. Two doors exited opposite sides of the room. Both were closed.

"I need to block that far door. Right?" Again Rad spoke softly but needed to make sure of what he was supposed to do.

Sparks answered, "Yes. Find two very heavy boxes. I'll help you place them in front of the door."

Rad tested several and found two that would work. Sparks and he secured the door and walked back over to Zeer.

Zeer looked at them both and knew that it was her time to act. They had thought about this for a long time. They knew someone with high-level clearance could enter this area, and it wasn't far from the main hall where the large meeting was being held. They felt this could work, but it was going to take some acting on Zeer's part.

"Here goes..." Zeer started walking towards the unblocked door to enter the larger room. Rad touched her shoulder for a moment, looked directly into her eyes and said, "You'll do great. We've got your back." They smiled at each other, and Zeer continued on.

At the door, Zeer stopped for just a moment, put her high-heeled shoes back on, straightened her clothes and shook her hair out. Standing up straight, she threw her shoulders back, licked her lips and opened the door. Light rushed into the smaller room and then dissipated. She had left the door slightly ajar so that Rad and Sparks could watch and come to her aid if necessary.

"Hi there boys!" Zeer spoke with a slight slur in her speech, doing her best to look sexy and sound just slightly tipsy.

Both men turned and stared at her. It was obvious that neither knew what to do for a moment. Then they seemed to recognize what was happening and started to enjoy the scene. One spoke up and said, "Hey there. What are you doing in here?"

The second guard figured it out and said, "Looks like you just came from the big meeting. Are people celebrating?"

"Yes, we are, and I came in here, because I knew I might get to see some strong, handsome guys." Zeer then gave them her best shy, yet alluring look, and walked passed the guards, putting a hand on each of their shoulders as she did so.

They glanced at each other, gave a small laugh and smiled. As she passed by, they turned and faced her and kept talking with her. They were very attracted and were enjoying the moment.

"How did you get in here?" one of them asked Zeer.

She giggled and explained, "A female friend let me in. She's part of the council and had the code. She was a bit drunk, too, and she'll be coming to join us in a few minutes, after she gets rid of her husband."

This made the two men even more interested. This could be an exciting night.

"We're both glad you dropped in on us. It's been pretty boring being on guard on a night when everyone else is having a big party."

The conversation continued. The men were facing away from Rad and Sparks and were completely focused on Zeer. This gave Rad and Sparks the opportunity to walk in quietly and stand just a few meters from the guards. Then Rad spoke. "Well, it looks like it's not going to be boring for you two much longer."

Both of the men jerked around and faced Rad, "What the

hell?" They then fumbled for their weapons in a panic. As they were trying to get their guns out, Zeer, now behind the men, clamped her fingers down extremely hard on the neck and shoulder region of both men. They collapsed in a heartbeat.

Sparks ran up and collected the weapons and gave them to Zeer. He smiled at her and nodded his approval. She smiled back.

Rad checked the door to the central core. It was locked. "Damn!" Rad exclaimed in frustration. He knew that this was the one door for which Sparks didn't have a code. Sparks tried the unlocking device that he'd used on the first door, but it didn't work. They had hoped this door would be open, because he'd found out that the guards sometimes used the computer room as a place to rest when they took breaks during their shifts, but not tonight.

Sparks went to plan B. "Okay, let's see if we can use this guy's hand print to get in."

They dragged one of the men near the door and together lifted his arm. Zeer grabbed his hand and placed it on the security pad. The lights flashed, and the door clicked open. "God, it worked! Okay, let's get them inside and get started." They were all relieved.

Inside, the room was dark and cool. They pulled the men inside with them and laid them face down where Zeer could watch them and stun them again if needed.

Rad and Sparks noticed the digital interface panel located in the center of the room. All Rad had to do was stand or sit in that area to begin to activate and control the computer with movements of his hands. He sat down, took some small hacking devices out of his backpack, and reached out to touch the interface.

It was amazing for Zeer and Sparks to watch Rad work. He flew through the interface, figuring out codes to hack through each layer of security with the help of the devices that he'd brought. The 3-D figures in the interface were swept aside, one at a time, as Rad moved deeper and deeper into the memory of the central system. He'd finally found the section where the plan to leave the Earth was located and within that found a sub-program entitled

"Pariahs." It took some time to unencrypt the program, but he was finally successful. "Okay, I'm in. I've found it. Let's see what they've planned."

It took Rad longer than they had hoped to find what they needed. Sparks and Zeer were getting nervous, and Rad had begun to cough as he worked. Sparks had brought more of the medicine, but he was worried about giving it to Rad. He knew that too much of it could cause some serious side effects. He really only wanted to use it once.

Rad was finally done. He had an angry and serious look on his face. "Okay, I'm going to have to delete this program." Sparks and Zeer stood closer to Rad and waited for him to continue. He spoke hurriedly in order to continue his work. "It's vile! We were right that the first part of the program contains the security for the Shelter. They did put a lock down procedure in that's set to activate when they leave to go to the rockets. That will occur right away. That's the first part that I'll get rid of. The second part will happen thirty days after they leave. They have millions of small drones ready to take off when the program gives the command. From the program notes, I can see that the drones will release a toxin that will kill every human left behind on the Earth while leaving all other life, the water and air, relatively untouched. It looks like they want to try to *reset* Earth. In the notes, it talks about wanting their ancestors to be able to come back to Earth some time in the distant future to re-establish human life and resettle after the Earth has had time to move back into balance. I've got to get this done!"

Zeer and Sparks felt the power of Rad's horrendous words. They were sickened. It was more than what any of them could have ever imagined, and it was only three days away. '*How could they do this?*'

Sparks spoke, "It's like they're trying to heal it so they can rape the Earth again at a later date. Do it Rad!"

Rad worked furiously. They all knew that they'd been in the room quite a while now and every moment brought them closer to danger.

"I've killed the first part of the program. The Shelter will not lock down. Now, the next part." Rad's hands were flying over the interface. He was close to deleting the destructive part.

Without warning, behind them, they heard a loud crash as a door flew open. Rad glanced up but kept working frantically. Zeer and Sparks hid behind the computer, their guns ready. The security guards on the floor started waking up, and there were a lot of other guards in the room now, along with one other person. Sparks recognized who it was. It was Harlequin. The guards were hiding and circling the room trying to surround them. Sparks and Zeer looked at each other and knew that they had to fight as long and hard as they could so that Rad had the time he needed to get rid of the program. The lives of every Terran depended on it. The two rose up off their knees, raised their guns and glanced quickly around the computer. As they did, they heard several shots ring out from above. Each felt a sting in their shoulder as they looked up and saw a solitary guard standing on a platform pointing a gun at them. They were already feeling numb and groggy as they quickly looked back at Rad and saw him slumped over in his chair, the interface still above him. Then Sparks fell on the floor near Zeer and lost consciousness. She, too, was losing control and crumpled onto the hard, cold floor. The last thing she remembered was seeing two cruel, demented eyes staring down at her with hatred and anger.

## 33
## The Room: Level 3
## End Game

Sparks and Zeer lay on the ground outside the Shelter. They both had awakened just as Harlequin and her guards had tossed them on the ground. Her last words were still clear and rang in their minds. "You god dam son-of-a-bitches failed! Now you'll die with everyone else. You will feel the death and destruction that you deserve, and you'll see yourselves and all of the Pariah wiped off the face of the Earth. Our ancestors will return and live and use the Earth again for their benefit, and you can't do a damned thing about it!"

Zeer looked with hatred at her and yelled, "Where's Rad? What have you done with him?"

"He'll be thrown out soon along with the rest of the trash!" Harlequin turned and walked back into the Shelter with her guards and closed the door.

Zeer and Sparks sat with their heads bowed, knowing that they had failed and understanding the dire consequences of that failure. They were in shock.

Sparks finally spoke, "Zeer, let's wait here. God, I'm worried about Rad. He was the one working with the computer. He was the one trying to destroy the programs. What are they going to do to him?"

"I don't know, Sparks. They'll probably keep him their while they check to see what he did. If they can't find out quickly enough on their own, they may torture him. I know Rad won't tell them anything. I'm afraid for his life."

They waited through the rest of the night. They had crawled onto an old dilapidated bench in the area and lay on the slatted surface, nursing the wounds where the guards had hit and kicked them. They didn't sleep, but nodded off here and there, trying to stay awake to help Rad when and if he came out.

***

The morning light was just beginning to spread through the polluted haze. Zeer had dozed off, with Sparks lying nearby asleep as well. Her eyes slowly opened. She sat up. Her side was aching from an especially severe kick to her ribs. She glanced around and noticed a lump on the ground in front of the Shelter. She got up immediately and ran toward it. It was Rad. She checked his neck and found a pulse. She then surveyed his body and found serious wounds everywhere. They *had* tortured him. He was unconscious and bleeding slowly from a brutal injury in his lower abdomen. She pulled back his shirt and saw a gash from some type of sharp object. She quickly yelled for Sparks. He was already awake and on his way over. She and Sparks ripped off pieces of their cleanest clothing and made a bandage for Rad. Just then, from behind, they became aware of several people coming toward them. The one in the lead was Zoe. She spoke first. "We thought something had gone wrong. You hadn't returned to camp so I brought some people to help."

Both Sparks' and Zeer's eyes teared up as they thanked Zoe and the others. They all worked quickly to make Rad comfortable and treat his wounds as best they could. Sparks asked Zoe if she'd brought one of the tri-bikes so they could use it to transport Rad back to the valley more quickly. She shook her head, apologized and explained that she didn't want to risk the noise. Sparks told her it was okay, and they began to carry Rad back to the mountains. They needed to get him there as fast as they could. It was where they had the best facilities to treat him.

Zeer walked up to Zoe and said, "Thank you, Zoe. Thank you for coming. He's hurt so badly. I don't know if he's...I don't know if he's going to make it."

Zoe had a very serious look on her face. "We're going to do everything we can, Zeer. Sparks is an excellent healer. Rad has a chance, though. He does." She put her arm around Zeer's shoulder, and they walked toward home.

***

Arriving in the valley, Zeer, Zoe and the others who were

carrying Rad took him to Sparks' hut and laid him on a table after covering it with a clean, sterile cloth. His wounds quickly stained the surface. Sparks asked everyone to leave except for Zeer and Zoe. He needed room to work. Zoe had become Sparks' nurse whenever he needed to treat someone, and Zeer stayed to help and be close to Rad. Following Sparks' directions, they carefully removed Rad's soiled and blood-stained clothing, allowing Sparks a good look at his injuries.

They were in the hut for several hours doing whatever they could to deal with his wounds and to try to determine how badly he was injured. He had multiple lacerations of the neck and head; his fingers and toes had been broken, and some type of device had been attached to his chest. They could see burns on his torso and more than one gash from a sharp object in his lower abdomen, probably a knife. He was in very bad shape.

Sparks had been able to stay the bleeding for now, but from the type and number of wounds that Rad had, Sparks believed that there was probably also internal bleeding that he didn't have the ability to treat. Zeer could see the extreme worry on Sparks' face and knew that Rad's chances of surviving were slim.

"It doesn't look good," Sparks told both Zoe and Zeer. "I don't have what I need to deal with the internal bleeding. I've done the best I can. I was able to give him a medication that should ease the pain and inflammation and slow the bleeding, but the only thing we can do now is stay with him, be here when he wakes up and hope for the best."

Zeer looked at Rad and thought of everything that he had been through and how much he cared for the Earth and the Terrans. She couldn't imagine losing him after all that they had accomplished and everything that had happened. "I'll stay with him. I'll let you know if I see any change. You two go get some food and rest."

Sparks knew that he couldn't argue with Zeer, so he just said, "Zeer, I'll get some food for you, too. I don't think any of us are very hungry, but we need to keep up our strength."

She looked up at Sparks, nodded and said, "Okay."

Zeer's eyes followed her two friends as they were leaving and saw them hesitate. Someone in an Earthen-colored robe entered the doorway. They all tensed, not knowing or recognizing who it was. The person pulled their hood down, and Zeer's eyes widened with surprise and relief. It was Fawn.

Immediately, Zeer ran to Fawn and hugged her and spoke through tears of worry. "Can you help him? They were incredibly cruel to him. He's in bad shape, Fawn. Can you?"

Fawn held Zeer, looking over at Rad's body on the table. "I'll try." That's all she said as she walked over to him, pulling back the sheet that covered him. "I'll need Sparks to stay for a few minutes to help me understand the severity of Rad's wounds. Then I'll need to be alone with him. Don't worry, I'll let all of you know more as soon as I can."

Zoe and Zeer left the hut, followed shortly by Sparks. He walked over to them and asked Zeer a question. "She went into Rad's clothing and took out some kind of ball that was in one of his pockets. What was that, Zeer?"

Zeer took hers out of her pocket as well. "It's an energy sphere that is tuned specifically to our individual bodies. We use it to travel, and I know that members of the Healing Cluster use them when someone is ill or injured to help them heal. I don't know a lot about it, but it's a very powerful tool. I can only hope that Fawn can use it to help Rad."

"Healing Cluster? What's that?"

Zeer, in her worry about Rad, had forgotten for a moment that she was not supposed to mention anything about Loon. She didn't think, though, that at this point it mattered very much. She just said, "I'll tell you later."

Sparks took the sphere to Fawn and then returned and sat down by Zeer and held her. Zoe left them and went to communicate about what was happening to the rest of the camp. Everyone was somber and quiet that night, thinking about Rad and hoping for his recovery.

***

Morning arrived, and Fawn had completed her work. She'd spent the whole night with Rad. She wasn't sure if she had been able to repair all of his injuries. Zeer could tell that Fawn was terribly worried, but she also knew that she'd done everything that she could.

Zoe was sitting with Rad now. The rest of them were eating what breakfast they could. Sparks had gathered all of the people in the camp together for the morning meal. He had a lot that he needed to tell them.

"I know all of you were worried when we didn't come back to camp yesterday, and I wanted to thank each of you for your concern. I want to also thank those of you who left camp and came to get us. It would have been very difficult to get Rad back here without your help. All of you – thank you."

Sparks continued, "We've been involved in something that you need to know about. Zoe knew generally what we were doing, but now I need to tell the rest of you. I'm sure you've all heard the rumors about the people who live in the Shelter leaving Earth. Well, it's true. They're abandoning our planet and all of us tomorrow morning." Everyone took this in, glancing at each other and murmuring. "They've been planning this for a long time, and you also need to know that the Visionary Council had a second part to their plan. No one, except their leaders, knew what it was, but it was rumored to be something that could affect the Earth and everyone outside the Shelter. We had to find out what it was. So, yesterday, Rad, Zeer and I went into the Shelter and snuck into the central computer core. Rad hacked into the system to find out what their plans were. We found that it was something horrible and decided to delete the program and stop what they were going to do. It took us too long, though. They found out, stopped us, threw Zeer and I outside and tortured Rad."

One man spoke up in a grave voice. "What's the second part of this plan?"

Sparks paused and then explained, "As I said, tomorrow they will leave Earth. Thirty days after that, the program that we were trying to delete will run." Again Sparks hesitated. He still couldn't believe this was going to happen and wished that he didn't have to give them this news. "Millions of small drones carrying a toxin will be released all over the Earth. The toxin will be short-lived, but it will kill every human left behind on the planet."

Shock lay upon the small gathering. There was not a sound as they took this in. One small woman spoke in a shaky voice, "How could...How could anyone do such a thing?" She fell to the ground. Her husband knelt down beside her. Dismay, astonishment and disbelief spread over the faces of everyone.

Sparks spoke again. "We do have one hope. It's not going to be easy, and I don't know if it will actually work, but after they leave, the Shelter will be left untouched. It will probably be locked, though, and have a lot of security measures in place to keep us from entering. We're going to try to get in with as many people as possible before the thirty days are up. Maybe we can still find a way to shut it down, but if not, at least we might be able to protect ourselves from inside. There are a lot of "ifs" in this plan, but it's our best shot."

The Terrans spoke up, "We'll help! We'll do whatever it takes. When do we start?"

"I know. Thank you. You're remarkable people - all of you! Right now, though, lets all hope that Rad recovers, and I want all of you to take care of each other and do what you can to prepare. That will include eating enough and getting your rest. One other thing, please don't tell anyone in the city yet. We'll need to see if we can get inside. If we're successful, then we can begin to move people into the Shelter in an orderly way. If we're not, we'll let them know what will happen. They'll have a right to know."

Everyone dispersed from the meeting, some to their huts and others just remained outside to talk or think. Thirty days. It was all they had.

***

A bright orange sun rose on the eastern horizon, attempting to burn through the toxic atmosphere of Earth. The sky was murky and russet, blocking the bright rays of the dawn and covering the camp with a heavy pall of uncertainty. No one had slept the night through as the reality of this particular morning had begun to sink in.

Some were doing their best to get the day started by preparing food and going about their morning chores. Others sat quietly with family or friends, wondering about the future and what would happen in the next few weeks.

Zoe was ladling tea from a large kettle to anyone that wanted some. This had become a tradition at the beginning of each day, and everyone appreciated Zoe for her care and her cup of tea. She kept glancing up toward the horizon in the east where the sun had risen. Sparks had mentioned to her that the launching area was located in that direction. She was watching for the first ships to leave.

It seemed incredibly surreal to think that a large group of humans would actually be leaving Earth to relocate and resettle on different moons, asteroids and other planets in the galaxy. Zoe knew that there were already people with settlements on the moon and on mars, but never had anyone attempted to live outside the Earth's solar system. It was beyond her imagination. She and most of the people on the planet had been doing their best for many, many years to simply survive.

She had just poured some tea when she looked up again and there it was - the first ship exploding into the sky - the first leaving Earth. The pot of tea fell from her grasp as she gasped and pointed. Others quickly looked at the rocket as it shot upwards and disappeared into the heavy smog. It only took a moment for it to be gone, but then she saw another and another and another. Everyone was standing, watching and listening to the constant roar in the distance, mesmerized and stunned that this was really happening. It brought Sparks' words into stark reality. They were *actually* abandoning Earth.

It went on and on for several hours. Sparks and Fawn were outside with everyone now watching the spectacle with sadness and worry in their hearts. Fawn knew the history of Earth and knew that all human life on Earth would be destroyed in a short time. She looked at Sparks and understood that he would do everything he could to help, but it was already written – already almost upon them. She reached out to him and put her arm around his shoulders – this man who cared so deeply and had worked so very hard.

At that moment, Sparks asked himself, *'What would happen to all the people that he had cared about so much, all the plans, the hopes and the dreams that he'd had for Earth?'* A small tear streaked down his face. He had to turn away. Anger began to sweep through him.

When Sparks turned, he noticed Zeer standing just outside his hut. He walked toward her and noticed that she, too, had tears streaming down her face, staining her clothes. Through her tormented grief, she looked straight into his eyes and spoke. "Rad is dead, Sparks. God, he's dead..."

***

*'It was too much. Too much!'* The people of the Shelter deserting the Earth and the Terrans in such a cruel way, the news of the oncoming holocaust and now Rad...their dear friend, a person who had meant so much to them, who had given his life in order to try to help them. *'It was too much to bear!'*

Fawn knew that she needed to help everyone gain some closure in order for them to make it through the next thirty days. Inside her chest, the pressure of what she knew and how little could be done was immense. It was an ache from which she might not ever recover. She had never, actually, traveled to this time in Earth's past. She had learned about what had happened here by watching the histories on Loon, listening to the historians and to her teacher, Shar. But actually being here, meeting and knowing the people and being involved directly were more than she could deal with. For Zeer and Sparks and for the people here in this camp, though, she had to remain strong. There was only one course that she could take. She knew what she had to do.

Zeer and Sparks were in bad shape. They had spent so much time with Rad. They were all so incredibly close and had bonded, not only because of who they were, but also because of living through this time together. Now, part of that bond had been broken. They couldn't believe he was gone.

Fawn spent some time with Sparks and Zeer, preparing a ceremony to honor Rad and hopefully help everyone that had known him deal with the tragedy. It wouldn't take long, but they all felt that they needed to do something. They needed to remember him together.

With Zoe's help, they brought a table out into the middle of the huts and placed pieces of wood around and under it. They covered the wood with a liquid that would enable it to burn fast and hot. They moved slowly, and none of them spoke a word as they went about preparing the pyre.

They carried Rad out and laid him on the table. All of the Terrans in the valley were gathered round. Everyone was solemn, mourning the loss of their dear friend.

Finally, everything was prepared and Fawn spoke. "Rad lays with us here on Earth, his home, his mother. To care, to empathize, to hope, to dream, to love were all part of who he was, and I can say that these important characteristics are in all of you as well. He came to your home and worked tirelessly. He gave up his life as your friend and fellow human. You, and the Earth, meant so much to him. You meant everything to him."

Fawn reached into her pocket and brought out a leather book, which she placed on the table beside Rad. She then grabbed a small knife and cut off a lock of his hair. She placed it in a container and gave it to Sparks and said, "For you. Keep it nearby, always, where others can see it and gain hope and strength from it." Next, she grasped Rad's energy sphere, which was lying in his hands and held it above him and said, "Now, remember what you see. Rad is not gone. He will always be with you." As she spoke, the sphere began to glow and an image of Rad was projected into the air above his body. He had an easy smile and a peaceful look on his face. It seemed that he was looking into the eyes of everyone there. The vision of Rad held for a moment and then dissipated, leaving only stillness.

After a minute of complete silence, Zeer and Sparks walked forward and lit the pyre. Everyone watched as the flames roared into the sky.

It was done.

***

A new day had arrived. Twenty-nine days were left. After the morning meal, everyone walked up to a high point above the camp and spread Rad's ashes on the ground overlooking the valley and the city below. They knew how much this place had meant to him, and this was where he should remain for millennia.

Fawn walked down from the mountain in silence with Zeer and Sparks. Each of them caught up in their own thoughts. They were thinking about Rad and about all of the people still living on the Earth. The situation was terribly dire, and they had little time to grieve. Plans needed to be made to see if they could get into the Shelter. Zeer and Sparks decided that they needed to go down to the Shelter today to see what could be done.

Before leaving, Fawn took Zeer and Sparks aside. She needed to talk to both of them. "Zeer, what I'm going to ask of you now is going to be extremely difficult. Please listen carefully before you answer."

With Sparks looking on, Zeer looked at Fawn warily and said, "I'll listen. What is it?"

"Sparks, I know how much you depend on Zeer. I know how you all have become so close, and with Rad being gone, you need to count on each other even more. Am I right?"

They both acknowledged the truth of this and Sparks said, "Zeer *is* extremely important to me."

Fawn continued, "Yes, I understand. However, I need to take Zeer home with me."

Sparks eyes widened, as he couldn't believe what he'd heard, and Zeer's anger flared as she spoke with furious conviction. "Absolutely not! Not now! What are you saying? How can you even think such a thing? You know how much work it will take to get as many people inside the Shelter as possible, and we don't even know if we can get inside in time!"

Fawn remained quiet as she listened and then said,

"Believe me, I know. But as I asked, please listen." With great difficulty, Zeer held herself in check.

After a pause, Fawn said, "You were allowed to come here to do what you could. What you've accomplished under the circumstances has been amazing, but there are also extremely important things that need to be done on Loon. We have plans for you that will allow you to have a critical impact on the development of the human race. The knowledge that you've gained through the Room, from living on Loon and by spending this time on Earth will be invaluable to that end." Fawn paused again to let both Zeer and Sparks think about what she had said. She then continued, "Zeer, Sparks has many good people that want to help and work with him. This is *their* time and *their* place in the cosmos - *their* moment when they need to work together to determine the future. I'll say again. It is *their* time. This is not *your* time. Your body and soul come from the future. That is where you belong. Please let me take you home."

Zeer looked directly at Fawn and unequivocally said, "Absolutely not! I will never leave while this is happening. Rad gave his life to help these people and to help the Earth. I will *not* do less! I'm staying!"

Sparks had been quiet and had listened carefully after the initial shock of what Fawn had suggested. He didn't understand everything that she was talking about, but he did understand her reasoning. He looked at Zeer, took her hand and spoke with a calm compassion, "Zeer, you are my friend, and I'm incredibly grateful for all that you've done for us. You, Rad and I, along with many of the Terrans, have accomplished so much together, but Fawn is right. This is *our* time, not yours. We need to write this history ourselves. We need to succeed, or not, on our own, and I believe that, with the help of all my dear friends here, we will succeed. Yes, Rad gave up his life for us, but even knowing Fawn for the short time that I have, I know that she would not ask this of you if she didn't have a good reason. Go home, Zeer. We need you to be there. If you can help make sure that nothing like this ever happens anywhere else, ever again, then you need to go. It's okay. I love you, dear friend. Go home to your time."

Sparks *was* her friend. He meant so much to her, and as she heard his words and looked into his eyes, she knew that what he had said was right. She then glanced back at Fawn and understood that Fawn would not ask this of her unless there was a good reason. Her heart stopped racing, and she then remembered what she had promised Fawn when she left Loon. She would come home when Fawn asked.

"God, this is difficult. I need to be alone for awhile." Zeer walked back up the mountain near Rad's ashes and sat down. *'In twenty-nine days, what will happen here? What will happen to these people, to Sparks?'* She just didn't know.

***

Zeer had remained on the mountain all the rest of that day. The word had spread around the camp about what was happening. Everyone came together and discussed the situation with Sparks. They decided to meet with Zeer on her return.

Zoe came forward and met her as she walked back into camp. It had obviously been a terrible day for Zeer. Behind Zoe, the fires were burning, and the people sat in a group with Sparks and Fawn. They all stood, and Zoe gave Zeer a cup of tea, held her hands and spoke these words. "Zeer, we love you. We love what you've done here, your passion and your care for us and for our world. We, and this Earth, are damaged. We don't know if we will survive, but we are determined to try. Fawn and Sparks are right. This is not your time. This is ours. We will either succeed or fail on our own. We want you to live and do good things for others. Your spirit needs to live on in your own time. I'll say it again, Zeer. We love you, but please go home."

Everyone behind Zoe walked forward and one at a time held Zeer close. Some spoke quietly to her and said, "We'll miss you, Zeer."

Zeer was overwhelmed. She stood and accepted everyone into her arms. When they were done, Sparks held her and asked, "So, my dear friend, do you understand how we feel about you and what we want you to do?"

217

Through her sadness and longing, through her desperation and fear and because of her love for them, she said, "I understand. I'll go home in the morning."

# 34
## Home

A month had passed since Zeer's return to Loon. Upon her return, many people on Loon, including her closest friends and the entire History Cluster, had welcomed her home. She had returned to her Cluster and had taken time off to reintegrate and recuperate from the unbelievably traumatic events on Earth. She spent time with Landree, Dominie, Brit and Shee talking, listening and doing her best to understand in her own mind what had happened and why. She deeply missed the people she had come to know on Earth, while understanding that those beautiful spirits were now gone and had been for hundreds of years. She thought of Sparks and her close friend and companion, Rad. The memories were still very raw and her sadness still present.

One afternoon, she contacted Landree and asked him to come to her apartment. She had decided that she needed to look back in time and view what had happened on Earth after the thirty days had passed. She still held out some hope that Earth's history had changed in some way. She knew that Sparks and the people of the city would do everything they could to avert the impending disaster that had been planned by the Visionaries, but she didn't want to go back to that time alone. It frightened her. She needed her old friend.

Landree arrived and asked her what she had on her mind. She explained, and he wondered, "Are you sure you want to do this? Maybe you should give it more time."

"Landree, I have to see what happened. I know that they probably weren't able to change anything, but I need to know."

They took out Landree's sphere, and he steered them back to Earth at a time that coincided with the end of the infamous thirty-day period. They both gazed wide-eyed, as the sphere showed them city after city and guided them across vast plains to mountainous terrain and deserts, solitary valleys, oceans and rivers. Nowhere were they able to see even one human alive. Patches of meager trees and plants still clung to life; water was as polluted and tainted as before; they gazed upon the same

219

atmospheric brown blanket that had enveloped the planet prior to the toxins release and saw raw areas of deforestation and huge open mines, which still festered like open sores on the planet's surface. But they saw not a single person alive. The humans that *were* visible were on the ground, still and dead. Silent and motionless figures lay in the cities, in small villages and along solitary, deserted trails and paths. Some remains floated in rivers, in the ocean or on beaches. It was desolation and death on a scale beyond comprehension.

Zeer couldn't look any longer, couldn't believe or understand how anyone could do this. "Why? Why, Landree?"

"I could list reasons, Zeer, but I really can't comprehend it either. I can only say that what happened on the Earth during that time was pure evil – an evil beyond anything that any of us on Loon could ever fathom. I am utterly and totally ashamed of the people who sent our ship into space, but I'm also very proud of how we have developed on this wonderful planet. We are not what the Visionaries would have expected."

They sat and held each other. They talked a while longer, then Landree left, and Zeer stood staring out upon her miraculous new planet – thinking about the people of Loon, the wondrous and diverse ecosystems, the rich plant and animal life and the Scree. This planet and *all* of the organisms that lived upon it gave her comfort and hope. She loved this place. She needed to heal.

\*\*\*

Several more months went by, and Zeer was doing her best to move on with her life. Each day she could smile a little more, was more engaged in her work and was able to spend more time with her friends. It had been quite a while since she had seen Fawn. Not only did she need time to get over what had happened, but the part that Fawn had played during Zeer's final days on Earth was something that she needed to put into perspective before she could talk with Fawn. In the final analysis, she had agreed with Fawn and Sparks and the others in the camp, but it had been an excruciatingly complex and painful decision - a decision that she would carry with her always.

***

There was hardly a time of day on Loon that didn't contain something memorable, no matter the season, but today was very special. It was a crystal clear spring morning. The air was fresh with the smell of green, and the warmth of the rays from the sun covered Zeer like a blanket, easing her into her day. She sat on her deck, looking at the new emerald green growth on the nearby trees and plants and the freshly budded flowers surrounding the History Cluster. The colors were vibrant and new, the view, spectacular. Her hands were cupped around a warm ceramic mug of tea. She had eaten and almost felt whole again. *'A healthy planet could heal a person,'* she thought. *'We are so tied to nature, to our environment.'* Zeer knew these things to be true.

As she drank some of the steaming liquid, she heard a knock on her door. She opened it. Fawn was standing there, waiting. Zeer didn't quite know what to say for a moment. Fawn spoke, "Can I come in, Zeer?"

"Uh, of course…of course you can. Let's go out on the deck."

They sat together. Zeer offered Fawn some of the tea she'd made and thought of Zoe. It had been some time since she had said that name to herself.

"It's been a long time since we've been together, Zeer."

"I know. I've needed time."

"I knew you would, and I've been busy. I hope it's okay for me to be here."

Zeer smiled at Fawn. "It's perfectly fine. I'm doing a lot better. It's good to see you."

"I'm relieved and glad you're doing better. I was very worried. How do you feel about being home?"

"Loon and all my friends here have helped me." Zeer thought for a moment and then spoke about what was on her mind. "I know you made the right decision, Fawn. It was just…just…very hard for me."

Fawn smiled at her and laid her hands in Zeer's. "It was so very difficult in so many ways. I wish things could have been different. That time in Earth's history was such a terrible, terrible time, but you, Rad and Sparks did so much to help. You had no way of knowing what the people in the Shelters were going to do. All of you did everything you could." Fawn then thought of Rad and said to Zeer, "I also want you to know that I, too, miss Rad, dreadfully, and the deep sadness in my soul for the Earth and its people is something that I have lived with for a very long time – ever since I first learned of it from my teacher, Shar."

"I understand, Fawn. I know it was dreadful for all of us. I just wish we could have done more."

"Well, there is more to be done. I have a lot to talk to you about, but first, I have a task that I need you to perform. Can you come with me to the Womb – the cave where you began your cycle here on Loon?"

"Yes, if you need me, of course I'll go, but...why?"

"I can't quite tell you yet, but I would like you to meet me there in seven days at this same time in the morning. I'm sorry that I can't say more, but I'll tell you everything then."

Zeer looked at Fawn, wondering what this was about, but she agreed to go. She wondered, *'Why was Fawn being so secretive?'* But then she remembered that this was just the way Fawn usually worked. She didn't want to share something until everything was in place.

# 35
## The Womb

The day had finally arrived when Zeer was to meet Fawn in front of the cave. The days and hours before their meeting had crept by with Zeer understanding that this was going to be an important day for some reason, but the "not knowing why" was almost unbearable at this point.

Landree had been outside waiting for Zeer when she left her apartment. He brought her to the cave, and they stood at the entrance waiting for Fawn. They had only been there a few minutes when Zeer heard something behind her and was surprised to see Dominie, Shee and Brit had arrived along with a few others whom she didn't know.

Just as she was about to ask why they were there, Fawn exited the entrance to the cave and stood in front of them. They all turned toward her as she spoke. "It is such a glorious spring morning, and I want to thank all of you for coming today." She paused for a moment while everyone there acknowledged her greeting. "Today is going to be a momentous day for all of us, and each of you have played a vital role in this. You have to know how much I value you and your help."

Zeer looked around and saw that everyone was smiling. "What's going on?" she asked. She seemed to be the only one there that had no idea what was happening.

"Zeer, please come with me." Fawn took her by the arm, and they walked and sat down just under the arched entrance to the womb. "The time has come for me to explain why you're here. I'm sorry we couldn't tell you before, but we needed to complete some tasks ahead of bringing you here. I can tell you that you have a very important part to play today."

"Well?" Zeer was more than ready to hear and motioned Fawn to please continue.

Fawn began, "When we were on Earth and Rad died, it deeply touched the people of Loon. He had worked so very hard during all of the levels of the Room, had learned so much and cared so deeply. We knew that he would have been an extremely important part of our community, just as you are. His death stunned us. It moved us to do something that has been forbidden in our culture since we first settled on Loon."

"What is that?"

Fawn cleared her throat and continued, "As you know, all of the people on Loon came from the original settlers that were created from the DNA of many renowned people that once lived on Earth. Once those individuals were raised to a certain age, their education began. The robots and computers on the ship that had brought them from Earth schooled them and taught them everything that they needed to know to survive on Loon. They were then sent to the planet's surface with supplies and structures to live in. These individuals developed the civilization that now exists on Loon."

Zeer stopped Fawn for a moment and asked a question that had been bothering her. "Yes, I know, but I have to ask you something. I know that your ancestors from that ship were educated from the biased views of the Visionaries from all the Shelters on Earth. Why is it that this culture is so very different?"

Fawn smiled at this and gladly answered. "Yes, we are, thankfully, incredibly different. We're this way because those that first settled here were extremely independent thinkers. They knew about what had happened on Earth. The Visionaries had kept nothing from them, thinking that they would just be grateful and except what they had done. They believed that if an Earth-like planet was found and a settlement established that the early settlers of Loon would simply live the way that the Visionaries prescribed and espouse the same philosophies about life. But our ancestors didn't! They studied carefully, observed the singular beauty of this natural world and decided for themselves what course they would follow. Also, I know that once they met the Scree and learned how to communicate with them that they were influenced greatly by their beliefs."

"I understand. Now...why am I here?"

"Early on, our ancestors decided that every living thing needed to live naturally within its biological limits. They were hopeful that they could enhance the quality of life of everyone on

Loon and that their people had a good chance to have very long and healthy lives, but they also felt that all life needed to cycle; it was important that everyone had a time and place where they should live, and that death was a very natural and essential part of living within an ecosystem. Because of these beliefs, they made a decision that they would allow scientific work to move forward on the study of DNA and gene therapies as well as reproductive studies for the health and diversity of our population, but they would not allow the creation of any cloned organism on Loon. We've always had the ability to create an exact replica of any organism, but living within the bounds of our own particular time and space was very important to the continuation and diversity of our species here and throughout the galaxy. We have always believed that everything must cycle."

"Fawn, I know that you're going somewhere with this. Could you please cut to the chase and tell me why I'm here?"

"Sorry, I had to share that with you." Fawn stood up and took Zeer's hand. They walked into the cave.

It was just as Zeer had remembered it – the warm glow, the scent of spices filling the air and the lush ground cloths covering the floor in the sitting areas. She could still feel herself waking here when she had first arrived on Loon. She thought of the ceremony that had initiated her cycle, and she remembered Dominie - his gentleness and his care.

Fawn watched and knew that Zeer was thinking back to her time here. She let her soak it in and remember and then she took her behind the sitting area and pointed towards the ground.

Zeer turned her head in the direction that Fawn had pointed. She gasped and fell to her knees in disbelief. This was not possible. There was a man lying naked on the ground on one of the ground cloths, a bowl of steaming liquid next to him along with an energy sphere that glowed and blanketed his body in subdued light. It was Rad!

He looked to be either sleeping or unconscious. His wounds were gone. His body was whole. Zeer turned to Fawn and spoke quietly with anxious wonder, "My god! Is he alive?"

"Yes, Zeer. He's alive but he hasn't been awakened yet.

That is your job."

"You cloned Rad?"

"Yes."

Zeer had deep concern in her voice as she said, "Fawn, he won't be the same person. It's not really Rad. It's just his physical body. This isn't right!"

Fawn waited for a moment to let Zeer's emotions settle and then explained, "Yes, it is Rad, Zeer. When I attempted to heal him on Earth, I carefully collected his DNA, and before he died, I used the energy sphere to scan and collect his core – his memories – his soul. I knew that the Science Cluster had the information about how to do this, so I learned from them before I left for Earth. I had hoped that I wouldn't need it, but it turned out that I did."

"So, this Rad has all of his memories - all his mannerisms - his basic nature is in tact? His very soul is the same?"

"Yes. That's right, Zeer. This *is* Rad."

"How were you able to do this when it was banned on Loon? How do the people feel about this?"

"All of Loon was informed, and without hesitation, they decided in this case to allow it. However, the only way they would agree was if he were brought back to the exact age where he was when he died, and that all of his memories must be in tact. Otherwise, they wouldn't agree."

"My god! I can't believe this!"

Fawn continued, "So the scientists worked incredibly hard and were successful. The fact that people on Loon have their own energy sphere, which is tuned specifically to them, was the only reason that this could be done. And, Zeer, we want you to help Rad. We want *you* to awaken him and help him gain some strength. We want *you* to be the one to initiate his first cycle on Loon."

Zeer stared down at Rad, "I'm not sure I know what to do. I haven't been trained to help someone cycle and start their life here."

"Whatever you do is what needs to be done, Zeer. The ceremony is a very individual thing. We know that you care deeply for Rad. You are already part of him, and that's going to be very important. Just make sure that you have him drink the warm liquid. It will help revive him and give him strength. The other part to remember is that in order to be fully open and ready to exist here in our culture, you must also bond with him in the deepest way possible. You know that is our way. It is how you started your cycle and how we bring all young people into our culture when it is their time. We do it with love."

Zeer nodded and walked slowly toward Rad. Fawn watched for a moment, turned and left the womb.

# 36
## Awakening

Somewhere in this bottomless night a small spark lay smoldering ever so slightly, almost losing its heat, barely clinging to the oxygen molecules providing for its insignificant existence. Then minute by minute, second by second, the flicker matured, almost imperceptibly. That glint, which had been so inconsequential seconds before, had now become an ember, an ember that continued to burn, sustained by hope and the unknown.

\*\*\*

His first thought bubbled up inside. *'What? Who am I? My name...My name is...Rad.'*

His breathing was extremely shallow, but on one particular inhalation, he smelled the strong odor of spices in the air. He breathed again a little deeper. The thick aromas etched themselves on his senses, his mouth began to water, and he ascended further from his shadowy tomb toward the light of life.

*'A dream. This has to be a dream,'* he thought, but then other feelings were growing and spreading through him. The nerves on his skin came alive to the warmth of the air encapsulating his body. It calmed and rested on him like a supple blanket. His head, arm and leg muscles twitched ever so slightly, communicating to him that they had been still far too long.

Rad's awareness began tugging and pulling itself upward, through the fog and haze of oblivion, escaping his long, deep sleep. He slowly licked his lips and moved his eyes back and forth, faster and faster, behind immovable eyelids, searching for the tiny patches of light that were dancing on his face.

His hands, back and legs started registering the cushioned, yet malleable cloth that lay beneath him. It cradled his body and lovingly reassured him with its touch. And then a sound bounced through the air, vibrating his inner ear and entering his mind. Someone was there.

Rad tried so hard to open his eyes and awaken himself, but his body was simply not ready yet. He relaxed again. *'Just let it happen,'* he thought. *'Just let it happen.'*

The touch came as a shock to him. He felt fingers sliding under his head, through his hair, working to gain support, then attempting to raise his heavy head, just a bit. A voice. A female voice spoke tenderly, but Rad could not understand the words. He then felt something against his dry lips. A small amount of warm liquid slid into his mouth. The muscles in his throat involuntarily swallowed. It was soothing. He took more. The taste and feeling of the warmth seemed to bring him closer to opening his eyes. He smacked his lips just a little and received more. He knew that he needed this food. He began to yearn for it.

Again he heard the voice, this time hearing his name. It touched him deeply. Someone was reaching out to him. Someone cared.

Whoever was there had stopped feeding him the broth. The sound of something being placed on the floor nearby echoed around the room. It sounded as if he were in a large space. His eyes cracked open slightly. The lids were heavy with mucous. It would take time to be able to see clearly. What he *could* see was only clouded shapes, some colors and the glimmer of lights around the room. He reached up to wipe his eyes, but a hand stopped him and positioned a warm, wet cloth on his face. He had never felt anything so welcome. The heated water caressed his skin and helped clear his eyes a bit, allowing him to see the outline of a person above him.

Zeer continued to use the cloth. Rad voiced his pleasure with a small groan rumbling up from his chest. He was working hard to wake up. Zeer lay the cloth down for a moment, brushed the back of her fingers over his face and caressed his forehead with a gentle kiss. The loving gesture led to Rad tilting his head slightly. He tried to speak but wasn't able to voice anything recognizable. However, Zeer thought she did notice that the right side of his mouth lifted ever so slightly into a miniscule smile. She recognized that look.

Rad desperately wanted to awaken now. He wanted to see

and talk and come completely out of this trance. When the fingers brushed his face with such care and the kiss had touched his forehead, he wanted out of this even more. Then something happened which took his breath away. The woman lay down next to him, her skin touching his, creating a cascade of feelings and sensations that were almost overwhelming. He relaxed somewhat when she wrapped her arms around him, holding him close and whispering his name in his ear. "Rad...Rad, I've missed you terribly."

He now knew and remembered. *'It was Zeer. Zeer!'* A tear of joy escaped his matted eyes and rolled down his cheek. The two lay together inside Loon's womb, wrapped within the brilliant light of their spheres, surrounded by love.

***

It had been about seven days since Rad's awakening, and he had recovered enough that Zeer felt that he could walk out of the cave into the sunshine. He was still weak, but the food and care that she had provided were definitely working. They had begun to smile and laugh and talk. Zeer had so much to share with him about Loon, and of course, they talked of his death, his rebirth and what had happened on the Earth. They could have stayed there longer, but it was time to get Rad into the sunshine and then Zeer needed to take him to the Medical Cluster to be sure that his recovery was complete.

They gathered their things to leave. Rad didn't have very much to take, just the clothes on his back and his energy sphere, which he clutched tightly in his hand. Zeer placed the items that she had into a bag and slung it over one shoulder. She reached her other arm around Rad. They looked into each other's eyes and Rad said, "Zeer, everything that has happened is beyond me, but I do know this, my dear and wonderful friend, I love you." Their lips pressed together, and they held each other close.

"I love you, too, Rad. I love you."

They both smiled as Zeer said, "Now, let's get outside in the sun!"

***

Even before they had completely left the cave, they heard clapping and people hollering their names. They walked out and couldn't believe what they saw. With each step, the roar grew louder and louder. Their closest friends were in the front of the throng, and they ran up to Zeer and Rad with tears in their eyes, hugging them in turn and wishing them well. They saw Brit, Dominie, Shee and, of course, Fawn and Landree. Zeer noticed that the leaders from every Cluster on Loon were there, many of her friends from the History Cluster and many more people that she had never met. The crowd was wild!

They had tables of food and decorations. There were children and families. People were standing as one, cheering and welcoming Rad to Loon. It was overwhelming for both of them after the quiet and solitude of the cave, but it also gave them strength. They couldn't stop smiling. Fawn walked forward and calmed everyone. "I want to thank all of you from the bottom of my heart for being here to welcome Rad and show him the spirit of our world."

The people clapped again and yelled, "Welcome home, Rad!"

Fawn held up her hand after the crowd had had time to express themselves and asked for quiet. She said, "I'm sure Rad and Zeer would love to speak to all of you and share their feelings, but they've both just been through a life-changing experience. I'm sure they're overwhelmed, and I know they both need some time." Rad and Zeer nodded and smiled in agreement. "I would like everyone to stay and enjoy the celebration and the beautiful day. Landree and I will take Rad and Zeer to the Medical Cluster to help Rad complete his recovery." Everyone there nodded with understanding and agreement and started to clap and cheer again.

Rad held up his hand, and Zeer helped him walk over beside Fawn. The crowd hushed again as Rad spoke. "As you all know, I don't have a lot of strength right now, but I have to say that

I am deeply touched and moved by your welcome and what you have done for me. You are remarkable people! Thank you! Thank you so much!"

The gathering of people from all across Loon smiled as one and cheered. They opened a path for them and watched as the two stepped up into the bubble-chair and floated into the sky with Landree and Fawn by their side. They all gazed down at the celebration, watching it disappear into the distance. Then Zeer, sitting beside Rad and holding his hand, pointed in a different direction and said, "Rad, look!"

Rad turned, stopped breathing for a moment and simply stared. "My god, this is a magnificent world!"

# 37
## Another Beginning

Landree and Rad had spent several months together on Loon. His first cycle there had been completed. His training had been very similar to Zeer's, although, no two persons' education was ever identical. His instruction had been lead by his interests and questions as well as by the important concepts that Landree had needed to teach him.

Together they had encompassed Loon, visited diverse biomes, shared ideas about the water, air and mineral cycles, worked to understand the balance of small and large ecosystems, studied plant and animal life across the globe and Rad had been taught a great deal about the history of the people of Loon. Also, they had discussed their culture, their beliefs and how they remained in balance with the natural environment. The final part of his training was meeting and learning from the Scree, just as Zeer had done.

After Landree and Rad were finished with their work, Rad took some time to simply live and be a part of this great planet. He went to each of the Clusters and decided the Science Cluster was the one that most interested him. He spent many hours with his old friends, especially Zeer, and his bond with her had grown and strengthened with each passing day. They deeply respected and loved each other. They both were in awe of this planet and its people. They could hardly believe they were here, and Rad was incredibly grateful just to be alive and have a chance to do more with his life.

\*\*\*

It had been a little over a year now since their return. One afternoon Zeer and Rad were in his apartment when they heard a knock on the door. It was Fawn.

"Hello you two." Fawn walked in and smiled at her two friends. "I've heard that your time with Landree was very productive, Rad. I've also heard that you've started working with the Science Cluster. I'm very proud of you."

"Thanks, but of course without you and many other people here, I wouldn't even have had this chance. It's been a joy, and the knowledge I've gained has changed my life. I can see why you love your home. The people of Loon are like a huge family, working, living and striving together, and Loon itself is such a fantastically beautiful planet. I'm blessed."

Zeer watched and listened as Rad spoke, nodded in agreement and added, "We're just glad you're here Rad. Everyone is. But, you'd better take better care of yourself this time around!"

They all laughed. Zeer was always giving Rad a hard time as well as caring about him more than anyone. "I will," he said. "I don't think anyone will ever let me forget that I've been given a second chance. I'd better not screw it up!"

It was fun sharing some time together and relaxing. They ate a meal and were watching the sunset when Fawn finally talked about the reason for her visit. "I need to let both of you know that the day after tomorrow there is going to be a gathering of all the leaders of Loon, along with Landree, myself, Dominie, Brit and Shee. We're going to get an update from several of the Clusters concerning Earth's recovery. We know its environment has made great gains since the disaster several hundred years ago. We have a lot to talk about and wanted to make sure that you both would be there."

Zeer was excited and said, "Absolutely!"

Rad added, "Of course! We wouldn't miss it for anything!"

"I thought that's how you'd feel." She got up and started to leave as she said, "I'll see you in two days."

***

Rad and Zeer walked into the meeting chamber, which was located in the Gathering Hall. Landree was already there. His energy sphere sat on the center table and was beaming a large projection of the Earth above their heads. The chamber reminded Rad of the layout of some of the Rooms on R-131. The Rooms where he'd joined his friends Tal, Simon and Vella and where he'd actually started this long, amazing journey.

"What are you thinking about, Rad?" Zeer wondered.

"Oh, I was just thinking of our last lifeglobe. Many of the Rooms had a configuration similar to this gathering room with the seating area and chairs forming a circle around the main viewing area. This just reminded me of those times."

"I know. I remember them, too. R-131 was the start of all this, wasn't it. Now here we stand."

Landree stood below them. "Rad...Zeer, please come down and sit near me."

They walked down toward the center area and sat at a railing, looking down on Landree. Zeer looked up at the projection of the Earth and asked, "Landree, is that a current view of Earth as it is now?"

"Yes. Can you believe it?"

Landree slowly spun the projection. The oceans were blue with light wispy clouds floating overhead. Areas of lustrous green were bursting from its surface. Snow-capped mountains jumped into view along with fast rushing streams and rivers that plummeted towards the seas. On the nighttime side of the globe, they could even see a few lights flickering. Zeer and Rad's eyes immediately focused on those lights and then they looked at each other. A huge question was poised on their lips.

Landree recognized their question before they spoke and remarked, "We have more to see, and we also need to listen to the research that has been done by several of the Clusters. They can tell us what is going on there in greater detail."

Their eyes were glued to this astonishing vision. What they remembered of the Earth when they were there before was vastly different from what they saw in front of them now.

Above where they sat, the doors had opened and many people were entering the gathering room. The seats were filling. This assembly was going to be held with a large number of people, some from every Cluster. Then Rad and Zeer saw Fawn, Dominie, Brit and Shee entering the room. They all walked down and sat near them. It was about to begin.

\*\*\*

For several hours, with some breaks in between the sessions, everyone there listened, watched, and learned about the current condition of the Earth. The real time view of the planet was zoomed in and out, rotated and placed at different angles as each Cluster began sharing the data that they had collected about various parts of the Earth. It *had* undergone radical, evolutionary change. Every perturbation that had damaged the ecosphere had diminished in intensity. The Earth, a living planet again, had healed itself more than anyone would have thought possible.

They also learned that the drones had not entirely wiped out the human species on the Earth. Some small, pocketed settlements had survived and after years and years had begun to stabilize. The future looked positive, and at this point, nature was still very much in control again, not the humans.

The sharing of data and ideas ended, and Fawn walked down to join Landree near the globe. Above them, the projection slowly rotated in the focus of everyone's attention. Everyone had been touched by what they had heard and shared. The room was hushed.

Fawn pointed towards the Earth and spoke to the crowd. "This planet spawned each of us. It is our original home. We owe her our lives. Our ancestors did their best to break her – almost completely destroying her ability to sustain life - but they failed. Corporate and individual greed, power and complete disregard for all life brought Earth to the brink of disaster. Any action that sustained the status and wealth of the powerful was lauded, while most of the inhabitants of the Earth were simply abused, used and tossed aside. So many suffered. This can never, ever happen again. The Earth *must* remain in balance. Man does not have the right to overpopulate or destroy their home for profit or for any other reason. As humans, it is our obligation to live within nature, not above it."

Fawn paused. The room's silence demonstrated everyone's agreement with her words.

She continued, "Now, we must act. We must share what we know and how our society has developed in a way that embraces growth and change, embraces education, science and technology, and yet has done all this without destroying or degrading our planet. We must pass this on. Landree and I have spoken with the leaders of every Cluster. We know that they feel the same as we do." Again, there was agreement around the room. "We all feel that we have an obligation to our birthplace – Earth – as well as to the humans there and throughout the galaxy. With both of these thoughts in mind, we will first of all be adding to Loon's diversity and its gene pool by slowly bringing selected humans to Loon from various lifeglobes. We will meet with the governing bodies across the galaxy and create an agreement with them, educate them and decide on the numbers of immigrants that will join us here on Loon. Secondly, we are going to be asking for volunteers from each of the Clusters to travel to Earth and join with the small pockets of population there. We will be asking you to share Loon's history with the Terrans and become a catalyst for a strong, eco-centered development there that will be healthier for the planet and for its people. As time passes, we should be able to return others from the lifeglobes to Earth as well. This will be a very slow and long project that we feel has the capacity to add sustained stability and balance to not only the human population throughout the galaxy, but to that ever-present need for balance between the environment that we live in and an organism's need to survive."

Applause started slowly and grew to a roar as everyone at the gathering stood and confirmed their excitement and support for this bold, incredible plan. Their hearts swelled with joy and pride at the prospect of helping to heal the stain on human history. Loon's people had much to give.

Landree spoke, "We know that the people of Earth will write their own story, and we have no desire to create another Loon. Loon is unique, in and of itself, just as all of us are unique. But, we can influence the healthy balance between a culture, its civilization and the environment. This time, Earth can be healthier, and its people can live happier, longer and more productive lives."

The applause continued as the gathering came to an end. There would be a meeting of all the Clusters to discuss the recommendations and to determine if the people of Loon agreed. There was a strong belief that they would and that many would volunteer to go to Earth to help. Plans needed to be made and a time frame set out.

\*\*\*

Zeer and Rad both asked to go to Earth and work. However, because of all that they had done, everything they had learned and because of their unique perspectives about the lifeglobes, the Earth and Loon itself, they had been assigned to teach the Earth-bound volunteers from Loon and design a course that would help them when they arrived. Within their lessons, they spoke of the incredible spirit of the people that they'd known on Earth. They also remembered individuals like Zoe and Sparks and many others that they had met and worked with. They taught about the Shelters and what they had done. There were many meetings and long hours of preparation, as the volunteer immigrants planned their journeys to Earth.

\*\*\*

Rad and Zeer asked two favors of Landree and Fawn before leaving Loon. They first asked to have the opportunity to visit R-131. They just wanted to see their friends again and visit their old home. They were given permission, with the understanding that they not divulge anything about Loon or their mission to Earth. That information had to be given out slowly and carefully. Rad and Zeer thought about this a while and decided that when they arrived on R-131 they would say that they had been playing and progressing through the levels of the old one's Room. This had been true and was something that their friends could understand. They could share some of what they had actually experienced that way and let them know that they would return in the future when they could. Landree and Fawn felt this was a good idea and agreed.

"And your second favor?" Landree wondered.

Zeer spoke for them. "We want to return to the city where we worked when we were on Earth. If we can, we want to find out exactly what happened to Sparks and the people of that time. We need to know."

Landree and Fawn glanced at each other and Fawn replied, "We thought that might be the case. Of course you can. We'll help you prepare."

# 38
## Earth

Placing the spheres back into their bags, Zeer and Rad, along with their team from Loon, stood gazing at their surroundings. The first thing that they observed was the clean air. There was a light breeze blowing down from the mountains that day. The sky was clear and blue with icy cirrus clouds floating high above their heads. Where there had been broken buildings and meager dwellings, dirty water, filth and so much human suffering before, now there was the green of lush vegetation and the sounds of birds in the distance. The buildings, structures and concrete had all been consumed and overrun by life.

There was a small population of humans in the area that looked to be living in huts - huts whose design seemed very familiar to Rad and Zeer. They looked very much like those that Sparks and Rad had constructed in the valley in the mountains hundreds of years before. They were larger, more beautiful and of a higher quality, but Rad couldn't help but notice the resemblance. Zeer noticed as well and said, "They look like our huts, don't they." Rad agreed and smiled.

None of the Terrans in the area had noticed the arrival of Rad and Zeer's group yet, which is what they wanted. They didn't want to just appear all of a sudden. Rad thought for a moment and whispered, "Let's move through the trees and go toward where the Shelter used to be. Maybe we can set up a camp there and decide on the best strategy for making contact with the Terrans. I think it was in that direction." It was difficult to tell if he was correct or not with everything being so much different, but Zeer agreed, and the team followed him.

Reaching the location where he and Zeer felt the Shelter would have been, they saw an area that was covered by a beautifully landscaped garden with flowers and plants, and in the center of it all there was a large sculpture made of wood. The sculpture was a spire with a massive, artistically carved base that narrowed as it soared skyward. Everyone gazed at it – their eyes wide with amazement. It seemed to go on forever until it touched the clouds. They looked around to make sure no one was nearby, then they all walked closer to get a better look. As they reached it, Rad noticed some words etched into its surface, and he read them quietly to his team.

"This sculpture, rising into the sky, is in remembrance of all of the Terrans who suffered so much here and lost their lives from the horrible holocaust that was perpetrated by the leaders of the Shelter. It is also here to help us remember Sparks and Zoe and all of those who worked so incredibly hard to help many Terrans survive. We honor, respect, love and will always remember. Without them, this small settlement would not exist. We would not be alive."

Through the tears in Rad and Zeer's eyes, they could see that the likenesses of Sparks and Zoe had been carved into the wood just above the writing. They reached out simultaneously and touched each of their faces; it was remarkable how much the carvings looked like them. They then knelt down, wept and remembered together. Their friends from Loon stood behind in silence, knowing this moment was precious to them.

After a long sigh, Zeer held Rad's hands in hers and looked at him. With a shudder, she voiced her fear, "Rad, I'm afraid."

"Why?"

"What about the progeny of the Chosen? What if they return as Harlequin promised? We don't know where the Visionaries finally settled. We don't know how their children's children developed or if their descendants still intend to return to Earth. I can still see in my mind the look of evil righteousness in Harlequin's eyes. I can still remember her words and her rage."

"Zeer, none of us knows the future, but that was so long ago. There's also a good chance that Harlequin's ancestors are just hanging onto life and simply living on some rock, just as we were before Loon."

She smiled and simply said, "We're home aren't we Rad."

As Zeer spoke, Rad immediately thought back to the lunar

planet that had been his first home. He had to smile a bit, wondering why that thought had come forward just now. In his mind's eye, he remembered clearly the moment when he had shut off the system in his suit and removed his headgear. He hadn't thought about it for a long time. He tried to remember what had driven him to do such a thing. Then it came back to him. It was simply the overpowering desire to experience and understand the sensation of standing outside with both feet set in the dirt on a planet without anything between himself and his world. Up until that moment, his existence had always been inside a bubble and had remained that way until he had been called to play the Room. That single, specific, defining moment on that one particular day outside on a lonely outpost in space was truly the instant when his life had begun. That was his birth.

Rad looked back into Zeer's eyes, kissed her, held her close and said, "Yes, we're home, and we're standing outside in the open air on this astonishing planet – alive and free."

# ABOUT THE AUTHOR

Bob Stegner grew up in Colorado and now lives in the Pacific Northwest. He has a master's degree in education and has been a "ski bum," a teacher, a published singer/songwriter and musician, has run his own school in Alaska, worked in educational technology and was recently employed overseas for five years. All of these experiences have added depth to his life and to the stories that he has to tell.

Visit Bob's blog at http://bobstegner.blogspot.com.

Made in the USA
Lexington, KY
15 July 2014